JUNKYARD DREAMS

JUNKYARD DREAMS

A NOVEL

JEANETTE BOYER

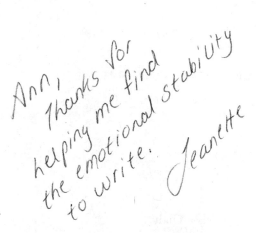

Ann,
Thanks for
helping me find
the emotional stability
to write.
Jeanette

UNIVERSITY OF NEW MEXICO PRESS   ALBUQUERQUE

Library of Congress Cataloging in Publication Data

Boyer, Jeanette, 1952–

 Junkyard dreams : a novel / Jeanette Boyer.

     p. cm.

 ISBN-13: 978-0-8263-3949-2 (pbk. : alk. paper)

1. Automobile graveyards—New Mexico—Santa Fe—Fiction.

2. Single women—Fiction. 3. Santa Fe (N.M.)—Fiction.

4. Real estate developers—Fiction. I. Title.

PS3602.O936J86 2007

813'.6—dc22

                    2006033223

Design and composition: Melissa Tandysh

To Jim
for his ongoing support through the years.

With thanks to the
Speed Humpsters Writing Group
for helping to shape the story

and to Beth Hadas
for taking a leap of faith.

|| **RITA** || Rita had pulled the transmission out of a Bronco for a customer earlier that morning. She was still wearing her greasy overalls when a black SUV turned into the junkyard. The people who visited her in search of salvaged parts typically drove older, less expensive vehicles. Curious, she watched to see who got out of the Land Rover, which somehow managed to gleam despite the dust it had raised barreling down the dirt road. When the door opened and Leroy Sena climbed down, Rita had a sense of time repeating itself. In high school, he'd owned a Camaro. It, too, had been black and spotless. Leroy had lots more money now, but he remained slick. Even his attempt to dress conservatively revealed his vanity—the lemon yellow shirt tight across his chest and the khaki pants hugging his butt.

"Rita, Rita! Looking good." Compliments spilled off his tongue like seeds off a dandelion. He advanced upon her, hand outstretched.

"I don't think you want to shake, Leroy." She held up her oil-smeared palms and smiled as he recoiled.

Quick as ever, he returned her smile. "You have to be the only woman who can look like a grease monkey and still come across sexy."

Rita knew she looked terrible, but Leroy wasn't the first man who'd made innuendos when she was gilded in grease. "You must like things kind of kinky."

He moved in closer and ran a finger across her cheek. "Smudges bring out the fire in your eyes."

Now she was the one to step back, pulling away from the warmth his fingertip had stirred within her. It'd been too long since a man had touched her, but there was no way she'd give in to Leroy. She'd watched him use too many women as a means of getting other things.

"How's your wife these days?"

1

"Still putting up with me." He had the grin of a self-satisfied man, a man who'd wheedled his way into more than one woman's heart.

"What can I do for you, Leroy? Don't tell me you're hunting a piece for that new Land Rover."

"It's a beauty isn't it?" Pride widened his smile. "I've come a long ways since my first car. Won't be needing to scrounge around for parts to keep this baby running." He shook his head, his arms folded across his chest as he stood looking over her junkyard. Wrecked vehicles stretched into the distance, row upon row of rusting metal. "Can't believe you held onto this place after your old man died."

"What else was I supposed to do? A high school dropout, no husband, and a kid to feed. I didn't have much choice."

"You could have sold the land and lived pretty."

"I do live pretty," she said. If she overlooked the junkyard and didn't turn around, the rest of her land spread before her with no sign of people. Juniper and piñon trees stood guard, scattered among the dips and rises of the panorama.

"Getting a little crowded." Leroy gestured at the houses behind her, ornate mansions in falsely modest earth tones. She used to think the junkyard would protect her, would keep anybody from wanting to live nearby, but as Santa Fe had grown, people had begun to move beyond town, creeping ever closer.

"I try not to look in that direction."

"Kind of hard to do, isn't it?"

"I manage," she said. His false empathy raised her guard. The last time he'd commiserated with her, she'd needed money to keep her father alive and Leroy had convinced her to sell the ridgetop that bordered her property to the north.

"Why barely manage," he asked, "when you could be wealthy?"

His own father had been regularly unemployed, the family poor even by New Mexico standards. As far back as Rita could remember, Leroy had worked, taking odd jobs as a little kid, bagging groceries at Kaune's as a teenager, vowing one day he'd be rich. How could she explain to him that money meant little to her except when there was too little of it? "What would I buy that I don't already have?"

"You could get rid of that old truck of yours, for starters."

Rita glanced over at the battered Dodge Ram that took her anywhere she wanted to go. "No payments, plus low insurance rates."

"Sell some land and you could afford car payments plus a decent place to live."

She saw the scorn on his face as his hand swept toward her small adobe. Trying to view it from his perspective, she noticed the way the tin roof slanted to the south, giving it a lopsided look, but she liked the irregularity, the handmade unevenness of its walls, the beckoning openness of its front porch. Granted, it could use some fixing up, but it served its purpose. "My grandparents lived in that house before they built the big one. It's where I grew up. Why would I want anything else?"

"That's the kind of thinking that keeps us Spanish from getting rich. Just because our families lived here for generations is no reason we have to hold onto the land."

"The land is intrinsic to who we are."

"Let me put it another way." He again indicated the houses behind her. "Your new neighbors are accustomed to getting things their way. It's just a matter of time before they see to it you're zoned out of business."

Rita had already recognized that possibility, but she wasn't going to let Leroy prey upon her fears. "If they succeeded, that would make my land all the more valuable, wouldn't it? I mean, who wants to live next to a junkyard? If I'm forced to go out of business, my property will be yet more desirable."

She immediately regretted the unintended sexual implications of the last word, as Leroy's eyes grazed her body, seeking out the curves under her baggy overalls. His voice lured her, especially when it went husky, as it did then. "You've always known how to play the game, haven't you?"

Standing on her tiptoes and leaning close, as though she were going to kiss him, she raised the middle finger of her left hand, the greasiest, and drew a mustache over his mouth. "You were always the bigger player, Leroy."

He jerked away, grabbing a handkerchief out of his pocket and rubbing it across his mouth. "Shit!" he said, examining his face in the side-view mirror of his car. "What did you do that for?" He spit on the handkerchief and scrubbed more vehemently at the mark, staining his skin a muddy red.

"Doing business with you is dirty, Leroy."

Her insult swept past him, brushing the anger out of his eyes. As though she'd complimented him, he smiled, a cockeyed smile bordering on a grin, with one tooth playing peekaboo. "I'm a player all right," he said, reaching into his back pocket for his wallet and pulling out a card. "Here's my new number. Give me a call when you change your mind." He opened his car door. "No sense being land rich and cash poor."

It wasn't until he climbed up into the Land Rover that she noticed his boots. Rita's own closet contained three pairs of fancy boots, but none were made out of the skin of a reptile. Snakeskin suited Leroy.

He raised swirls of dust as he drove away, bouncing over the bumps and racing toward town. She knew he'd be back. Not today, and maybe not for several weeks, but he would return, determined to buy more of her land, just as he had the ridgetop. Her eyes followed the brown cloud raised by his car until it disappeared in the distance.

Dust clung to her body. She would have liked to take a shower, but she had a trailer hitch she wanted to finish welding before the day got any hotter. Ten o'clock and already the June sun had a harsh glare, burning the earth. They needed rain desperately, but there wasn't a cloud in the sky. A dry winter followed by a dry spring had left her hungering for moisture. It would be hot in the welding shed.

Despite the discomfort of sweltering under her leathers and hood, Rita enjoyed welding. It thrilled her to take what appeared to be nothing and make it into something. Inured to the noise and fumes, she bent over the trailer hitch with her welding gun. When she finished, and lifted the hood off her face, she jumped at the sound of a voice.

"Feels like the devil's workshop in here." Parker stood in the wide doorway, the sun shimmering like a halo around his curly hair. "Sorry, didn't mean to startle you." He came over and laid a hand on her shoulder.

At four foot eleven, Rita had grown accustomed to having to tilt her head to look into people's faces, but she could never quite get used to the way her son towered over her like a benevolent giraffe. It didn't seem that long ago that she'd had to lift him to reach the cookie jar in the kitchen. Now here he was, twenty-four already, a man, not a child. Only the light brown curls remained the same, softening the sharp angles in his face. He had a wiriness akin to her own, but with a grace she attributed to his father, an Anglo who'd swum through her life with the ease of a fish.

"I thought you saw me come in," he said.

"You know how I am. I get so involved when I'm welding that I wouldn't notice a thunderstorm unless lightning struck me." Her eyes finally having adjusted to the shadows, she saw that he had four or five hubcaps cradled in his arm. "What about you? Got a new sculpture going?"

It fascinated her the way he turned discarded junk into pieces of art. Her father would have loved the irony.

"If you don't need them, I want to try something with these hubcaps."

Rita checked first to make sure they weren't from a model popular with low-riders. "They're all yours."

He shifted the hubcaps to his other hand. "Wasn't that Leroy Sena I saw with you?"

Unaware that Parker had been poking around out in the junkyard while she and Leroy stood talking, she wondered if he'd been close enough to overhear them. "How do you know Leroy?"

"He's a regular at the restaurant."

"A regular at Santa Café? Guess he finally hit the big time." She started taking off her leathers, but Parker didn't leave.

He shifted the hubcaps again, clutching them to his chest, the clanking metal echoing in the room. "So why was he here?"

Rita bent over to pick a piece of slag off the floor, collecting strength to confess. "He'd love to buy more of our land."

"Well, I'd love to sell some of it." Parker kicked a second piece of slag over to her as though they were playing a game. "But not to Leroy Sena. The guy's got a reputation for buying low and selling high. Hits up a lot of old-timers, folks who don't have a clue how valuable their property is."

"I know what our property's worth and I'm not about to let him buy it." Lifting her head, she met Parker's eyes. She loved her son, but they disagreed on what it took to sustain a person. He thought money alleviated all your problems; he didn't understand that without the land she would have nothing. "I'm not selling to him or anybody else."

Parker shrugged, moved toward the doorway, then paused, once again a shadow against the bright light. "If the price goes up high enough, I might consider selling my half."

She watched as he shifted the hubcaps, holding them closer to his chest, as though embracing them. And in that embrace she saw how greatly he loved his art and the extremes to which he'd go to support it. Whereas she had only her land. Without it she'd be as rootless as a tumbleweed.

|| **JOE** || Life felt like it was zipping past, rushing by him before he could grab hold of it. The sensation of time running out struck Joe especially hard as he paused in front of Mrs. Padilla's house. He still thought of it as hers, though she'd been dead almost a month now. Like blaring trumpets, daylilies blazed alongside her fence. He missed seeing her out there in her faded floral housecoat. With her stick legs and curved back, she'd reminded him of a sandhill crane, gingerly picking her way through the yard. Each step had required a deliberate effort as she bent over her flowers, calling them her beauties, coaxing them to flourish even in this summer of no rain.

Now her house sat empty and he couldn't help reflecting on his own mortality. Thirty-nine, divorced, no children, both his parents already dead. What mark would he leave? Even Mrs. Padilla's beloved garden would disappear all too soon.

As he stood there, staring at the vacant house and the forlorn flowers, a shiny black Land Rover pulled in front of the detached garage. Probably a real estate agent, come to put up a for sale sign. Saddened to think of somebody else living there, Joe resumed walking.

"Oakes, hold up a sec."

He turned to see a Hispanic man coming down the sidewalk. Built like a bull, slim in the hips, he had a chest and biceps that strained against his black silk shirt. He also wore a familiar smile, one that offset his imposing muscles. "Leroy Sena," he said, holding out his hand. "We met at a city council meeting."

Joe thought back to a few months ago when he'd had to assure people in a residential neighborhood that his rental business wouldn't attract a high volume of traffic. Leroy Sena had sat next to him and been first on the night's agenda with a request for a zoning variance.

"Morning," Joe said and exchanged a firm handshake. Knowing Leroy speculated in land, not houses, he wondered what brought him to Mrs. Padilla's.

"My mother lives around the corner," Leroy said, as though sensing the need to explain his presence.

Joe liked Mrs. Sena. She'd welcomed him to the neighborhood with a bowl of posole the day he moved into the small adobe near hers. Several months later, after he'd knocked down walls, put in new windows, and expanded out back, she and Mrs. Padilla had appeared at his door and asked for a tour. They'd teased him about a single man adding a second bathroom, but oohed and aahed over the modern kitchen.

"So you're the realtor for Mrs. Padilla's house?"

"Yes and no. I'm the executor of her will." His news surprised Joe. In all the times they'd talked, Mrs. Padilla had never mentioned Leroy.

"I haven't put the house on the market yet," Leroy said. "That's why I wanted to talk to you. Save us both a bunch of money if you make a bid up front."

Although Joe lived in the neighborhood, he'd never considered it for a commercial endeavor. A quick glance explained why. Chain-link fences and iron bars on windows did nothing to inspire businesses to locate there. The houses sat so close together thieves sometimes walked over the roofs to reach a heist. "Outside of my own house, I only renovate places downtown."

"This neighborhood's going to catch on before you know it. Close enough people can walk to the plaza. The ideal thing for vacation rentals."

"Sorry, it's just not the kind of thing I do."

"It's all legit," Leroy said, misunderstanding him. "I don't need to do a public listing of the property, as long as I get fair market price."

Joe looked at the house anew, debating whether Leroy would sell it for little enough to warrant the risk. Despite the peeling stucco, the arched portal made an inviting entryway and he knew the interior also had its charm. But the neighborhood itself had too few attractions, and fear of losing money held him back. "I'm sure it's a great deal, but I don't handle vacation rentals."

"Why not? In this town it's one of your better investments."

"Yeah, but it's also a headache. Hoping the tenants are reliable, cleaning up every Monday one checks out, and then having weeks go by when you can't get anybody to rent it."

"You know Mike Daily?" Leroy asked. Joe nodded his head. Daily owned some of the most lucrative real estate in town. "He has a vacation rental one street over. Only rents on a monthly basis and right now he's got a couple staying there for the entire summer."

"What about the other months?"

"Claims the place is never vacant. You should talk to him, see how he does it."

"So why don't you offer the property to him?"

Leroy's face reddened. "My mother wants you to have it. Says you respect the neighborhood."

No wonder Leroy had blushed. He didn't look like the kind of man who'd let his mother dictate his decisions. Yet Joe could easily see Mrs. Sena cajoling her son into doing whatever she wanted. She had a sweet persuasiveness, inviting you over for bizcochitos while asking if you'd mind taking a look at the peeling linoleum in her tiny bathroom and seeing if there was anything she could do about it that wouldn't cost much money, eventually nudging you into remembering that you had just enough tile left over from an earlier project to redo the floor for her at no charge. "She's probably hoping I'd keep Mrs. Padilla's garden alive."

Leroy chuckled. "I'm sure Mom would be willing to give you advice on how to do it."

Joe looked at the daylilies again. He would have to hire a professional landscaper to maintain the garden, but maybe it would be worth it. Like Leroy said, if it went well, he could make more with a vacation rental than with an office lease. He ran some numbers through his head, calculating the mortgage payments versus the rental income, taking into account the cost of the renovations. His own house he'd done himself, shuffling his belongings from room to room as he undertook each one. With this, he'd need to hire a contractor and move fast, try to catch the opera and Indian Market crowd.

"A hundred and twenty." He knew it was low, but he also knew Leroy wanted quick cash, could smell it on him like a stallion nearing a mare.

"Hundred thirty-five and you got yourself a bargain."

Joe's heart raced, giddy with the speed of the transaction. If he wasn't careful, he could acquire a taste for high stakes. "Hundred twenty-two and that's it." Shocked at his own audacity, Joe held his breath, waiting to hear if Leroy would go that low.

Leroy grinned. "My mother was right. You're good." An enormous grasshopper plopped down between them, and Leroy smashed it under his boot. "I'll draw up the papers this afternoon."

Suddenly panicked by the quickness of it all, Joe scrambled for time to reconsider. "I have lots to do today," he lied. "Let's meet tomorrow morning." That way he'd have a night to mull it over, make sure he wasn't getting in too deep.

III

The old wooden floors squealed when Joe stepped into the front room. They were badly scuffed, but not warped. Perfect for refinishing. And the kiva fireplace was definitely a plus. Even in the middle of summer, he could smell the lingering sweetness of burning piñon.

He loved the house, but still had his doubts. No matter how nicely he fixed up the place, the barrio would deter most tourists. And if he renovated it beyond the area's price range, he'd never be able to sell it and recoup his money. A hundred and twenty-two thousand might be cheap, but after awakening several times during the night, Joe had called Leroy first thing in the morning and asked for another day to think over his offer. A few minutes after he'd hung up the phone, Mrs. Sena appeared at his door with a key. "Go look at it again. You won't be able to say no."

As soon as he walked into the house, the tenseness left his body, like he'd stretched out on a comfy couch and had the whole day to kick back. Even vacant, the place had a coziness that made you want to snuggle up in it. Light flooded the front room, and a breeze came through the open door. He turned at the sound of footsteps on the brick walkway.

The morning sun highlighted Chloe's blonde hair and glazed the smooth planes of her cheeks. Her skin radiated youth. Eleven years separated them, but mutual passions bridged the gap. "Hey, hand-some," she said, bounding up the porch steps, her kiss welcoming.

"Um, lavender." He pressed his nose against her neck, where the soap's fragrance lingered in the hollows of her collarbones.

"You're lucky I don't stink of horse." Her eyes moved over the house. "So what's going on?"

"Come inside and tell me how you feel about this place." Old houses fascinated her almost as much as they did him, both of them loving the sense of previous lives worn into the grooves. Furthermore, Chloe had a keen instinct for sound business decisions.

Anxious to hear her opinion, Joe fingered the coins in his pocket as she walked into the center of the front room and spun in a circle, her arms wrapped around herself. When she stopped, she gave him a dizzy grin. "Feels like an adobe hug."

"Is it too small? You think people will find it claustrophobic?"

"The right people will love it." Chloe wandered into one of the two tiny bedrooms. He stood in the doorway, watching her caress a deeply recessed windowsill, her long fingers dancing across the surface. Her face exposed a wistful longing. "Too bad you only do office rentals. This would make the perfect romantic hideaway."

He'd had the same thought. The house might sit in the middle of a barrio, but it spoke of warmth and love. A honeymoon cottage was how he was thinking of advertising it.

"Come see the kitchen." He took her hand and they crossed the hallway into a room that overlooked the backyard, which held even more flowers than the front. As he'd expected, the splash of colors caught her eye.

"What an exquisite garden!" Chloe opened the door and stepped out onto the small deck.

He came up behind her and put his arms around her waist, resting his cheek alongside hers. "Beautiful, isn't it?"

"Whoever did this was an artist." She kissed his cheek before slipping away down the steps and into the garden. Floating over to a peony bush, she bent to smell it. When she lifted her head and turned to look at him, he again saw the longing in her eyes. "Looks like too high maintenance for you."

"Maybe not." He joined her in the garden. Pulling out his pocketknife, he cut one of the raspberry-colored peonies and held it out to her.

She took the flower and smiled. He would do anything to have her continue to grace his life with that smile. "I'm thinking of hiring a landscaper to keep up the grounds, and gambling on long-term vacationers."

Her fingers ruffled the flower's petals. "Think it'll work?"

"The realtor swears this will be the next boom area, but I'm not entirely convinced."

Chloe's lips scrunched together, unsuccessfully repressing a proud smile. "Remember how you didn't want to rent to me, convinced my gallery would fail because it's so far off the beaten track?"

He doubted he'd ever forget the day they first met, her self-assurance winning more than his willingness to give her a lease. "I never expected to see tourists at that end of town, clutching their little Chamber of Commerce maps, wandering onto side streets to track you down."

"You have to trust people, Joe. They'll go out of their way if you offer what they want."

"Yeah, but your situation is entirely different from mine. You're selling a product, not a getaway."

"Either case, location is crucial." Chloe gazed across the chain-link fence at the neighbor's yard, which held a broken-down swing set and a rusting chile roaster. "Nothing offensive there, but not exactly picturesque either." She pointed her chin at the opposite yard, where the clutter of broken, discarded things grew higher than the weeds. "That place, on the other hand, is a downright eyesore."

"Exactly the kind of thing I'm worried about. I mean, I can build a coyote fence to block all that out, but it's essential that anybody staying here feels safe."

"It isn't a particularly dangerous neighborhood, just a little rundown. Not quaint, but different from what most folks have at home. Plus, downtown is walkable from here."

"Yeah, that's what the realtor pointed out, too."

Chloe's eyes swept over the garden and then the house. "You could turn this property into a showpiece. I think you should go for it."

"And if it bombs?"

She closed the distance between them in two steps, rubbing her nose playfully against his. "I'll still love you."

"Will you?" Losing money would be bad enough, but his biggest fear was losing her. Putting his arms around Chloe, he pulled her closer.

She moved her lips against his ear. "You have to take a few risks now and then, if you want to come out ahead."

Like too much wine, her kisses emboldened him, made him reckless, kindling a heightened sense of possibility. "I'd risk anything to keep you around."

|| **PARKER** || Moving with the quickness of a dancer, Parker circulated among the restaurant's patrons, careful never to appear rushed, lingering where necessary while constantly aware of the need to keep things flowing. If somebody in college had told him that he'd return to New Mexico and wait tables, he would have scoffed. He'd had dreams of the high life, fantasies of himself as a big-name artist, one who ate in places like Santa Café, instead of working there, relying on tips to afford his dreams.

He bustled from the patio into the bar with a drink order. "Two Chilitinis."

Jake nodded and deftly poured chile-soaked gin into martini glasses, propping a chile in each of the drinks. "Been nonstop tonight."

"Makes the time go faster."

"And the wallet get fatter." Jake slid the glasses across the bar.

"Party of three in the corner," the hostess told Parker as he passed by her with the drinks. Glancing over, he saw Leroy Sena with a woman from the city council and a well-tanned man in a salmon-colored shirt and plaid golf pants. Leroy gleamed with the smugness of a rooster who'd just won a cockfight.

When Parker approached the table, Leroy spoke first. "Hey, Parker," he said, as though they were close friends, "this is Drew Stinson." He nodded his head at the man sitting next to him. "He just bought the property across the road from the junkyard."

The city council member tried to shush him, but Leroy only raised his voice. "Going to divide it into three-acre lots with some of the poshest houses in town. A gated community."

Drew Stinson scooted his chair a couple of inches back from the table, distancing himself from Leroy. Yet Parker suspected that without Leroy the man could never have bought the property. It had sat abandoned so long that Rita figured whoever inherited it had forgotten about it. She'd be furious when she found out Leroy had tracked down the absentee landowner and finagled a deal.

The city council member, a woman whose name always eluded Parker, murmured something about the approval for the subdivision not being quite final.

"They'll break ground for the first house next month," Drew said with the certainty of a man who bought whatever it took to accomplish his goals.

"What can I get you folks to drink?"

"Bring me a Scotch," Drew said.

Leroy made a show of pulling a cigar from inside his jacket. "It's a special occasion. We'd like," he said, placing his hand over that of the city council member's, "a bottle of your Mumm champagne." The woman slipped her hand out from under his, looking around to see if anybody had noticed them. Parker excused himself to get their drink orders, but as he turned away, Leroy tugged at his sleeve. "Tell Rita her property just got more valuable."

Parker didn't bother to inform Leroy he owned half the property. Few people knew. Not that it mattered. His piece lay behind Rita's, with no public access. Much as he'd love to sell it, nobody would want it. On the other hand, if they sold the entire parcel—thoughts of how much their land might be worth crowded into Parker's head, pushing aside everything else. He detoured into the bathroom, splashed cold water on his face, gripped the sink and stared into the mirror, reminding himself he needed to focus on a winsome smile and prompt delivery of customers' orders.

Hurrying into the kitchen, he saw Drew Stinson standing at the bar, talking to Jake. When he came back out, Drew cornered him. "Leroy says your mother owns the land across the road from mine."

Parker held two bowls of rapidly chilling soup. "That's right," he said and moved to walk around him. Drew laid a hand on Parker's shoulder, restraining him while slipping a business card into his shirt pocket. "He says she'll never sell. I don't have a problem with that. My clients will think her old house is kind of cute, but I'll pay a bundle for you to get rid of that junkyard."

It wasn't until they'd closed for the night, and Parker sat in the kitchen eating a slice of chocolate gateau, that he pulled out the card. It made a clear statement: "Drew Stinson, Developer." No convoluted words disguising the facts. The man was in the business of buying and developing land. He had a local number and one in Scottsdale.

"What you got?" Jake asked. He held a couple of brandy snifters and raised a bottle of Remy-Martin in a questioning gesture. They were the last two in the restaurant and Parker nodded his assent to a drink. It was their little ritual, his and Jake's, finishing off the evening with a soft blurring.

Parker held up the card. "Know anything about this Drew character?"

Jake sat down and poured them both a glass of cognac. "Supposedly he just sold a three-acre lot on the edge of town for three hundred and seventy-five thousand dollars."

"Right across the road from the junkyard."

Parker had only seen people in movies sputter their drinks, but Jake, who usually showed the utmost protocol, sprayed cognac down the front of his shirt. "Why would anybody pay three hundred and seventy-five thousand dollars to live out there? No offense, Parker. I like your sculptures, but your mother's junkyard is hideous."

"Maybe they bought it sight unseen."

Shaking his head, Jake again raised his glass. "Why is it that the folks with no taste are filthy rich, while we artistes are constantly broke?" He took a whiff of the cognac, sighing appreciatively before sipping it. The brandy softened the pinched look around his eyes, eyes that had peered through years of cigarette smoke and sordid stories. Already in his mid-thirties, he had a weary cynicism that Parker recognized would pervade his own life if he, too, had to continue supporting his art by working in a restaurant.

Parker flicked Drew's card with his finger. "If I understood him correctly, he's willing to pay so nobody has to look at the junkyard."

"What's he going to do? Build a ten-foot-high wall?"

"Don't think so. Sounds like he wants to buy the business and get rid of it." Parker pressed his thumb against the plate, picking up a few last chocolate crumbs and putting them into his mouth.

"Better give that one some thought. It might sound like an easy way to make money, but how are you going to make sculptures?"

"No way I'd stop sculpting."

"I'd be careful if I were you. Eyesore that it is, that place feeds your art."

Exhausted from the night's work, Parker rolled his neck to ease the tension in his shoulders. The junkyard might be his main source of materials, but he could find supplies elsewhere. For now, he was curious to find out what Drew wanted and how much he'd pay to get it.

Driving home, he tried to calculate what the business was worth. He really had no idea of its value. Rita had a few classic automobiles that presumably would sell for a pretty penny if they ever found any buyers. The other vehicles would probably be assessed by bulk weight. Compacted together and shipped off to a metal salvage yard, they wouldn't bring much. Yet, to get paid to dispose of what amounted to nothing but trash seemed like an incredible deal.

Slowing down, he turned into the dirt driveway that lay between his mother's house and the junkyard. His headlights swept over the bumper of an old Buick and for a second he saw it as the reclining body of a woman. He dropped his speed to a bare crawl, letting the image of a new sculpture play in his mind as he drove on back to his place. Last week he'd found a corroded set of bed springs out by the old landfill and carted it home, not sure what he'd eventually use it for. Now he envisioned the bumper arranged seductively on the bed. Excited by the idea, he wanted to turn around and pull the bumper right then, but that would set Rita's dogs to barking and awaken her. He'd have to wait until morning.

III

Parker lay in bed gazing up at a water stain in the corner of the room. Some mornings it looked like a map of Texas; other days it reminded him of a giant amoeba. Today it proclaimed how shabbily he lived, holed up in a tin box, the wind whistling through the cracks. Usually he congratulated himself for buying an old trailer and not paying rent, but then he'd go through spells like this morning when he felt imprisoned by his poverty. Rather than think about it too much, he kicked back the covers and sat up. As he put his feet on the floor, he saw a scorpion scurry under the dresser, taking refuge in the dark.

What had possessed him to leave LA for this? He glanced out the window at the desert's emptiness, the answer to his question. He'd felt too penned in by the city, crowded, pushed to the edge. And his art had felt too contrived, too slick. So here he was, back home, in the middle of nowhere. Living next to a junkyard. A rusted heap of inspiration. Jake had been right, though, in reminding him he needed the place. Where else would it occur to him to transform a bumper into a woman?

Eager to see if the idea would work, Parker stood up and stretched, his hands brushing against the ceiling. Cramped though his lifestyle might feel at times, creating sculptures excited him as nothing else ever did. Money might entice him, but he would never give up his art for it. He simply needed to find a way to have both.

The phone rang, and he bumped his toe against the door jamb as he hurried into the kitchen to answer it.

"Hey, bro, it's Ramón. Sorry if I woke you up. Your mom's not back from Mass yet, and I got a piece I want to buy."

"We're not open on Sundays."

"For me she is."

True enough. Matter-of-fact, Rita would open the place for anybody who happened by when she was there. But that didn't mean Parker wanted to be at people's beck and call, especially not after a late night at the restaurant. "You and your damn cell phone," he said. "Don't you know it makes you look like a drug dealer."

"Who says I'm not?"

Parker laughed. Ramón might cultivate the tough look of a cholo, but he made good money as a technician at the lab in Los Alamos. "You're no more a drug dealer," he said, "than I'm a pimp. I'll be over in a few minutes, vato."

He found half a mug of tea and inspected it for mold before sticking it in the microwave. While the tea warmed, he got dressed, slipping his feet into yesterday's dirty socks. He'd meant to do laundry this morning, but it would have to wait. He pulled on his steel-plated boots and grabbed a pair of leather work gloves. As soon as he finished with Ramón, he'd yank off that bumper he'd seen last night and reshape it into a woman's body.

Parker headed out the door and angled across the land. His trailer sat behind a rise and he couldn't even see the junkyard until he'd crested the hill. He paused a second, as he often did, impressed that a junkyard could look so orderly. Shortly before his grandfather died, Rita had rearranged everything into neat rows, separating the different makes of vehicles. Abuelo had teased her about giving the place a woman's touch, but admitted it made it easier for customers to find what they were looking for. Parker missed the old man and his humor that had cushioned the sharp edges of their lives. Even after all these years, stepping into the junkyard felt to him like entering an amusement park, a place he'd played since he was a child.

He went through a fence of old tractors and horse trailers, past a section of Volkswagens, and made his way toward the Impalas, Ramón's enduring predilection. Sure enough, there he stood chatting to his wife Teresa, who waved when she saw Parker approach, her red fingernails ablaze. She no longer wore the high curled bangs favored by most of the girls in Española, but like Ramón, she flashed the local style. Her silver blouse glittered above her tight jeans as she gracefully maneuvered among the cars in her high heels.

"There's the slacker," Ramón called out, trailing behind her, carrying a side-view mirror.

Teresa kissed the air next to Parker's cheek, sparing him the mark of her lipstick, while draping him in her flowery perfume. "Long time no see."

"Where are the girls?" Parker asked. Even when Ramón came by himself, he often brought his two daughters, carrying one in a snuggly and holding hands with the other.

"They're over at my mom's," Teresa said. "We didn't want any distractions."

"Is that all you're buying?" Parker indicated the mirror in Ramón's hand. "Hell, you could have walked away with that and nobody would have known."

Ramón rubbed his thumb over the stub of hair he'd recently grown in the dent of his chin. "Know why I gave up trying to talk Rita into computerizing her inventory?"

It took Parker a moment to get the connection, then he laughed. "She might know every single piece that's out here, but she'd forgive you for taking a mirror. Hell, you low-riders are the ones who keep her in business."

Teresa sat on one of the Impalas, impatiently jiggling her foot. "That mirror's not what we really came out here for. We want . . ."

A chorus of barks interrupted Teresa's explanation. Two dogs raced toward Rita's truck as she drove into the junkyard. She got out and played with the dogs, her feet entangled with theirs as her hands held cookies just out of their reach, finally tossing one to each of them. The black Lab and Lhasa apso trailed behind her as she walked down the aisles, making her way toward the Impalas. "Looks like a party," she said.

Her own outfit, Parker thought, lent a festive air to the place. She had dressed up for Mass in turquoise boots, a black velvet skirt, and a turquoise blouse set off by her grandmother's concha belt. A modest outfit, really, but she looked stunning. And incredibly young. It was no wonder guys in high school had razzed him about having such an attractive mother.

"Look who's decked out for a party." Ramón whistled his approval.

When Rita shrugged off the attention, Parker took her hands and twirled her around in a two-step, the dogs barking and trying to join in the dance. Rita threw back her head, her hair coming out of its clasp, streaming behind her. Ramón pounded out a beat on the car and Teresa sang "Nunca Te Olvidare," prompting them to keep dancing. When they finally stopped, Rita fell against Teresa, the two of them giggling like teenagers.

"Girls, get a grip! We have business to conduct," Ramón said. "I'm here to buy a couch."

Rita lapsed into a chortle. "Since when does this place look like a furniture store?"

"Told you she'd think we were crazy," Teresa said to Ramón.

"Wait'll they hear about it. Parker, you're going to love this. The other day, we seen a . . ."

"Saw," Teresa corrected him.

"She's trying to improve my English." Ramón put an arm around Teresa's waist. "We seen this couch made out of an old Cadillac with fins."

Teresa lightly elbowed him in the ribs, while rolling her eyes at Parker and Rita. "It was the coolest thing, but we couldn't afford it. So Ramón said he'd make us one."

"I know the couches you're talking about," Rita said, "but the guy who does them took the trunks off every single one of my Cadillacs."

"Since when have I been a Caddie man?" Ramón scoffed. "We want to do it with an Impala."

"Should have known," Rita said. She looked out over the cars. "There's that white one you used the hood from. It even has fins."

"I don't want white," Teresa whined.

"Easy enough to paint it a different color," Ramón said, already striding down the row. Teresa hurried to catch up with him, thrusting her hand into his.

Parker watched them turn down a side aisle, Teresa's silver blouse blending in with the chrome.

"They make a good couple, don't they?" Rita said.

Teresa pointed out a metallic blue Impala, and Ramón shook his head, running his hands over the white one's fins, demonstrating why his choice worked better before listening to her counterarguments. Parker envied the intricate balance they'd forged with their lives. He'd yet to meet a woman who tolerated, much less accommodated, his lifestyle.

"Looks like the white Impala's the one," he said, as Ramón gave them a thumbs up and walked back toward his truck. He never visited without bringing his torch. He once told Parker that Rita's junkyard was like a holy place to him, one of the last of the "you-pulls," an altar to the god of men who still worked with their hands.

"I bet half of Española would go up in arms if you ever tried to close this place," Parker said.

"Why would I ever close it?"

Although she barely made any money on the junkyard, he knew

she maintained the place as a testimonial to her father, a living museum in his honor. "You may not have a choice," he said. "Junkyards are being forced to close all over the country."

She tossed her head the way an upset horse might, her mane of hair swishing from one side to the other. "Leroy warned me some of the people moving in might try to zone me out of business, but . . ."

"Leroy would say anything to get you to sell him more land."

He hadn't realized how vehemently he'd spoken, how angry he was, until he saw Rita tilt her head, narrowing her eyes, as though to peer inside his mind, seeking the information he was withholding. "Don't give me that look," he told her. "You know it's true."

"It doesn't matter. They're not going to force me off my land. I was here before any of them were."

Parker doubted historical precedence would grant them a right to stay in business. He gazed across the junkyard, watching as Ramón carefully cut around the gas tank, avoiding an explosion. Other than Parker, he was the only one Rita let get near a fuel line with a torch. Modern junkyards touted themselves as recycling centers, but in reality, they were all land mines, seeping lethal chemicals into the soil. People routinely had them condemned as environmental hazards. It was just a matter of time before they were forced to close the place. "What if somebody paid you to get rid of the junkyard?"

Rita snorted. "If a frog had wings, it wouldn't bump its butt on the ground."

"Sometimes frogs turn out to be princes."

Before he could say more, she lifted her chin, pointing it at him. "I see you got your gloves with you. Planning on pulling a piece?"

Parker looked down at the gloves in his hand. Art was to him what the land was to her—a sanctity. His mother might outwardly appear a Catholic, but Parker knew her to be a true pagan. Nature was her religion, and walks her prayers. For years, she'd wandered freely over this land. How could he tell her that soon a gated community would sit across the road from them? She would feel caged.

"I'm thinking of doing a nude," he said.

"Really?" Her eyes sparked with interest. "When you say *a nude*, do you mean a naked woman?"

"Naked as any seductress can be when she's made out of a Buick bumper."

Rita picked up the mirror Ramón had left on the hood of the car. She twirled it in her hand a moment, looking at Parker thoughtfully, then raised the mirror in front of him, the sun glinting off his reflection. "You'd be as hard-pressed as Ramón if I had to shut this place down."

Confronted with the sight of the stubble on his face and his uncombed hair, Parker snatched the mirror out of Rita's hand. In that instant, though, he also caught a vision of yet another sculpture. A child with a mirror for a face. His mind scrambling to make the vision more concrete, he stood up, staring unseeingly across the junkyard, until he noticed Ramón beckoning to him, gesturing for help with dragging the tail end of the Impala over to his truck.

Parker didn't want to admit it, but his mother was right. Just as Ramón depended on the junkyard for parts, he needed it for the visions it inspired.

|| **RITA** || With one foot on the porch floor, Rita kept the hammock swaying back and forth as she read a novel about a young widow struggling to run a farm in the Appalachians. Looking up from the book, she stared out beyond her yard with its lilac bushes long past blooming and the penstemons only now beginning to open, on over toward the Sangre de Cristos, which had already lost what little snow the winter had brought. Her mind roamed the land while, at the same time, seeing the characters in the novel. Though not a widow, she knew what it was to feel totally alone. Men had from time to time taken up space in her life, mostly in her bed, and occasionally to go out dancing, or sit in the kitchen, talking into the late hours of the night. A few had even wanted to live with her, but none had provided the closeness she longed for. Friendships had eluded her, and books only went so far toward filling up empty afternoons when it was too hot to weld and she had nothing else to keep her company.

At the sound of an approaching vehicle, Rita set aside the book, grateful for the interruption. Except for her dogs, she hadn't spoken to a soul all day. The white truck, however, passed her driveway and pulled onto the land across the road. Annoyed to think it was a couple of target shooters, she watched as two men got out of the truck, went around to the back, and removed surveying equipment.

"No!" she shouted.

Neither man heard her. One proceeded to set up a tripod, while the other counted paces, measuring off feet as he walked east.

Rita sprung out of the hammock, her book falling onto the porch. So this was what had prompted Leroy's visit last week! Obviously he'd known somebody was planning on building over there and had hoped to con her out of more land before she learned of its increased value.

She charged down the steps, Flojo and Loca at her heels. Sensing her agitation, the black Lab charged ahead, the Lhasa apso scrambling to keep up with him. They tore through the scattered penstemons, past the front hedge of lilacs, on across the dirt road, barking at the surveyor by the truck.

"Whoa, lady, call off the dogs!" The man picked up his tripod and held it in front of him, the skinny metal legs an inadequate shield. Although Rita guessed him to be in his late twenties, the red splotches of fear on his pale cheeks made him look all of fifteen.

"They won't hurt you." She snapped her fingers and both dogs sat at her heels.

The other man, a little younger and a lot more assured, came forward, pointing at the tripod and laughing. "Put down your weapon, Hank." He knelt in front of the dogs and roughed them behind the ears. "If it isn't Beauty and the Beast. My little girl would get a kick out of these two."

His ease with the dogs deflated Rita's anger. After all, these men hadn't bought the land; they were simply staking off the perimeters for somebody else. Maybe it wasn't even a done deal yet. Maybe the owner wanted to put the property on the market, and nobody would buy it because of the junkyard.

"You're Parker Vargas's mom, aren't you?" The man at her feet stood up and held out his hand. "Frankie Tapia. Me and Parker had a welding class together at Santa Fe High."

It wasn't a name she remembered Parker mentioning, but she shook his hand, liking his open smile. Compact and slightly bowlegged, he had a self-satisfied manner, without the false swagger common in so many young men. "So what're you doing out here?" she asked.

"Trying to get a job done," the other man said, pointing at the truck with his tripod. A sign on the door designated them as part of Tierra Survey Co.

Frankie bent down to reach under a piñon. Pulling out two sticks, he whistled and threw them. He watched as the dogs ran after the sticks, laughing when they veered in the opposite direction to chase a startled jackrabbit. As the dogs disappeared into the distance, he sighed. "I hate to see this place get built up. My brothers come target shooting out here. They're going to be pissed when they find out they can't."

Rita wouldn't miss the sound of bullets or the threat of being accidentally shot while out walking. The absence of target shooters, though, meant the arrival of houses. "So somebody bought this land?"

Hank had finally come out from behind the tripod. Reaching through the open truck window, he grabbed a clipboard off the dashboard and read the worksheet to her. "Drew Stinson, Developer." Adjusting the baseball cap that sat backward on his head, he added, "Supposed to be six hundred and forty acres."

"A square mile," Rita said. "Just like what my grandparents had before they divided it between their two sons." She peered toward the Sangre de Cristos, trying to remember if her grandparents had ever mentioned who'd lived here before. During her many walks over the land, she'd never come across signs of an old homestead. What she had found was enough prickly pears to make several jars of jam, a clump of evening primrose, an enormous piñon entwined with a juniper, like lovers embracing on a hilltop, an occasional condom, bullet casings, broken beer bottles, and busted bags of rotting trash. Despite the litter, the place had beauty, rising higher than her own land, rolling toward the mountains like waves toward the sun.

Often, when she set off on her walks, she'd head over here, the distant peaks calling her. Both her bedroom and living room windows looked out this way, affording her a view of open countryside, countryside that all too soon would give way to houses, marching toward her like tanks.

Hank set up his tripod again, and Frankie gave her an apologetic look. "The town keeps getting bigger and bigger. It's like there's no place left for us to go."

"Do you have any idea," she asked, "how many houses they're planning on building?"

"He's dividing it into three-acre lots."

Quick to do the math, her voice croaked, jammed in her throat. "Two hundred and thirteen houses!"

Frankie extended his hand, palm turned down, as he might do to calm a snarling dog. "Nowhere near that many. Lot of the land is unbuildable, so this guy's designing it for folks with horses."

She'd seen it elsewhere. People working in town and living out in the country on a piece of property just big enough to include a horse corral, but little else. "Everybody wants to be a cowboy, but without the cows."

"Yeah, my wife does mortgages at the bank and she calls these kind of places ranchettes."

"Ranchettes," Rita repeated the word, picturing individual horses penned up here and there, a chain of fences stretching across the land, closing her out. "I used to think the junkyard would prevent anybody from wanting this property."

"Not many places left to build if you want a large lot. And you can't beat that view," Frankie said, gesturing toward the mountains.

"Yeah, but anytime they watch the sun go down, they're going to have to look over at my pile of junk. And they're not going to like that."

"Shit out of luck. Excuse my language, but that's what I'd tell them. They don't like your place, they don't have to live here."

Rita wished it was as simple as he made it sound, but she suspected Leroy was right, that these people would find a way to put her out of business. "I should let you get to work," she said to Frankie. "Will I be in the way if I take a walk out here?"

"Better do it now, while you still can. Before they start putting up their No Trespassing signs."

Tears swam in her eyes, giving everything the blurred appearance of being underwater. She called out for the dogs, who came with the quickness of endless affection, panting with excitement and thirst in the heat of the day. It was her least favorite time to walk, when the sun bleached the color out of everything. But it was useless to attempt to do anything else. She was too agitated to sit still and too preoccupied to weld. Her feet would find the way, carrying her over the land, calming her soul.

But it didn't work. She couldn't pass by a flat spot without imagining a house and a corral. All too soon, the dull afternoons she had lamented would fill with racket. People would come and go, driving up and down the road, with visitors arriving at all times of the day, shattering the quiet and offering little, if anything, in the way of companionship.

|| **JOE** || After running the roller down the last strip of unpainted wall in Mrs. Padilla's living room, Joe glanced over at Chloe, who hummed as she finished the brushwork on the windowsill. A headband lifted her hair away from her face, highlighting the curve of her cheekbones and the long lines of her neck. At moments like these, when he stood back observing her, he couldn't believe his fortune. Like the tide, she had swept into his life, lifting him on a wave of happiness.

"Hey, you," she said. "You're supposed to be working, not daydreaming."

"I was taking an appreciation break." It was what he tended to say whenever she caught him staring at her, never admitting that he feared the day the tide ebbed and she drifted away from him. Instead, he behaved like a photographer, taking mental snapshots of her beauty, framing the moments he had with her. "Standing there, with the light in your hair, you're absolutely radiant."

She turned away to look out the window, as though he'd praised not her, but the sunlight. "It's a gorgeous day, isn't it?"

The front door stood open, letting in the sound of two girls giggling as they rollerbladed past the house. It was the kind of weather that drew people outdoors, and he felt guilty about Chloe spending the day inside helping him. "You should have gone hiking," he said, secretly glad she hadn't spent the day with her friend Lacy, a woman who flirted with men the way cats played with mice, amused to see them suffer. Lacy was the kind to encourage Chloe to drop him.

"Lacy and I can go hiking next week." An impish smile on her face, Chloe sashayed over to him, the paintbrush still in her hand. "No way I would have passed up this opportunity. It's the closest I'll ever come to being a painter." She touched his nose with the tip of her paintbrush, then kissed him.

Her mouth tasted of the strawberries they'd eaten earlier. He wanted to go on kissing her but broke away when he heard a truck pulling into the gravel driveway. "Sounds like the landscaper finally showed up."

The unreliability of Santa Fe workmen irritated him. The renovation was taking way too long. Instead of painting, he should have been renting the place by now. If only he hadn't let the contractor talk him into replacing all the windows. Yet, as he turned to glance out the front, he had to admit the clear glass was a vast improvement over the old streaked panes. New windows and fresh stucco definitely made the house more suitable for the high-rent market. But it had cost him far more than he'd intended to spend. And then the landscaper, the cheapest he could find, kept delaying the coyote fence. "I was about ready to give up on you," Joe said, as the screen door opened.

But it was Leroy Sena, not the landscaper, who stepped inside.

"Looking good." Leroy gave a whistle of approval. His eyes took in Chloe, and Joe's grip tightened on the paint roller until Leroy finally moved his gaze around the rest of the room. "Man, I never would've thought these old wood floors could get that kind of shine."

Chloe laid her arm across Joe's back, enfolding him in her warmth. "Joe has a knack for bringing out the beauty of a place."

"He definitely knows how to find pretty assistants." Leroy extended a hand toward Chloe, oblivious to how his words had made her dig her fingernails into Joe's shoulder. She ignored Leroy's waiting hand, her one holding a paintbrush and the other remaining on Joe's shoulder.

Awkwardly, Leroy let his hand fall back to his hip, rubbing his palm, unsure how he had dirtied it.

"Leroy, this is Chloe. She owns the New Visions art gallery."

"Where I sell paintings. It's only in my free time that I paint houses."

Not one to wallow in a faux pas, Leroy strolled over to the kiva fireplace, where he propped his forearm on the mantel. "Have to say, you've done a fine job on this place. It's an asset to the whole neighborhood."

"So what brings you by?" Joe asked.

The question seemed to discomfit Leroy. He leaned down and picked a piece of invisible lint off of his slacks. Then he looked back up and flashed his crooked grin. "Heard you've already got renters lined up for next week. Wondered if you'd like to look at the house of another one of my mom's friends. Guy needs to be in an old folks' home. He'll let the place go real cheap."

Leroy acted so friendly, but his underlying motives gave Joe the creeps. It was as though he couldn't wait to hustle his mother's friend into a nursing home so he could profit from the man's demise.

"I thought land was your thing, not houses."

Shrugging, Leroy gave another one of his ingenuous smiles. He had an overlapping front tooth that buckled his lip with a simple charm. "You know my mom. Always conning people into doing favors for her."

Although Chloe hadn't left his side, Joe felt her restlessness. They had hoped to finish painting in time to go horseback riding.

"I've got all I can handle with this house, Leroy."

Nodding his head, Leroy continued to stand by the fireplace. Joe could almost see his mind searching for another tactic. "You're right," Leroy finally said. "Land is my thing. Let me know when the two of you are ready to build a house, and I'll get you a deal on a great piece of property."

Joe didn't know if it was because Chloe's hand had remained on his shoulder all that time, but Leroy addressed them as a couple, assuming they would have a home together. Joe would have liked nothing better, but the one time he'd broached the idea with Chloe, she'd come up with excuses for them to maintain separate residences. Yet now her fingers lightly stroked his ear, as though encouraging him to listen to Leroy.

"On the whole, Joe and I tend to prefer old houses, but I'd love to have a piece of land. Someplace where I could keep my horse."

Leroy actually rubbed his hands together, as though it were a done deal. "I have some terrific places I could show you."

"Any with an old adobe house we could remodel?" Chloe asked. Joe couldn't believe her, stringing Leroy along, playing him like a fish on a line, as though seriously considering his proposal.

Leroy, of course, held on, taking it as far as he could go. "Plenty of crumbling adobes around, but they're usually either huge ranches or sitting on ugly property. And what's the point? I mean, why do all that work on an old place instead of having one custom built?"

"Renovation is nothing," Joe said, "compared to the work involved in building a new house."

"Yeah, but the advantage is you could design a house just the way you want it. And the properties you could choose from!" Leroy shook his head, as though overwhelmed by the choices. He directed his gaze at Chloe. "You say you want to keep your horse on the property? I've got places where you could ride like the wind. Land you'd want to live on forever."

Chloe whirled around to face Joe, her hair swirling past her headband, rimming her face in a cloud of golden fluff. "It could be fun to build our own place, couldn't it?"

She held the paintbrush in the air, as if she were about to paint a picture of the ideal life. A painting with a horse, a house, the two of them, and maybe even a couple of children. The image dazzled him. He had to remind himself how quickly she could seize hold of an impulse, and then, just as suddenly, abandon it. She would rush ahead impetuously and he would follow, enthralled by her enthusiasm, only to have her abruptly turn in the opposite direction.

"It'd be expensive," he reminded her.

She dabbed his nose again with the paintbrush. "Lighten up! What do you think banks are for?" She spun around to face Leroy, clasping Joe's free hand around her waist. "Wednesdays are the only day I can get away from the gallery. Can you show us some property next week?"

"Let me check," Leroy said, reaching into his back pocket and pulling out a day planner. Joe suspected he took longer than necessary to look over his calendar, wanting to give the impression he was a very busy man. "How about ten o'clock?"

Chloe shook her head. "I promised a friend I'd go hiking with her in the morning. How does four look?"

Leroy ran his finger down the page, as though working his way through a list of obligations. "Let's say four-thirty." Having learned from his earlier mistake, he made a point of handing his card to Chloe. "Why don't the two of you meet me at my office, and we'll take off from there? I already have a place in mind for you."

"Can't be too pricey," Joe said.

"Don't worry. I've got lots you can afford." He addressed Joe, but winked at Chloe. "See you both next week." Whistling, he walked away from them, the screen door swinging back and forth behind him a couple of times before settling shut.

Chloe leaned her head back against Joe's chest, her cheek alongside his chin. "Wonder what he'll find for us."

Joe lowered his nose to her neck, seeking her lavender scent beneath the paint fumes that had made him lightheaded. "Think you're really ready for us to buy a house?" he asked, his lips brushing her ear.

She rubbed her face against his chin, then turned around within the circle of his arm. "I didn't know I was until Leroy suggested it." With a light laugh, she stepped back. "A true salesman if there ever was one."

Joe chewed on the inside of his cheek, his teeth mashing the pulpy skin. He should have known better than to trust one of her whims. For a moment she had succumbed to Leroy's persuasiveness, but she would never carry through with the idea. Sharing a mortgage would mean giving up too much of her freedom.

Chloe reached over and stroked his cheek, putting a stop to his nervous habit. "Leroy's right, though. It's time we had a place together."

"You didn't use to think so."

She made an arc in the air with the paintbrush like a rainbow spanning the room. "Something about this place brought it home to me. Back when you were still uncertain whether to buy it and you invited me over. I remember walking through these rooms, seeing the garden, thinking of the woman you said had lived here from the time she got married until she died. That's when I realized I wanted us to be brave enough to try to make a go of it. To quit holding our distance because we're afraid of being hurt like we were in the past."

Joe wanted to be brave, to believe again in love that lasted forever, but his ex-wife's face reappeared in his mind telling him she was leaving him for another man. "Maybe we should just move into this place. See how we do."

"It's too small, Joe. It would be like saying we didn't dare hope for anything bigger from life."

Joe twirled the paint roller, the paint long since dried up on it. Sharon had nearly bankrupted him when she left. It scared him to think of going deeply into debt for something that might ultimately fail to keep Chloe in his life.

"We have to be willing to take a chance, Joe."

He thought back to the day she had first seen this house, recalling the wistful expression on her face, the longing he had sensed in her but couldn't identify. Chloe waited for him to speak. He noted the tenseness in her shoulders, the way they had tightened like a harness. There she was, asking him to do the very thing he had wanted her to do—make a deeper commitment to their relationship—and he hesitated.

"You really think there's a bank out there that'll give us a big enough loan to make us landed gentry?" he asked.

"Small-time landed gentry, but, yeah, I think somebody will give us a line of credit."

His arm had begun to ache from holding the paint roller. He went over to the other side of the room and laid it in the tray. Then he crossed back to Chloe and cupped his hands under her elbows, anchoring her in his palms. "So you really want us to buy a house together?" he asked.

Solemnly, she nodded her head. He sometimes teased her about her Midwestern earnestness, yet it was part of what he loved about her. "Looks like your roots have come back to claim you," he said. "Abandoning the big city life of downtown Santa Fe to live in the country."

Chloe pressed her forehead against his, rubbing noses with him. "You mind?"

Her reluctance to ask for more than he could give provided the faith he needed. "You're the woman I love. How could I mind?"

"I mean do you mind that living in the country might mean building a new house instead of fixing up an old one?"

"You're asking a would-be architect if he'd mind designing his own home?"

"You sure?" She pulled back, the question hovering on her lips.

Joe bent to kiss away the doubts. Sharon had never cared what he wanted; she'd bulldozed ahead with her own plans, regardless of his needs. "I can't think of anything I'd rather do than live with you in a home we'd built together."

Chloe sighed. "Maybe Leroy can find us a piece of land with a view from here to eternity."

|| **RITA** || Rita lay in bed the morning of her uncle's auction, the day when he would relinquish the last vestiges of ever having ranched. He'd sold the cattle earlier in the year, shortly after his heart attack, but he'd held onto the equipment. The empty calving pens and waterless troughs lent the land a ghostly appearance. All of it would disappear today, leaving little sign the Vargases had run cattle on their property for close to a century. Carlos and his wife would remain as long as their health allowed, but Rita knew it was just a matter of time before their children sold the land. And then she would be surrounded by houses on three sides, only the ridgetop to the north preventing her from being completely boxed in.

"Stop feeling sorry for yourself," she commanded aloud, forcing herself out of bed. It was getting late, and if she wanted to walk, she needed to hurry. Overdue to wash laundry, she had to resort to a fancy black lace bra and matching panties, remnants of her last romance. If she ended up in the emergency room, the incongruity of her undergarments would come as a surprise to the medical staff. She pulled on yesterday's jeans, a faded Cowgirl Hall of Fame T-shirt, and red hightop tennies that had turned rosy brown from walking the land. Quickly brushing her teeth, she saw that an uneasy night's sleep had tangled her long hair. Too hurried to comb through the snarls, she pulled it back into a ponytail. There wouldn't be anybody at the auction but a bunch of ranchers, men dulled by work and too worn-out around the edges to interest her.

Grabbing a banana, she went out the back door, Flojo and Loca right behind her. They had made this walk numerous times, down the driveway that led past the junkyard, around the hill that hid Parker's trailer, and west to the house her grandparents had built when their family outgrew the one where Rita now lived. Her father used to say his truck knew the way by heart, so often had he driven it, particularly after his wife ran off, leaving him with an infant to raise on his own.

Now she was the one to travel the road regularly, pounding out by foot what everybody else tended to drive. That morning she walked it at a particularly fast pace, upset at the thought of eventually losing her uncle's home as a destination. She had almost no photographs of her grandparents, but she viewed the land like a family album, something treasured over the years and passed down through the generations. Unfortunately, three of Carlos's sons had professional jobs elsewhere and would just as soon sell the place. And Alejandro, who would love to live there, couldn't afford to buy out his brothers.

Rita arrived at the ranch slightly short of breath, the dogs racing toward the water bowls on the porch. Several pickup trucks already sat in the yard, men shaking hands and ambling off to check out the equipment, five or six of them clustering around the hay baler.

"There you are," Elaine said, the porch door banging shut behind her. "Just called over to your place to see what was holding you up." Years of working outdoors had hardened her aunt's face, and her bristly iron-gray hair did nothing to soften it.

"Looks like plenty of buyers," Rita said, having long ago learned to ignore Elaine's seemingly critical remarks. Her words might sting, but with one exception, she had always been good to Rita.

"We'll find out how much buying they do, or if they're only here to gawk." Elaine trotted down the steps. "Come see El Rey. I've got him where he's not spooking so much."

Sensing that the invitation was for more than looking at a horse, Rita followed her aunt through the corral and into the hay-scented stables. They stopped at the stall of a chestnut stallion, and Elaine reached up to stroke the horse's nose. "See how much calmer he is?" El Rey reared back and Elaine tugged on the halter, bringing his face close to hers, soothing him with softly spoken endearments. Then, as though still talking to the horse, she said, "Leroy Sena was out here yesterday."

"Yeah, he was out at my place a couple of weeks ago."

"Man's like a water witch, but with a nose for land. He wants the far pasture."

As though El Rey had kicked her, the news knocked the air out of Rita, leaving a sharp pain in her chest. Although she had braced herself for the fact that eventually the ranch would go, she hadn't expected it to happen before her uncle died. Like a prisoner thrown into a small cell, she began to pace, walking over to the bushel basket by the tack room, bringing back an apple for El Rey, then returning to the tack room and taking down a currycomb, only to rehang it, looking up to find her aunt watching. "He wants the pasture by the BLM land?"

Elaine nodded. "Says people will pay a lot to have their house next to a greenbelt."

"That's Leroy for you," Rita said, her voice a high pitch that made El Rey prick his ears and toss his head nervously. "He'll find an angle to sell anything."

"You wouldn't believe how much he offered."

"An honest realtor would offer you even more." She hated the idea of them selling any of their land, but if they were going to do it, she'd just as soon they got a high price for it. At least it was the far pasture, at the westernmost end of their property. But it was all happening too quickly. Houses were going up around her faster than she could keep track. This must be what it felt like to live in a country undergoing an invasion, besieged by the enemy, the troops drawing a stranglehold around you.

"Elaine, old girl!" A loud voice shot through the stables, causing El Rey to snort and paw at the ground. "What's this I hear about you buying a Spanish Barb?"

At first, Rita could see nothing but a silhouette of a short man in a cowboy hat. But as he drew closer, the hat came off, and a red-haired man held out his hand. "Pat Archuleta," he said. "My wife and I run into Elaine all the time at horse shows."

"You here to talk horses, or buy equipment?"

"Órale, Elaine. Can't a man do both?"

Rita immediately liked Pat for his ability to roll with her aunt's brusqueness. Maybe it came easier to ranchers, people accustomed to those who used words minimally. As the two of them began to discuss horses, Rita excused herself.

When she left the stable and walked out into the bright sun, she blinked, squinting at the sight of yet another short, red-haired man. This one leaned against the corral fence talking to Elaine's old pinto. He wore jeans, but with a silver ranger set rather than the plain belt adorned by a big buckle that most ranchers favored. The rolled-back sleeves of his denim shirt revealed arms lacking the nicks and scars of outdoor work. A small gathering of freckles skipped along the top of his cheeks and over his nose. Oblivious to her presence, he kept murmuring to the horse.

"Rita," her uncle called out to her from the group of men by the hay baler. She waved, and Carlos walked toward her with the gait of a robust man. Nobody meeting him for the first time would guess he'd had triple bypass surgery last winter. He clasped her hands, swinging them lightly in his, the texture of his skin as worn and crinkled as a pair of old leather gloves. "This is the day," he said merrily. Her uncle had worked hard all his life, but his eyes held the twinkle of somebody who'd found joy despite adversity. "After this I can officially say I'm no longer a rancher, but a farmer."

"Speaking of which, how are those exotic eggplants doing?" Although she teased him about raising designer vegetables, it awed her how casually he'd set aside years of ranching, work she knew he'd loved.

"Helluva a lot easier than cows. Vegetables don't talk back." He laughed, clearly pleased to have this second lease on life.

"Carlos!" From behind her boomed a voice she instantly recognized as Pat Archuleta's. "What's this I hear about you selling your best pasture?"

Her uncle rolled his lower lip between his teeth and gave her an apologetic look. "It's not a done deal yet."

"It's okay, Tío," she said. "You need to take care of yourself, not me."

"Escúchame," Pat bellowed, coming between them. "I want you to sell that land to me so I can get the BLM grazing rights."

"Hell, Pat, I didn't even know you were interested."

"You bet I'm interested. That's prime rangeland you've got."

If Pat bought the land for grazing, it wouldn't be developed. For a moment Rita got excited, then she realized no matter how low a price Leroy had offered, it was more than any rancher could afford. Cows didn't make the kind of money yuppies did.

Carlos propped a foot on the corral fence, and gnawed on his lip as he looked off in the direction of the far pasture. "It's good grazing land all right. Thing is, no rancher can pay me what this guy can." He turned around and gave Rita a wink. "But I'd much rather see cows out there than houses."

"Maybe you ought to consider a conservation easement," said the red-haired man on the opposite side of the corral gate, moving away from the horse to join them.

Pat punched him lightly in the shoulder. "How many times I gotta tell you, Miguel? Folks around here can't afford your environmental crap."

The man held out a hand to Carlos. "Miguel Archuleta. Pat's politically incorrect brother."

Rita heard sadness beneath his joke. His eyes held a longing for something that didn't exist.

"You the lawyer he was telling me about?" Elaine asked, walking up behind them.

Miguel looked at Elaine, a wry smile tugging at the corner of his lips. "If he told you about a city slicker who can keep your land from being developed, then yeah, that's me."

"How can you keep the land from being developed?" Rita asked.

Carlos put his arm around her. "Miguel, this is my niece, Rita. She's got a new housing project going in across the road from her."

"You somebody else who'd rather see cows than houses?"

His words carried a mix of the northern New Mexico lilt and an educated refinement. He stood only an inch or two above her, his eyes taking in her measurements too, and she wished she'd taken time to comb her hair. "I'd like to keep the land as free of people as possible."

"You don't like people?"

She bristled at the teasing tone in his voice. "I find a lot of people obnoxious."

"A lot, as in lots of people are obnoxious, or you find it obnoxious to have lots of people around you?"

"Lawyers! That's who I find the most obnoxious. The way they dissect a person's words until there's nothing left but a mutilated corpse."

Pat roared, his laugh as loud as his voice. "She nailed you, Miguel!"

He thumped his brother on the back. Then he touched the brim of his cowboy hat, tipping it to her uncle in a gesture of respect. "Carlos, I can't give you top dollar, but I can give you a fair price for that pasture. What do you say?"

Carlos shoved his hands into his back pockets, his elbows sticking out like sharp signposts. "I don't want nobody out there running lawn mowers, that's for sure. I'd give it to another rancher before I'd sell to a developer."

"Now we're talking," Pat said with a big grin.

Miguel held up his index finger, as he might when addressing a jury. "What's to keep Pat from turning around and selling to a developer further down the line and making a big profit?"

"Shit, bro. You know me better than that."

"I do. But do these people?" Miguel moved his cupped hand in the air, indicating Carlos and Elaine. "How do they know you won't decide you need the money?"

"They've got my word."

The credibility of somebody's spoken word obviously didn't amount to much for Miguel, a man who made his living twisting words into new meanings. Rita saw the scorn on his face, the scorn of somebody who'd long ago lost the notion of trust.

"Te creo, Patricio," Carlos said. "I know you've got ranching in your blood, just like me, and you'll work the land until you can't." He took his hands out of his back pockets, hitching up his jeans as he did so. "I looked into one of them conservation easements," he said, turning to Miguel. "Don't do me no good. Means our kids can't sell the place after we're gone."

"That's the whole point. It protects the land well into the future."

Elaine stubbed a cigarette out on the corral fence, the smoldering butt creating yet another black mark among the multitudes she'd previously left on the wood. "We didn't work all these years for nothing. We want our sons to have the money."

Carlos rubbed a thumb over the arthritic knuckles of his gnarled right hand. "Nobody wants to ranch no more. Work's too hard. Your brother's the last of a dying breed."

At that point, the auctioneer, a professional out of Durango, came over and asked if they could get started. He'd listed the sale on the Internet, and Rita saw license plates from Colorado, Oklahoma, Arizona, and Texas in the yard. Ranchers might be disappearing, but those remaining banded together. She respected them and their families. There was an honesty in their way of life missing in most people's work.

As Rita followed her uncle and the auctioneer across the yard, Elaine came up beside her and snarled, "You know he's only selling to Pat because of you."

Rita's back stiffened, but she ignored the pain, reminding herself that her aunt lashed out when threatened. Nine years ago she had kept her husband from helping Rita when she most needed it, stopped him from loaning her money, thus forcing her to sell the ridgetop. But Elaine had held him back out of fear, not anger. She had worried that Rita would come to depend on them too much. It had taken Rita years to understand that. She stopped walking and looked into the fading blue of her aunt's eyes and saw a woman trying desperately to hold on to what she loved. "I think he's doing it for all of us. Not just for me, but for you, your sons, your grandkids, and for himself. It's a chance to pretend the land is still ours before we lose it completely."

|| **JOE** || "Where in the world are you taking us, Leroy?" Joe leaned forward, thrusting his head between Leroy and Chloe, who sat in the front seat of the Land Rover. Having already shown them property in Tesuque that they couldn't afford, Leroy was now driving west of town, raving about how they were going to love some new place specially developed for equestrians. "You didn't tell us it was across the road from a junkyard!"

"Relax. In no time, that place will be gone." Leroy whisked a hand in the air, like a magician who could make the whole mess disappear.

Joe looked out the window at row after row of mangled vehicles. "What are we supposed to do? Pretend it's not there? Shoot, I didn't know there were enough people living in the entire state of New Mexico to pile up that much junk."

"For some reason, junkyards have always fascinated me," Chloe said. "I used to visit one with Daddy. The owner would let me ride with him on the front-end loader. It had a forklift that could turn over a truck. I loved it!"

"Yeah, but you wouldn't want to look at one every day."

Chloe shrugged. "I don't know that it would bother me."

Lifting his head, Leroy caught Joe's eye in the rearview mirror. "Like I said, you don't have to worry. The developer is going to pay to get rid of it." The words rankled Chloe. Joe could see it in the way her eyebrows drew together, but before she could say anything, Leroy pulled off the road. Leaving the junkyard behind them, he parked facing the Sangre de Cristos. "How's that for a spectacular view?"

Not waiting for an answer, he opened his door and urged them out of the car. A pending thunderstorm charged the air with electricity. Joe paused to take in the smell, admiring the deep emerald of the piñons and junipers against the dark sky. Having grown up in the East with big leafy maples, he craved the sight of trees. Earlier, Leroy had suggested a piece of property south of town, but Joe had immediately nixed the idea, disliking the area's flat, treeless plains. This spot, though, had what he loved about northern New Mexico's land-scape—soft hills jeweled with greenery.

"This is gorgeous," Chloe said. Just then the sun broke through a spot in the clouds and streamed down on the land in front of them. "If I were a mystic, I'd say the heavens were telling us this is the place." She clasped a hand over her mouth, laughing at herself. Shaking her head, she said, "But I'm just a woman who loves beautiful things and I sure wouldn't mind owning a piece of this."

"You're the first people I've brought here. It's not even officially on the market yet."

Joe had participated in too many real estate deals to fall for Leroy's pitch of exclusivity, but he liked the idea that they could choose any site they wanted. One hill to the south particularly drew his eye, the way it resembled a reposing elephant. He hadn't expected to respond so well to the idea of living out in the countryside, but as his eyes traveled over the open sweep of land, his mind quieted. In town, he felt energized, but never at rest. Much as he loved the constant buzz, it also drained him. Here he could retreat, take time to slow down, recharge.

"It'd be an incredible area to ride," Chloe said. She grinned at Joe. "You might even have to get a horse."

"We'll see," he said, unconvinced. Horses drew flies and dropped shit. He really preferred not to have one close to his house. Fortunately, Leroy had said they would have the option of boarding Chloe's horse at a central stable. "Where's that stable going to be?"

Leroy indicated a dip in the land where the hills seemed to gather in a circle. "Right over there with trails taking off in all directions. Only for residents and their guests. That's the best part. This is going to be a gated community."

Leroy thought he was making a strong selling point, but Joe knew he had just killed Chloe's interest. She might openly confess to being a materialist, but she abhorred the idea of gated communities. As somebody who, as she put it, had pulled herself up by her high heels, she hated anything deliberately intended to exclude people. He saw her mouth scrunch up, ready to insist they look elsewhere. With her hands on her hips, she scowled, but then her attention shifted, and she tilted her head, staring at something behind Leroy. She pointed at a ridgeline in the distance. "Who owns that?"

Leroy turned around to see where she pointed. "That hill?" He threw his shoulders back, and Joe half expected him to imitate a rooster's proud call. "Interestingly enough, I do. It's too steep to build on this side, but I can drive you around to the other side and show you the one lot that's left. Terrific spot, has the . . ."

"I don't want to live on the other side; I want to live on top."

Leroy's mouth churned, making a couple of complete circles. "I can understand the attraction," he said. His lips scrunched and churned again. "Problem is, there's no place to ride horses."

"Bet I could arrange to board down here. I could even jog down, it's so close."

"Must have incredible views," Joe said. "But it doesn't look wide enough to support a house."

Leroy pulled out a pack of gum and offered it to each of them before sticking a piece in his mouth. "It's deceptive from this side. You could actually put four houses in a row up there. Help diffuse the cost."

"A developer might, but that's not what I do."

Leroy squinted his eyes, as though calculating Joe's capabilities. "You said you didn't do vacation rentals either, and I hear you've already got clients lined up for the next three months in old Mrs. Padilla's place."

Santa Fe was a small town, but it still amazed Joe how quickly news spread. "Beginner's luck," he said. "Things will slow down in January."

"Depends how good of a ski year we get. You fixed that house up classy enough, you should be able to rent it year round."

"Joe's the best," Chloe said, reaching across to stroke his cheek. Her eyes briefly tangoed with his, before turning back to Leroy. "What is it you're suggesting he do with that hill?"

Though the sun had again disappeared behind the gathering clouds, Leroy took a pair of sunglasses from his shirt pocket and put them on. Then he pointed at the eastern end of the ridgetop and slowly ran his finger westward through the air. "A premium spot like that will sell for top dollar. To pay for it, you'd probably want to put in three more houses, with yours sitting at the western end."

Chloe's eyes followed Leroy's hand as it traversed the ridgetop, her tongue duplicating the move across her lower lip. Whenever she concentrated fully on something, that tongue of hers would work its way out of her mouth. Normally Joe found it an endearing habit, but today it irritated him. She was being childish, succumbing to Leroy's ploys as easily as a kid watching a TV commercial for the latest fad toy, clambering for something she hadn't even known she wanted.

When she looked back at Joe, she had the flushed cheeks of somebody high. "It'd be the best of both worlds. We'd live in the middle of all this beauty without being totally isolated."

"That's right," Leroy said. "You'd have neighbors without being hemmed in like you are in town. All it takes is a little ingenuity."

"Ingenuity I've got, but I don't gamble with high stakes. There's too big a risk of getting stuck with three lots nobody wants to buy."

Giving his gum an extra loud snap, Leroy started to say something, but Chloe spoke first. "Let's go take a look at it before you say no. If it's as amazing as I think it is, we'll have an easy time selling the rest of the property."

It was her use of the word "we" that led Joe to reconsider the idea. Chloe had an instinctual feel for what sold well. If she thought the ridgetop had the potential to attract buyers, maybe they could swing it after all.

Leroy herded them back into his car, talking about the advantages of the ridgetop's location. "Just a hop and skip into town, yet you're living in complete tranquility."

Chloe turned around in her seat to face Joe. "Just think what it would be like to live up there. We'd see the sun as it rose in the morning and then watch it set again in the evening, with the mountains all around, embracing us."

The rapture on her face seduced Joe. What was a little debt compared to the immense happiness she brought him?

Leroy drove back toward town and then north to the other side of the ridge, where an affluent neighborhood lay at its base with half a dozen houses scattered on the hillside itself. As they ascended past the last house, with no road ahead of them, Leroy switched to four-wheel drive and proceeded overland. He patted his dashboard. "Best realtors have SUVs so they can take their clients to the prettiest properties." The light-handed remark couldn't cover the fact that building on the ridge would entail the additional expense of putting in a road. Joe had no idea how much that would cost, but he would definitely have to find out before he gave the place further consideration.

The Land Rover groaned as it struggled up the steep incline. When they reached the top, Joe and Chloe simultaneously gasped. It was far more stupendous than anything Joe had imagined. Outside the car, they held hands, speechless, as they took in the 360-degree views. The town of Santa Fe nestled slightly south of them, with the Ortiz Mountains and the Turquoise Hills in the distance. "You can see all the way to the Sandias in Albuquerque," Chloe marveled.

Joe hadn't wanted to be smitten, had hoped something would detract from the hill's magnetism, but as they stood there, he knew this was where he wanted to live for the rest of his life.

Chloe hooked her arm in his as they walked away from Leroy. "I had thought I wanted a big piece of land so I could have Speedo with me," she said. "But now that I've seen this, I don't need to see anything else." She stopped and looked at him, a seriousness deepening the brown depths of her eyes, pulling him toward her. "I want us to make a home for ourselves here."

On the drive up the hill, she had asked Leroy which school the kids in the area went to, murmuring that the one he named was the best in town. They had never broached the subject of having a family. Joe knew Chloe liked kids; she couldn't meet one without engaging the child in play, but she had also made the gallery's success a priority in her life. Whereas he couldn't even pass by a kids' soccer game without wishing he had a son or daughter. If Chloe was willing to build a house with him, would she also be willing to have his children?

"I'd like that," he said. Maybe after they dared live together, they would find the courage to marry and raise a family.

They walked back to ask Leroy the price. "Six hundred fifty thousand," he said. "And that's firm. No negotiating on this one." Joe felt his dream ripped away from him faster than it had appeared, like the ropes of a hot air balloon burning his hands as the basket lifted into the sky, floating high above him.

But Leroy kept on talking. "Once you put in a road, and clear space for the lots up here, you should be able to get two hundred K for each of them. Basically pay for the place."

"Why would anybody pay two hundred thousand for a small lot up here, when they can get three acres below for three seventy-five?" Joe spit the words out, angry at Leroy for stringing them along, letting them fall in love with this place and then jerking it out of their reach.

Leroy took off his sunglasses and used them as a pointer, indicating the land that lay below them. "The views down there are nothing compared to the ones up here. Up here you feel like you're on top of the world. People pay a lot for that feeling."

"He's right, Joe." Chloe traced a finger over his jaw. "I'm going to let you two discuss the details, while I check out the spot where we want to put our house."

Neither man said anything as she left them, Leroy watching her, until she was out of earshot. "You can do this," he finally said to Joe. "But it'll take a bit of finessing. Legally, it's only wide enough for a driveway to one house. Quirky rule on the city's part. A road has to be a few inches wider than a driveway. Theoretically, that eliminates the possibility of three other houses up here. But I've got a brother who works for the city and will get it approved for you."

"Wait a minute. I'm already having enough trouble convincing myself to do this, and now you're telling me it's illegal?"

Leroy put back on his sunglasses, his index finger pushing them into place, then scratching the bridge of his nose. "More a matter of working around a stupid law."

"The law's there for a reason."

"Sure it is. Can't have whole hillsides sliding down on the houses at the bottom. But if you can put in a driveway to your house at the end, why shouldn't it serve three more houses too?"

He couldn't fault Leroy's logic. If the regulation stipulated a width that accommodated a driveway, it should suffice for the other houses too. "Be my luck I'd get caught."

"No way. My brother does this stuff all the time. Only way anything gets built around this town."

Joe knew some developers paid under the table to squeak past certain regulations, but it violated his sense of ethics. He'd always done his renovations strictly to code. Yet the arbitrariness of this particular rule tempted him to circumvent it.

A raven flew overhead, its wings outspread as it coasted by, floating on a current of air, letting the wind carry it along freely. Joe envied the playful bird, wishing he didn't have to struggle so hard for all he had.

"Tell you what," Leroy said, "I'll arrange a meeting with my brother and have him show you how we can get away with this."

As a man who prided himself on the caliber of his work, the idea of getting away with something bothered Joe. The very words implied a shoddiness that undermined the hill's grandeur. His eyes wandered over the Jemez Mountains, moving on to Wheeler Peak north of Taos, circling south, around to where Chloe stood at the western tip. The expansiveness made him giddy. The ridge curved in such a way that four houses would form half an arch, none blocking out the views of the other. And a road along the edge would easily provide access to all of them.

"I'd need to check out the regulations to see if it would work."

"No problem. We can head over to city hall right now."

"Not today. Tomorrow." Joe looked at Chloe, waving her hands and shouting out that she loved the place. "And this has to stay between the two of us. She can't know it isn't legit."

"Got you," Leroy said, grinning with a complicity that made Joe uncomfortable.

Even more than he did, Chloe would abhor the idea of cheating. It was part of what he loved about her, her straightforward honesty. On the other hand, if he could put four houses up here without causing any serious environmental damage, why not bend the rules a little to bring them both the happiness they deserved?

|| **RITA** || The dust rose under Rita's feet, clinging to the cuffs of her jeans as she walked home from the auction. The cicadas had begun their summer drone and the dogs hung close, panting in the heat, while Rita's thoughts turned to Miguel Archuleta, questioning why she had an ongoing attraction to people gifted with words. Often inarticulate herself, she easily mistook eloquence for sincerity. She had loved Brad Parker's verbal dexterity, the way he had wooed her with dreams. But then he just as adeptly sidestepped her when she got pregnant, saying she couldn't prove the baby was his. She had given his last name to their son so that everybody would know, but it hadn't eased her sense of betrayal.

Now here she was, as though she'd never learned her lesson, mooning over another smooth talker. During a break in the bidding, Miguel had spoken fervently about the need to pay homage to their heritage, and at least, if not continue the occupations of their ancestors, respect the land that had sustained them all those years. While listening to him, she'd noted that his red hair gave him a fiery look, like a Viking warrior with a Latin's passion.

"Stop it!" she said aloud. Forty-one years old and she was carrying on like a teenager, inventing romantic heroes. Miguel was a lawyer, not a warrior. He was a man out to earn a living, not save people or court lovers. Probably married to some Anglo woman.

The sight of a BMW nestled against Parker's trailer pulled her attention back to her surroundings. A well-tanned man with sandy brown hair nodded attentively as Parker pointed at his studio. She started to cut wide, not wanting to interrupt a possible sculpture sale, but Flojo and Loca took off running toward Parker, and the man gestured with his head in her direction. Parker raised his arm and halfheartedly motioned her over.

Rita could tell he didn't really want her there, but it was too late to pretend she hadn't seen the invitation, and so she wove her way through the half dozen metal sculptures in front of his trailer. "Rita, this is Drew Stinson. He . . ."

"I've been eager to meet you," the man said, his mouth spreading into a big smile that revealed perfectly white teeth. He wore a shirt the color of lime Jell-O, cool and green on a hot day. His name hummed in her ear, reminiscent of a song she couldn't fully recall.

"Why is that?" she asked him.

"I've been talking to your son here about a deal I want to make you."

"I don't believe in deals."

"Now that's a new religion," the man said, his mouth opening into a laugh, ready to swallow her. "Can't say I've ever met anybody who didn't believe in deals. Wait'll you hear what I have to offer." She raised her hand, holding it out like a stop sign, but he proceeded anyway. "Beautiful land you've got here. I bought the piece across from your house. Some of the prettiest property around."

His words barely registered as she finally recognized who he was—Drew Stinson, Developer. The man who would soon make her world immensely more crowded, her mind far less settled. The enemy. She couldn't help seeing him any other way.

"What do you want from me?" she asked.

Her directness made Drew flinch, but he quickly flashed his pretty teeth in a big smile. "Seems a shame to clutter such beautiful scenery with a junkyard. I was going to pay you to get rid of it, but then your son mentioned an alternative."

Rita had forgotten Parker's presence and turned to find him rubbing a nearby sculpture as he might a talisman, his thumb running back and forth over the top of one of the horseshoes that formed a bowlegged cowboy.

"I told Drew we'd prefer to keep the business, but we could move it back here where nobody would see it."

"Why should we hide the junkyard? It's nothing to be ashamed of."

"Come on, Mom." Parker rarely addressed her as "Mom" unless he wanted something. "This way we make a little money and still keep the junkyard."

She stared at him until he grew uneasy. He picked a pebble off the cowboy's hat and tossed it from one hand to the other.

"I have no interest in moving the junkyard. It's too convenient where it is." She wasn't about to traipse back to Parker's place every time somebody turned down her driveway. And she detested Drew Stinson's arrogance, his thinking he could move people around like chess pieces.

"You may want to reconsider," Drew said, reaching into his back pocket and pulling out a news clipping. "This is an article about a junkyard in Tucson that was forced to close recently." He held the folded piece of paper out toward her, but she refused to take it.

"I don't need to read anything to know about people imposing their dictates on others."

"You misunderstand me, I . . ."

"Do I? I doubt it. You may have convinced my son that you've got a bargain to offer us, but I'm not that naive."

Drew smiled, those shiny teeth of his lined up on his face like little soldiers. He reached into his back pocket again, pulling out his wallet this time. "I understand how hard this is. We all have our emotional attachments."

Rita saw his mouth form the words, heard the implied sincerity behind them, but couldn't imagine Drew forming a close bond with anything other than money.

"Here's my card," he said, slipping it into her hand. "When you're ready to make the change, give me a call and I'll write you a check. Enough to pay somebody to do the moving and still leave you with a tidy sum."

He turned to Parker, giving him a chummy clap on the shoulder. "See you later." He raised his hand in a half wave and got into his car. The tires spun in the sand a moment, then gained traction as he backed up and lurched forward, settling into a smooth ride across the bumpy road.

Rita and Parker silently watched the BMW disappear around the hill that hid her house from his. The hill that could conveniently hide the junkyard. "You really want me to do it, don't you?"

Parker gave an ugly snort of a laugh. "It's stupid not to. His clients put you out of business, where will we be?"

"Same place we are now. Living on our land." She tore the business card into shreds and placed them on the brim of the metal cow-boy's hat.

"Don't you see?" Parker said. "It's an easy chunk of money for nothing. You heard him. Enough to pay somebody else to do the dirty work and still have cash left over."

She could understand the appeal, the fact that they would come out ahead financially. Parker was too young, too swayed by what money could buy, to understand an erosion of dignity. "Do you remember the day that Texas oilman drove out here and wanted to buy the weather vane off the top of the house?"

Parker puffed up his cheeks and let out a loud, exasperated breath. "How could I forget? A hundred dollars sounds like a lot of money to a little kid."

"But your abuelo told the man even if he offered a thousand, he wouldn't part with it because his father had made it." Personally, Rita found the weather vane quite ugly, a misshapen bull cut from an oil drum, an object she would have gladly parted with. She'd been about the age Parker was now and longed for things they couldn't afford. "I begged him to sell it. I was dating Jimmy Jaramillo in those days, and wanted to look good. It'd been ages since I'd had a new outfit. And you were growing faster than I could keep you in clothes. It seemed like winning the lottery to have a complete stranger walk up and buy something we didn't need."

Parker resumed rubbing his cowboy sculpture. "Antique weather vanes are popular these days. You could still probably get a couple hundred for it."

"I'm older now. A new outfit isn't going to win me a boyfriend. And that weather vane is your artistic heritage. Your great-grandfather was the first in the family to make a metal sculpture."

She knew the comparison might offend Parker, but the rigidity in his jaw loosened and he smiled. "Hope you think a little more of my work than you do of that hideous bull."

"Parker, I've supported your art since the day you welded Muffler Man. Now I have to ask you to try and support me in this." She opened up her arm, sweeping it outward in an effort to encompass all they could see. "With so many houses going in around me, it's like I'm being imprisoned. I have to do what I can to feel that I am still a free person, a woman with an ability to shape her own life. I don't want anybody to buy my acquiescence."

"Muffler Man. I'd forgotten all about him."

People only heard what they wanted to hear. He'd tuned out the rest of what she'd said, only picking up her reference to his work. It was useless trying to explain her despair to him. "How could you forget Muffler Man? He's standing at the end of the driveway, beckoning people to come to the junkyard. You pass by him every day."

"You know how it is. You see something every day and you're blind to it."

"Is that why you're oblivious to the beauty of our land?"

His lips tightened into a grim line and he bent down to remove a small dried-out bush that had gotten tangled up at the base of his horseshoe cowboy. "I know a guy who makes sculptures out of tumbleweeds." He lifted the rootless, withered plant and shook it at her. "Is that what I have to do? Become some kind of nature artist to convince you that this place means something to me too?" He tossed the weed and stood up, furiously dusting off his hands. "I came back here, didn't I?"

"That you did."

He shrugged his shoulders. "This place is my inspiration. Without it I have nothing. But I have no interest in being a starving artist. I don't see why we can't move the junkyard back here."

"Because we'd have to get permission from the city to make the road back here a public access, and once we do that, there's nothing to stop you from selling your land."

He took a step back, as though she'd slapped him hard, sent him reeling with her words. "Is that what it is? You think I'm calculating ways to sell my land out from under you?" The stunned look on his face made her feel as though she indeed had hit him. He sounded five years old. "Where would I go if I sold my land?"

"You could buy a little place in town."

"And live with the same choked feeling I had in LA? No thanks."

His answer confused her. "You talk often enough about letting go of part of the property."

"Sure I do. But it's just talk. If I learned anything in LA, it's that I can't make art without this place."

Rita wanted to believe him. Did believe him. But she also knew how hungry he was for recognition. He loved his art, but he wanted the external signs of success. Somebody more clever or more desperate than either Leroy or Drew Stinson might convince him that money was worth more than the room to do what you loved.

|| **RITA** || Sundays were the worst, coming home from Mass to nothing. The emptiness of the day hung heavier than the heat, clinging to Rita with a tenacity she couldn't shake. If Ramón hadn't called to ask if he could stop by, she would have escaped to the mountains and hiked in the cool air. Instead, she sat on the front porch, nursing an iced tea. She pressed the cold sweating glass between her breasts, shivering at the relief and regretting that it had been so long since a man had placed his hands there, or anywhere upon her body.

Spotting an advancing cloud of dust in the distance, she stood up, grateful for Ramón's arrival. But as the truck got closer, she saw that it wasn't the Ford he always borrowed from his brother-in-law. The grillwork indicated an old classic, a rusty '52 Chevy somebody probably wanted to restore. She would let whoever it was search the junkyard even though it wasn't officially open. It would provide another diversion in an otherwise aimless day.

The truck pulled into the driveway and stopped next to the house rather than continuing over to the junkyard. It took her a moment to recognize Miguel when he stepped down, wearing a blue bandanna around his forehead.

"You lived in California so long, you look like a Chicano gangster."

Miguel grinned sheepishly, nudging the bandanna with his thumb and then gesturing at the truck. "No air-conditioning in that sucker."

Rita realized she, in turn, must look terrible in the heat, wearing a pair of baggy shorts and a frayed T-shirt, her hair haphazardly pinned up to get it off her neck. "Fifty-two, isn't it?"

The question failed to divert Miguel's attention toward the truck. His eyes did a quick tour of her messy hair, past her sloppy clothes, and then paused at her feet. "I wouldn't have pegged you as one for pedicures."

She tucked a foot behind her calf, wishing she could hide both feet, but she had on flip-flops and the red toenail polish drew attention. "Not much point in painting my fingernails since they're always dirty."

"It's not like running this junkyard is all you ever do."

"Don't fool yourself." Her intelligence sometimes attracted men like Miguel, men with education and money, but they quickly outgrew any initial interest in her, dismayed by her lack of sophistication. She didn't want to go through that again. "I'm nothing but a wrench-wielding wench."

"One with a wicked way with words." His lips buckled as he tried to conceal his smile. "You're far more than the grease monkey you make yourself out to be."

"Not really," she said, barely able to speak, his praise coursing, with a delicious shiver, through her body.

His eyes played a moment upon her mouth then moved beyond her. "Did your grandparents build that house?"

She looked behind her at the curved lintel and the billowed walls, the lines as beloved as the wrinkles in her grandparents' faces. "Hard to imagine anybody working that hard these days, isn't it?" she said.

Ignoring the question, Miguel came up the steps, brushing by her and sticking his head into the open doorway like a country boy who hadn't learned to hide his curiosity. Craning his neck, he peered at the ceiling. "I wish it was still possible to find vigas that thick. You're lucky to have such a great house."

"Yes and no. It needs lots of work that I can't afford."

He leaned back against the door frame, bent a knee, and rested a foot on the wood. His casual posture gave the impression it was his home as much as hers. "You could do a lot of the repairs yourself and cut costs."

"Says the high-powered attorney who undoubtedly pays to have somebody else do his home repairs."

Miguel shoved both hands in his pockets. "I'd be better off paying somebody else to do it, that's for sure. You should have seen the storage shed I installed behind my house in California. It was so crooked it looked like it had survived an earthquake."

Many men, upon learning of her trade, boasted of their own manual skills, as though compelled to compete with her. She liked that Miguel readily admitted his own ineptness. "Some people are good with their hands, others with their minds."

He grinned. "Was that a backhanded compliment?"

"You're obviously intelligent. Too bad you weren't smart enough to avoid going into law."

Although he had red hair, Miguel's eyebrows bordered on brown, barely notable until he raised one, as he did now. "You really have a thing against lawyers, don't you?"

"Not my fault the profession attracts a lot of sleazy people."

Miguel's boot slid down from the door frame and he straightened his back, his posture proud. "I admit to pulling a few smooth moves from time to time, but I do it with integrity."

She saw the sincerity in his brown eyes and backed away, afraid of where trusting him might lead her. "So, you here for parts for that truck?" Not waiting for an answer, she started down the stairs.

But Miguel didn't follow her, and when she glanced over her shoulder she saw him still standing in the doorway. "That truck is only one of the reasons I'm here." He rubbed a thumb over a gouge in the wood. "I belong to a motorcycle club. We're having a benefit dance next Friday to buy school clothes for needy kids. I wondered if you would go with me."

"You ride a motorcycle?"

"Yes," he said, coming down the steps and sitting on the banister, close enough she could feel his breath when he spoke, like a sage-scented breeze blowing lightly on her forehead. "I have a Harley. It's what some of us lawyers do with our excess money."

"Shit, how many vehicles do you own?" He'd left the auction in a relatively new Toyota pickup, shown up here in a classic Chevy, and now he was telling her he had a Harley too.

"Well, let's see, there's the mandatory Porsche and the Lear jet." He raised both eyebrows this time. "Or do planes count?"

She wanted to think he was joking, but suspected he was making light of the truth. "How rich are you?"

"Would you like to see my bank statement?"

The amused expression on his face stirred a mixture of emotions in her stomach. She kept trying to keep a bit of distance between them, yet something drew her toward him. "Looks to me like you're already parading the fact that you make a lot of money."

He grinned. "I should have you pay my bills. Maybe you could find money I didn't know I had."

"Obviously you're not suffering."

Something hooded his eyes, a darkness she'd forgotten she'd seen when she first met him, a shadow of hidden pain. "How little you know," he said.

Preparing to apologize, she rested her fingertips on his forearm. He twitched and jerked away from her, but not before she had felt the sun's heat upon his skin. "Tell me what it is I don't know."

"Nothing to tell. I don't have a Porsche or an airplane. The Chevy belongs to my dad. He's had it sitting out in the barn for years, and I'm fixing it up for him. Keeping myself out of trouble." The pain remained visible in his eyes, drawing her nearer with his vulnerability. "What about you?" he asked. "What's your vice?"

"Sleeping with men I barely know." She flounced the rest of the way down the steps, not sure where she was headed.

He came up beside her and briefly encircled her wrist with his hand, just long enough to stop her flight and to send a quiver racing across her skin. "I'm only suggesting we go dancing. Nothing else."

Her hand atingle, she brushed the hair out of her eyes. "Friday or Saturday?"

He let out a breath, as though he'd been holding it. "I'll pick you up at seven on Saturday."

"Tell me where it is, and I'll meet you there." If he drove her home, it would be too easy to invite him inside. In her loneliness, she slept with men she barely knew, but they only filled the emptiness in her bed, not the void in her life.

He nodded his head, as though he heard her thoughts. "Seven-thirty at the Eagles' Club."

"Wings of Hope?"

"Who else would do something like this, plus line up a great salsa band?"

Rita loved salsa music, the way it quickened a pulse deep inside her. "Are you a good dancer?"

His eyes roamed over her hair the way some men's fingers had, then came to rest on her face. "I'm not the best, but I'm decent."

"Decent is fine," she said, thinking of all the word implied. The best dancers had too often proven the worst lovers, too self-centered to treat her decently. "As long as you know how to lead."

"Ah, but can you follow?"

Before she could answer, Ramón pulled into the driveway. "Whoa, a fifty-two!" he said, throwing open his door, jumping out, and striding over to where they stood next to the truck. "Is this yours, bro?"

"Nah, it's my old man's. But he lets me fool around with it."

"Miguel, this is Ramón, the local low-rider king."

The men shook hands in some complicated fashion she'd never gotten the hang of, but which it pleased her to see Miguel knew. Ramón was like an adopted son and, for some reason, she wanted the two men to like each other.

"I'm an Impala man myself," Ramón said. "But I love the lines in these old Chevys."

"Yeah," Miguel said, stroking the front fender. "Reminds me of those voluptuous actresses from the fifties."

"You men and your vehicles!" Rita snorted. "Give me a truck that takes me where I need to go without breaking down and I'm happy."

"Ah, Rita," Ramón said. "Where's your sense of style?"

"Lost with my youth."

The three of them wandered out into the junkyard. Ramón headed for the Impalas. "This is impressive," Miguel said. "You've got it all sorted by vehicle make, don't you?"

"Rita has the neatest junkyard in the state."

"Apparently not neat enough for my neighbors," she said, anger rasping her voice.

"What neighbors?" Ramón asked. "This is a dead-end road. The people south of you never have to drive out here."

"A new development is going in across the road. Expensive homes for people who don't want a view of a junkyard."

"Tell them to go to hell." Ramón raised a fist in the air. "Screw them. They don't like it, they don't have to live here."

She saw Miguel listening intently, waiting to speak. "Rich people arrange things to suit them. They'll contest you as an environmental hazard."

Rita slumped against the hood of a nearby Oldsmobile. "That's what I'm afraid of."

Ramón kicked at the Oldsmobile's front tire. "What do you mean an environmental hazard? Hell, I work at Los Alamos. The lab's got radiation leaking all over the place. What's Rita got? A few automotive fluids seeping into the ground? They can't close this place because of that."

"It's been done before," Miguel said, "but usually within a city." He looked off toward the mountains. "You've got some chance of winning because you were here first."

Ramón peered at Miguel, his thumb rubbing at his goatee. "So how come you know so much about all this?"

"It's my specialty. I'm an environmental lawyer."

"I thought that was something only gringos did. Saving land for nature freaks."

Unfazed by Ramón's remark, Miguel sat down next to Rita on the Oldsmobile. "La tierra is an equal opportunity employer."

Ramón spat on the ground. "That mean you're going to represent Rita?"

She immediately raised herself off the car, extending her height to all four feet eleven inches. "I can't afford a lawyer, Ramón."

He jerked his head in the direction of his beloved Impalas. "What am I supposed to do without this place? Me and all the other low-riders? Not to mention the poor Mexicans driving cars held together with baling wire, and the teenagers fixing up hand-me-down family fall-aparts, or the old hippies with their VW vans, and the folks with gems like that fifty-two Chevy truck. What about all of us? We need you to keep this junkyard going. There's got to be a way we can save it."

"Where am I going to get money to pay a lawyer?"

Still sitting on the Oldsmobile, Miguel stretched out against the front window with his hands behind his head. "I'm a big believer in bartering," he said. "I'm going to need lots of parts for that Chevy."

"Not enough for me to buy your professional advice."

"Hold on, Rita." Ramón started rocking back and forth on his feet, gearing up to the idea. "It's not just Chevy parts. You can pay him in Impala parts too, and then he can pay me to do bodywork on that truck."

Miguel nodded. "Like the viejos used to do. No money crosses hands but everybody gets paid."

"What color you want that truck?" Ramón asked him.

"Cherry. My old man wants cherry red."

"What's he got in mind for the interior? I've started playing with old serapes for upholstery. It gives . . ."

"Slow down!" Rita stamped her foot. It irritated her the way men could maneuver around a woman as though she didn't exist. "What kind of legal services are we talking about here? If this goes to court, there's no way I can trade enough parts to pay for Miguel's time."

"Did you see the tailpipe on his truck? He's going to need some serious welding work done too. It all adds up. Besides," Ramón squinted at Miguel, "you must do a little pro bono work now and then too."

"I'm not a charity case, Ramón. Don't go begging free handouts for me."

Miguel sat up, putting his feet back on the ground. "Fact is, I do throw in some pro bono work from time to time. I'd just as soon do it for the Vargases as anybody else." Before she could protest, he stood up, barely taller than she. "Don't forget what your tío is doing for my family. He's letting Pat have that grazing land below market value. This is a way for us to repay the favor."

It was true that her uncle would lose money selling his back pasture to Pat, and thus it seemed fair that Miguel charge her less than normal for his professional counsel. What worried her was what she, in turn, might lose in the exchange. She cherished her independence too much to give it up, even for this man.

|| **JOE** || Always punctual, and even more so when nervous, Joe arrived fifteen minutes early for a meeting at city hall with Leroy and his brother. Reading the postings on a bulletin board for the third time, he turned at the sound of raucous laughter and saw the two men stepping out of the elevator. Gilbert resembled a plumped up version of Leroy, padded with excess pounds instead of hard muscles, but their smiles were identical, even down to the crooked front tooth.

"Come in, come in," Gilbert said, ushering them into his office. Unlike Leroy, whose every move was steered by ambition, Gilbert had a casual ease, as though his plump body were a ball that rolled through life. Joe could see how Gilbert's good nature had helped him rise so high in city government.

His well-appointed second-floor office had a view through the leafy tops of cottonwoods. The greenery of the trees struck Joe as a rebuke, reprimanding him for daring to break environmental regulations. "I'm not willing to do this if it entails serious erosion," he blurted.

He heard the door close behind him. Then Gilbert crossed over to the window and adjusted the blinds, closing off the view. "Sit down, sit down," he said, motioning Leroy and Joe to take seats across the desk from him. "What a day! Not even noon yet, and already I've met with half a dozen developers. Town's growing faster than I can issue building permits."

Leroy leaned across his chair toward Joe. "This department is so busy," he said in a confidential tone, "they don't always have time to see that everything is up to code."

"We do our best," Gilbert said, "but sometimes things slip by us."

Joe felt like he was playing a role in a gangster movie, listening to innuendos about the Mafia's ability to help him. "I intend to do this as close to code as possible."

"Sure you do," Leroy said. "But be glad that ridgetop falls within city limits, or you'd have to deal with the county."

"From what I've heard they have more lax standards."

"Not really," Gilbert said. "They've got their rules and we've got ours. It's all a matter of what you want to accomplish."

"Besides, Gilbert's a lot easier to deal with than the county guys, if you know what I mean."

The implication outraged Joe. He had no intention of greasing palms. "I plan on keeping this as above board as possible."

"Sure you do. It's just that . . ." Leroy stopped at the sight of Gilbert shaking his head. It wasn't until then that Joe pegged Gilbert as the cautious younger brother, the one who reminded Leroy when he'd stepped over a line.

"Lot of developers," Gilbert said, "think they can buy my favor." He ran his tongue over his top teeth like somebody savoring the lingering flavor of a good meal. Joe suspected Gilbert welcomed any perks that came his way and wasn't above accepting a bribe, but he also recognized when insisting upon one could backfire on him. "You don't need to pay me to get your subdivision approved, and you're smart enough to know that." Gilbert leaned back in his chair, wiping what appeared to be pastry crumbs off the front of his shirt. "Thing is, Joe, I believe in helping out family when I can. My brother's got an eye for valuable real estate, but he doesn't always develop its fullest potential."

Leroy indicated the wall behind Gilbert's desk where a large map detailed the increasing density of the city. "When I bought that ridgetop, there wasn't even a road to it."

Gilbert spun his chair around to look at the map, then chuckled. "But Leroy had a girlfriend in the public works department, and she . . ."

"Hey," Leroy said, cutting him off, "don't go giving out secrets."

Gilbert winked at Joe. "My brother has a way with women. Gets them to do things for him they wouldn't do for anybody else."

Scratching at his neck, as though the particular woman still gave him an itch, Leroy said, "Point is, we got a road out there, but I could only sell lots on the hillside. Nobody who could afford to build on top would settle for a small lot." He quit scratching at his neck and gave a triumphant grin. "But that was back before so many people started building second homes in Santa Fe."

"Second, third, fourth, and even fifth," Gilbert amended.

Joe looked from one brother to the next, trying to follow the leap in their conversation. "I don't understand."

"Rich people," Gilbert said in a slow, patient voice, "typically want enormous houses, unless they're only going to live in them for two or three weeks out of the year. Then they like something a little smaller. More manageable."

"Which is where you come in," Leroy explained. "You can sell lots on that ridgetop to people who want to live here part of the year. The kind of people who want classy neighbors and a place big enough to throw garden parties and invite family for the holidays, but small enough for easy upkeep when they're away the rest of the year."

No denying that Leroy had great marketing strategies, but Joe distrusted him. There had to have been another reason he'd only sold lots on the side of that hill and not on the top. "I think there's more you're not telling me."

The two brothers exchanged glances, Gilbert lifting his shoulders as though asking permission to speak. When Leroy hung his head, Gilbert cleared his throat. "Lot of Leroy's troubles stem from women. He caters to them too much. Like the woman who sold him that ridgetop. They've known each other since they were kids. She didn't want anybody to ever build up there. And Leroy, being the nice guy he is, went along with the idea. But that was a long time ago and she never returned the favor when she had a chance, so he figures he doesn't have to respect her wishes no more."

"So now you're using me to get even with her?" Joe had to laugh at Leroy's shamefaced expression. "Look, I don't mind reaping the benefits of your revenge, but I need to be convinced this subdivision is going to work."

"Why wouldn't it?" Leroy asked.

"Well, for starters, I want to be sure putting four houses up there won't cause a problem with runoff. I don't want to end up like that eastside developer who got sued by the people at the bottom of the hill because their houses were flooded with sewage."

Gilbert reached to the side of his desk and picked up a rolled sheet of paper. "Let me show you how this can be done without causing any undue erosion." He slid the rubber band off the paper and unrolled it, smoothing it flat with his soft, puffy hands. "This is just a mock-up," he said, his fingers gliding across a layout of four building sites. "See these numbers?" He pointed to degrees written below the sites. "Those are slope inclines. They fall just below the maximum limit. If the hill was any steeper, you couldn't build even one house up there. As it is, you'll need to put in containment ponds to prevent runoff, but that's a standard requirement these days."

"You're saying I can put in four houses and still abide by the new escarpment ordinances?"

Again Gilbert seemed to look at Leroy for approval to speak. This time Leroy was the one to clear his throat before talking. "Like I already told you, there's one small problem. We don't have quite enough clearance for a full-sized road, but Gilbert knows a way around that."

Gilbert hunched over the map, resting his stomach against the desk. He tapped the last site, the one at the western end, where Chloe wanted to live. "Naturally, this is the best spot for a house, the place anybody would choose if they were the only ones building up there." He lifted his eyes from the paper to make sure Joe was following what he said. "You apply for a building permit for that site, say nothing about any other houses, and put in your driveway. Afterward, you apply for a permit to subdivide the lot and put in three more houses. The road is already in place; nobody stops to question its width. Simple as that." Gilbert leaned back, the chair creaking as he did so, his plump hands folded together with the index fingers pressed against his lips like the steeple of a church.

"What if somebody discovers the road isn't as wide as it's supposed to be?"

Before Gilbert could say anything, Leroy trailed his finger across the driveway drawn on the paper. "We're only talking a couple of feet. Who's going to notice?" His finger moseyed along the ridge, stopping at the western tip. "You and Chloe put your house here, and before you know it, you'll have sold the other lots, no questions asked." Leroy turned to his brother. "You should see what this guy's done with old Mrs. Padilla's house. Plus his girlfriend owns an art gallery. Between the two of them they'll build something so fine that people are going to jump at the chance to live next door."

Gilbert began rolling up the paper. "Like Leroy said, it's only a matter of a couple of feet. Somebody would actually have to measure the road to know it wasn't the full width."

"Is it wide enough for a fire truck?" Chloe had alluded to their having three bedrooms, evasive about how they'd use them all. He didn't want their children living someplace unsafe.

"Wide enough for a hippopotamus and a moving van to boot." Gilbert stood up, signifying the end of their meeting.

But Joe still had reservations. "How wide is a road nominally supposed to be?"

"Nominally?" Gilbert seemed uncertain of the meaning of the word.

"What's the narrowest road the city allows as opposed to a driveway?"

"Eighteen feet for a driveway; twenty-four for a road."

"Six feet difference," Joe mumbled. "The height of a man."

"Trust me," Gilbert said, pointing at him with the rolled up plans, "you won't be the first, or the last person to do this. It's a common device for getting a subdivision approved on a hilltop." He walked across the room and put the plans with several other rolls of paper on a table by the window. Then he raised the blinds and the light hit Joe in the eyes, forcing him to look the other way.

Leroy leaned against Gilbert's desk, gazing at Joe. "Nobody will hesitate to approve your plans. You've got too good of a reputation in this town."

"And I've worked hard to earn that reputation. I won't risk it all for something shaky."

"Shaky? You can't get any more solid. I'm giving you a chance to live in the house of your dreams."

"It's a beautiful piece of land and I'm sure you won't have any trouble finding somebody to buy it." Joe put his hands on the armrests and pushed himself up out of the chair. "I'm not comfortable with the idea of manipulating the rules to suit my needs."

"Whoever builds up there is going to have to skirt around the same problem," Leroy insisted. "Why shouldn't you be the one to benefit?"

"Leroy." Gilbert's pillowy voice enfolded them like a marshmallow. "Let the man have some time to think it over. We're talking a big commitment here." Gilbert nodded his head at Joe. "Why don't you drive out there and check the place over again. You'll see what I mean about there being plenty of room."

There was something about the way he offered it as a suggestion, rather than forcing the issue, that appealed to Joe. "I wouldn't mind taking another look at it."

"Be my guest," Leroy said. "Take Chloe with you when you go. Think about what you'll be throwing away if you don't grab that piece while it's still yours for the taking."

Joe bristled at the implication he'd lose Chloe, too, if he didn't buy the ridgetop. Leroy knew how to get to him. Sleazy though the two brothers were, they reminded Joe of Mrs. Sena when she'd persuaded him to do her bathroom, nudging a little here and there until finally he'd agreed. But this wasn't a matter as simple as laying down some tile; he had to be more cautious with her sons.

"I'll do that," he said. Then Joe strode over to the door and opened it. "But, in the meantime, you should keep your eye open for another buyer." He stepped out of the office and closed the door on the two men, leaving them to ponder his unwillingness to grab the opportunity they had presented.

How could he walk away from the chance to afford a home well beyond his usual means? Joe wished he didn't have ethical qualms, but morality had guided him all his life. It was why he had married Sharon when she told him she was pregnant, dropping out of architecture school to work for her father, trying to make her happy after she miscarried. Only to have her leave him for a cardiologist, complaining that Joe earned too little money. Now he had an easy chance to bankroll a dream, and he hesitated.

Outside, in the bright sunshine of midday, Joe fumbled in his pocket for his sunglasses. Before he absolutely nixed the deal, he owed it to Chloe to look at the property again. Thing was, he reminded himself as he got into the car, unlike Sharon, Chloe loved him not for what he could buy, but for who he was—a man of principle.

His old Honda lacked enough clearance to drive overland to the property the way Leroy had in his Land Rover, so Joe parked by the last house on the hillside and began walking to the top. Although he used the treadmill at the gym three or four times a week, he felt out of shape as his legs strained to make the climb. When he finally reached the top, he paused to catch his breath, once again awed by the view. Even in the glare of the noon sun, the place beckoned to him with its trees and its sense of being on top of the world.

As he stared off toward the end of the ridge where Chloe wanted them to build, he thought about last night's dinner. After leaving Leroy, they had gone to their favorite Italian restaurant, where Chloe couldn't stop talking about the house. "Our kitchen has to be big," she said. "You know, the old-fashioned kind, large enough for people to hang out while we cook." She fished a pen from her purse and excitedly began to sketch a kitchen layout on the white sheet of paper atop their table. At first, he'd watched her awkward attempts at architectural renderings, while she explained that she also wanted the kitchen to face east. Finally, he took the pen from her and situated the kitchen so that they could watch the sunrise as they had their morning coffee. Then he added a living room with a large window looking west so they could see the sunset. By the time the waiter brought their salads, Joe had covered the table with possible floor plans.

It thrilled him to hear Chloe use the words *we* and *our*. She had always asserted her independence with such ferocity that he had resigned himself to being lovers with separate domiciles. To have her suddenly want to live with him intensified his determination to own an especially nice home. He stared beyond the spot she had selected, scanning the Jemez Mountains as though the answer to his dilemma lay in the distance.

Then he pulled out a tape measure and laid it down on the ground. The places Gilbert had designated as building sites were readily apparent—big areas that curved to the south. The road would run the northern edge. The dropoff was so steep that in a couple of places it barely allowed for even the eighteen feet required of a driveway. Rarely was there a twenty-four foot clearance. Putting the tape measure back in his pants' pocket, Joe eyeballed the discrepancy and had to agree that most people wouldn't notice it, given the overall curvature of the ridgeline.

A raven flew past him and he wondered if it was the same one he'd seen his first day there. As Joe watched the bird soar on an updraft, his own spirit joined in the flight and, in that instant, he knew he, too, would float on the good fortune that had come his way.

Turning to leave, he saw a woman with a black lab and a little fluffy dog walking up the other side of the hill, the side where the junkyard lay. He gave a friendly wave, but didn't stay to meet her. He was too excited to do anything other than rush to tell Chloe of his decision to go ahead and build their home on the ridgetop. Waving once more at the woman climbing the hill, he hurried down the opposite side.

|| RITA || Although she'd told Parker a new outfit wouldn't win her a boyfriend, Rita had succumbed to the urge to buy one for her date with Miguel. The dress had a tight bodice and flared out below her hips in swirls of red and black. Surveying herself in the hallway mirror, she decided she looked good for a woman of forty-one. A fan of wrinkles appeared at her eyes when she smiled, but they lent distinction to her face. And her hair fell around her shoulders like a cape of black velvet. "Well, Mr. Archuleta, this is what you get for a dance partner." She spun in a circle, watching the dress billow and then drape against her legs. "Still sexy after all these years."

Giving each of the dogs a cookie along with her usual command for them to behave while she was gone, she slipped a small purse on her shoulder and went out to her truck. The music of the Gipsy Kings accompanied her as she drove into town, their guitars stirring movement in her body. She tapped the rumba beat on the steering wheel, coming as close to dancing as she could while seated. Miguel was the first man to excite her since she'd broken up over a year ago with a married lover who'd intrigued her more than anything with his unavailability. Whereas Miguel she found interesting in and of himself, and that scared her. After spending so long alone, she felt too easily susceptible to the lure of romance.

Parking a couple of blocks down the street, she walked to the club, her red cowboy boots drumming against the sidewalk. She charged up the front steps, not seeing Miguel until he reached out and took hold of her arm, turning her toward him. "Slow down. We've got all night."

His face had the eager flush of a man pleased to see her. He wore a loose-weave beige shirt and fitted black jeans along with boots as well-worn but lovingly tended as her own. She caught his eyes admiring the way her dress molded her breasts. Flustered, she muttered that she needed the restroom.

"Let's go inside," he said, flashing their tickets at the door. "I'll find us a table. What do you like to drink?"

"A Dos Equis for starters and then water." When she danced, it took too much alcohol to quench her thirst and she hated being drunk.

"Una cerveza and lots of water chasers is right up my alley," he said, clearly pleased they were in synch on that issue.

Escaping to the bathroom, she dug around in her purse. Although she rarely smoked, she considered having one to take the edge off, then squelched the craving, not wanting to stink of cigarettes. Instead, she joined a row of women at the mirrors, all of them peering at their reflections, desperately covering over any signs of imperfection, emphasizing whatever could pass for lovable. Rita reapplied her lipstick but resisted the urge to fuss with her hair, telling herself Miguel found her attractive enough or he wouldn't have invited her there.

About two hundred people filled the main room, their voices overriding the sound of the musicians tuning up their instruments. Rita saw half a dozen familiar faces, mostly men who'd used the junkyard, and one former boyfriend with his latest fling, a blonde who glared at Rita. Her behavior reminded Rita why she had no close women friends. She had no patience for female cattiness, the competitive play for male attention. Only women sure of themselves, like her favorite cashier at Albertson's, who stood by the bar waving at her, earned Rita's attention. She returned the wave and then located Miguel on the far side of the room. Despite his shortness, he stood out among the crowd with his red hair. It took her a while to move through the clusters of people, but she finally reached the little round table he had secured. When she sat down across from him, they both sighed, as though she had journeyed a long distance and he was relieved to have her back.

"You look stunning in that dress."

"It's the old Cinderella trick. Put her in a nice dress and even a scullery maid looks good."

Miguel squeezed lime into his beer then lifted it to hers in a toast. "To magical transformations."

She clinked his glass. "Don't forget that at midnight I go back to being a grease monkey."

"Slippery and elusive."

The words indicated a desire to know her better, which made her skittish. She brought the glass to her lips, the beer warmly sour. She would no more fit into his world than her foot would into a glass slipper. "Not so much slippery and elusive," she said, "as dirty and dull."

"I don't find you in the least dull, and you clean up quite nicely."

Rita knew she looked good, but remembering the row of women in front of the bathroom mirror, desperately doing what they could to attract a man, she also knew looks alone would not hold Miguel's interest. "Best way to sell a lemon of a car," she said, "is to give it a fresh paint job."

Miguel took a sip of his beer before responding. "Why do you insist on denigrating yourself?"

His remark dumbfounded her. It had never occurred to Rita that she tended to put herself down. "I just want to be sure you don't get the wrong impression. I spend most of my days wearing dirty overalls and working up a sweat. I'm not some feminine thing with a high-powered career."

"Thank God! I had my fill of those in California." He gazed across the room, while looking elsewhere in his mind. She presumed it was a woman he saw, the one who caused the pain that now ravaged his face. Ghosts made for tough competition. She would have to find out if she stood a chance against his memory of another woman.

Shaking his head, Miguel took a big swig of beer and smiled, forcing himself back into the present. "I think it's fascinating that you've opted to run a junkyard."

"It was hardly an option. I took what was available. Nothing admirable about that."

"There you go again."

It took her a moment to grasp what he meant. She shrugged. "I wouldn't want you thinking I'm more than I am."

"What you are is pretty incredible. There probably isn't another woman in the country doing what you are."

"Nobody else desperate enough." She ran a finger around the rim of her glass, raising a squeak. "I was a high school dropout when I started helping my dad run the place. A teenage mom. Too dumb to do anything else."

Miguel sat back in his chair, and stretched his feet out toward hers, crossing one leg over the other. The man had an amazing talent for appearing totally at ease in the most awkward situations. "The fact you work with your hands doesn't mean you aren't intelligent."

"Wasn't that a double negative?"

"Which makes a positive; i.e., you're a smart woman."

"But uneducated."

His hand fell to the table, hitting it with a thump, a light rebuff. "Do you know how many of my old friends treat me like I'm a leper because I have a degree? I'd like to think you're different."

Rita well knew what it was to be an outcast, but she'd never thought in terms of people being rejected because they'd succeeded rather than failed. Miguel wanted her to empathize with his plight, but she couldn't, not after how she had hungered to go to college. "Some of us can't help but feel inadequate around people with more education. Like we're not as smart."

"Having a degree won't turn a moron into a genius. Intelligence is an innate quality. You're very possibly smarter than I am."

"More clever perhaps, but hardly smarter."

The band announced its first song, and Miguel threw up his hands, as though conceding defeat, but she saw the smile he tried to repress. "I have no idea which of us is smarter, but you're definitely prettier."

Rita stood up as the band opened with one of her favorite salsa tunes. "Let's find out which of us is the better dancer."

When Miguel took her hand, she felt a tremor pass through his body, as though he, too, was nervous about where this night would take them. "I'm no John Travolta, but I've been told I'm not bad."

He was too modest. Though he lacked the flair of the showier dancers, Miguel had fluidity. His hand on the small of her back, he led with a light touch, his fingers whispering along her spine. She wanted him to continue strumming her body all night long. As it was, they danced the entire set, not stopping until the band took a break.

They made their way back to their table, bumping against other flushed couples. Rita lifted her hair off her neck and fanned herself with the cocktail napkin. "Why don't they open the doors?"

Miguel reached across the table and brushed some stray hairs off her cheek. She wanted to press his fingers against her skin, but he retracted his hand, holding one of her grandmother's silver combs out to her. "You were about to lose this."

Rita started to put it back in her hair. "Don't." His plea stopped her hand midair. "I mean," he stammered, "they look like family heirlooms. Those combs . . ." He searched for words. "You wouldn't want to lose them." His bumbling speech, so unlike his usual articulateness, baffled her. Then he reached over and removed the remaining comb, his fingers briefly trailing through her hair, raising currents throughout her body. "Wear it down." And with those words she understood that like every man before him, Miguel loved her hair. He touched it with a reverence that gave her an inkling what it would be like to be adored.

"Rita, Rita, long time no see," Leroy's voice graveled behind her. She felt his hands momentarily clasp her shoulders, as though asserting a claim, before he came around holding out a hand to Miguel. "Leroy Sena. You must be new in town."

Miguel crossed his arms over his chest, his hands tucked away. "My family's been around a while. Up in Rio Arriba county."

Rita loved the way he trilled his "r." He slipped into the local Hispanic accent as quickly as some people switched from Spanish to English, blending the line between the two. "Leroy, this is Miguel Archuleta."

"Not Pat Archuleta's brother, are you?"

"That's right. The black sheep of the family. The one who got away, only to come back home with his tail between his legs."

Rita hid her smile in her water glass, amused by the way Miguel could play self-deprecation to his advantage. She wasn't sure of his strategy, but she suspected he'd come out the winner of any round with Leroy. Leroy was no dummy, but he had more shrewdness than he did intelligence.

"I don't know what your stake in it is," Leroy said, "but your brother is sitting on one of the prettiest pieces of property in northern New Mexico. I'm ready to give him top dollar anytime he's ready to sell."

Miguel stretched his arms over his head, yawning, as though the subject bored him. "The ranch belongs to my parents, and after they die, it goes not only to Pat, but to the rest of us sibs. Five all told. You don't stand a chance of getting us to agree on what to name a dog, much less selling the family property."

"You say that now, but people change." Leroy turned to Rita as the band started a new set. "This one's mine." Before she realized what he was doing, he'd lifted her up out of the chair and pulled her toward the music.

She started to refuse, but then remembered how thrilling it was to dance with Leroy. They'd never slept together, but from time to time, over the years, they'd engaged in some incredibly sexy maneuvers on the dance floor. Tonight he moved with a passion that incited her own. She knew it was Miguel she wanted, but Leroy aroused her love of dancing. Like pieces of a puzzle, they fit together, their bodies inseparable from the music. People stepped back, clearing more room, stopping to admire them. There was even a round of applause when they finished. Leroy raised her hand in the air with the triumph of a victor. But it wasn't until she saw Miguel intently studying them that she realized Leroy had proven himself a contender.

Rita declined Leroy's invitation to dance again. With her dress clinging to her damp legs, she hurried back to Miguel. Gone was his relaxed pose. He sat upright in the chair, his back rigid as a steel plate. "You two must have quite a history together."

Only once had Rita tolerated a possessive boyfriend, and then not for long. But Miguel's jealousy didn't strike her as the kind that bound a woman to him. She sensed that he mistakenly thought she and Leroy were lovers. Several people, including Leroy's wife, had made that assumption upon seeing them dance together. Miguel's irritation showed that he wasn't, as she'd feared, interested in her merely as some quirky character. He had reacted as somebody who wanted more from her and was upset to suddenly discover she might be unavailable.

"That's right," she said, "Leroy and I go way back. All the way to first grade, when I had to scrub the cafeteria tables as punishment for pushing him off the swings."

She stared as a pink tide swept across Miguel's cheeks, a ghastly color combination with his red hair. He laughed. "Sounds like a troubled relationship."

"Leroy has never done anything to endear himself to me, but he's a terrific dancer."

"As are you. Totally uninhibited."

Now it was her turn to blush, as she recalled the words of a one-night stand, a man she'd met at Rodeo Nights, who'd later told her he'd known she'd be great in bed after seeing the way she danced. "It's where I cut loose," she said.

"And the rest of the time?"

She could feel the blush deepen, her face growing hotter. "The rest of the time, I'm that woman who owns a junkyard and does little else other than take long walks with her dogs."

The pain again clouded his eyes. He gave up any pretense of hiding his suffering. "Gets lonely after a while, doesn't it?" he asked.

"That it does," she said, laying her hand upon his, preparing herself for him to pull away immediately. Instead, he turned his hand over and ran his fingertips across her palm. She lost awareness of everything but the small area of skin he stroked, his fingers sliding between hers, clasping her hand.

The band slipped into a slow song, a sad melody about heartbreak. Miguel stood first this time, still holding Rita's hand. She had yet to discover how strongly some other woman had a hold on his heart, but when he slid his hand across her back and pressed her chest against his, she longed to take that other woman's place.

|| JOE || Moonlight filtered through the curtains and covered their bodies with patterns of lace. Lulled by the afterglow of making love, Joe traced the floral design shadowed on Chloe's hip. Sex brought him a repose like no other, a quieting of his mind and a stillness in his body. A light breeze lifted the curtains and blew through the room. "That feels good," Chloe murmured. And he didn't know if she meant his caress or that of the breeze. She turned toward him and brushed his lips with hers. "When are you going to call Leroy?"

A spasm torqued Joe's neck, constricting the muscles in his shoulders and back. "Not any sooner than I have to."

"What's the point of waiting?" Chloe trailed her fingers across his chest.

Distracted by the sensations she aroused, Joe almost slipped and told her he resented Leroy for conning him into doing something illegal. "Things come too easily for that man. Look at how quickly he seduced you with his ridgetop."

Chloe's fingers coursed down through his chest hairs, over his stomach, pausing below his navel, making his blood surge. "Yes, but ultimately he brought us closer, didn't he?"

Joe rolled over on top of her, putting an end to her words with a kiss. Her mouth opened to his, her breasts arching up against his chest. His kiss moved down her neck.

After they had again made love, as he lay spent, staring up at the ceiling fan, Joe said, "In the morning."

"What?"

"Tomorrow morning I'll call Leroy and tell him we want to buy the ridge."

Chloe wrapped her legs around one of his, snuggling up against him. "I love you, Joe," she said into his neck as she slid into sleep.

The words "I love you, Joe," sang in his ears like a soft hymn. Ever since they'd talked of building a home together, she'd become increasingly generous with the refrain, sprinkling it here and there throughout the day, like a benevolent rain falling on his thirsty soul.

Listening to the evenness of her breathing, Joe envied how quickly she could drop off into sleep. As a child, he'd believed a bogeyman resided under his bed, waiting to grab him if he dared to get up during the night. As an adult, it was hidden worries that lay waiting to seize him in the dark. Tonight they strapped him in the bed with the fear of getting caught with an illegal subdivision.

At some point, when he wasn't looking, sleep overtook him. He awoke the next morning to the sound of Chloe in the kitchen singing.

"Going to build a house, going to build a house, going to b-u-i-l-d," her voice stretched out the word, then rushed ahead, "a house." She routinely made up new ditties to go with old melodies and whenever he heard her sing, Joe knew she was in high spirits, but these particular lyrics made him uncomfortable.

Chloe had a staunch honesty that brooked no deviance. When clients offered to pay her cash for a piece of art, thinking she'd lower the price and keep the sale off the books, she'd tell them it didn't matter whether they paid by cash, check, or credit card—the price was the same. Minor though it was, if she learned about the fraud involved in their affording the ridgetop, she'd insist they not buy it. Joe had considered finding another place, but he knew nothing in their price range would enchant them as much. He hated keeping secrets from her, but he had to if he was going to provide the home they'd envisioned.

Chloe came waltzing into the room, wrapped in a bath towel and carrying a cup of espresso. "Brewed especially for you, sir," she said, sitting down on the edge of the bed and holding the coffee out to him like a gift to a god. The prospect of the house had given her an additional radiance. She tilted her head to the side, her blonde hair sweeping across her bare shoulders as she peered at him. "Why so thoughtful?"

He reached up and touched the glow in her cheeks. "Just thinking how lucky I am to have you in my life."

"We're both lucky. We finally got it right this time." Chloe's last two lovers had both been artists. One had partied too much and the other had played around. Joe worried that he, to the contrary, would eventually bore her with his steadfastness. Loyalty he could provide, but not high drama.

Chloe abruptly rose from the bed. "I need to get dressed. I have a client stopping by in a few minutes." He watched as she pulled different outfits from the closet, spurning three before selecting a linen sheath. He never understood how beige, normally such a dull color, could come alive on Chloe. She slipped a couple of bracelets on her arm and went into the bathroom. From where he lay in the bed, he could see her face reflected in the mirror. She fussed with her hair longer than usual, then hesitated between two lipstick colors.

"Who is this client?" he called out to her.

"A venture capitalist from LA. Just bought a place out in Tesuque."

"So what makes him so special that you have to open early?"

He saw the pout on her lips as she applied a pale pink. "He's on his way to the airport and wanted to take another look at a sculpture he's considering buying. Potentially a very big sale. It's worth the trouble."

Joe took another sip of his coffee and got up. "I'll scramble us some eggs."

She again fussed with her hair, draping it behind her ears then shaking it free and fluffing it with her hands. "Don't bother making any for me. He's bringing bagels and coffee."

"I thought this was a business meeting, not a breakfast date." Joe pulled on his pants, irritated by his own pettiness.

The phone rang and she raced to get it. "Hello," she gushed, turning her back to him. "Oh, hi." Her voice was that of a woman anxious to please. She opened her dresser drawer and pulled out a scarf. "That sounds better." Listening to whatever it was the person had to say, she draped the scarf around her neck. "We'll discuss it." She turned to give Joe a thumbs up sign. "Don't worry, he'll get back to you later this morning, Leroy."

Joe stood holding his shirt, curious about what Leroy wanted. Chloe hung up the phone, a bemused expression on her face. "You were right to make Leroy wait. He got so nervous, he lobbed twenty-five thousand off the price."

"You mean, now, instead of six fifty, it's a mere six hundred and twenty-five thousand?"

She lifted his shirt from his hand, slipping his arms into the sleeves and doing the buttons. "Isn't that why you postponed calling him?" she asked. "Expecting him to make us a better deal?"

She would think less of him if he admitted that cold feet, not cleverness, had caused him to delay contacting Leroy. "I can't find my belt," he said, and bent down to look under the bed.

"It's in the other room, remember?" When he'd come over last night to tell her of his decision to go through with the development of the ridgetop, she'd opened an expensive bottle of Cabernet. They'd been sitting on the couch, debating how big a master bedroom they should build, when she began removing his belt.

Recalling the ensuing foreplay, Joe laughed. "That house," he said, "has been the best aphrodisiac." He retrieved his shoes from under the bed and sat down to put them on.

Chloe ran a finger along the edge of his ear, tickling him. "Wait until the actual building begins. We'll be at it all the time."

Her smile promised passion, and the softness in her eyes hinted at an intimacy beyond the physical. Jealousy might strangle his mind from time to time, but Joe knew Chloe loved him. If she left him, it would be because he had disappointed her in some fundamental way, not because she had fallen for somebody else.

"Look out, Leroy!" Joe said. "Chloe and I are ready to conquer your ridgetop." He stood up, wrapped his arms around her waist, and swung her in a circle.

"Put me down, silly," she said, laughing and regaining her footing. "I need to get busy and make some money if we're going to pull this off." Walking over to the dresser mirror, she rearranged the scarf around her neck, then turned to see how the dress looked in the back before slipping into a pair of high heeled sandals. "Wish me luck with this guy. He can afford to buy more than one piece." She gave Joe a quick kiss, then hurried through the kitchen into the gallery at the front of the house.

Joe left via the back door, walking through the garden and out the side gate. A Mercedes convertible pulled up in front of the gallery, and the man inside passed a hand through his hair, checking in the mirror to assess the ruffled affect. Joe told himself any man would want to look his best for Chloe, and he forced himself to continue walking down the sidewalk without looking back. Yet he could hear the man whistling, his footsteps rushing up the flagstone walkway, with Chloe calling out a warm hello.

|| RITA || Pale light bathed the room, awakening her gently. She stretched and then sank deeper into the bed, remembering her evening with Miguel. He'd walked her to her truck after the dance, pausing by its side to comment on the beauty of the stars. His face within inches of hers, his breath brushing against her lips, he'd almost kissed her.

Rita sighed and the dogs whimpered, ready for her to get out of bed and start the day. Instead, she drifted away in reverie, lightly running a finger over her mouth, imagining Miguel's lips against hers. There was a luscious sensation to delaying a first kiss, a luxury she had not allowed herself in years, prolonging desire, holding it at bay, savoring the yearning.

Flojo barked impatiently, adamant that she stop her dalliance and tend to him. "Jealous, old boy?" she asked, scratching him behind the ears as she threw back the covers. "Don't worry. You'll always have a place in my life."

Slipping into an oversized T-shirt and a pair of flip-flops, she went outside with the dogs and set the hose on a low trickle below the apricot tree. A sweetness from the ripening fruit permeated the air. The sun fell softly on the snapdragons by the back door, stirring the bees to buzz. A solitary butterfly, black stripes bold against pale yellow wings, fluttered among the flowers. Rita took in the morning's warmth like a deep hug. Closing her eyes and lifting her face to the sun, she smiled in appreciation of the day's simple beauty and how easily it satisfied her. After so many failed romances, she should know better, but the prospect of drawing close to a man filled her with content.

So content that she found herself actually humming as she went back inside to pull on jeans and tennies for her morning walk prior to Mass. The walk was her form of worship, yet she went to church every Sunday. She liked the notion of a day of rest, a day reserved for things other than work. She joined people at Mass out of respect for an old tradition and to experience a sense of community. Even as a child she'd been a loner, a bit of a misfit, living at the junkyard with a father who made no effort to find another wife. Older women looked upon her with sympathy, forgiving her oddities, blaming them on her lack of a mother. Lace mantillas over their heads, they moved their lips in hushed whispers when she entered the church alone, undoubtedly offering up extra prayers on her behalf.

Yet Rita felt glorious that morning, her hair gathered at her neck in a big barrette and cascading down her back. She wore a simple white dress she'd found at the Salvation Army, its straight lines concealing the curves of her body and forcing her to take shorter strides. It suited her mood, unhurried and almost virginal. She sat in a middle pew, where a family of tourists dressed in shorts pressed against her. The two children gaped at the cathedral's high ceilings, while their mother sang in a clear soprano voice along with her husband's resonant baritone. Rita, usually off-key, rarely sang, but she joined them in the last hymn, her happiness spilling over into song.

Leaving the cathedral, her sandals click-clacked, echoing the lightness of her spirit. Outside, people mingled, chatting with each other. Rita paused to put on sunglasses, the sun now high enough to glare. Across the way, she saw Leroy introducing his wife to an Anglo couple. The way he beamed convinced Rita they were clients. His wife gave them an ingratiating smile and then excused herself to visit with somebody else, leaving Leroy free to work his charm. Rita immediately marched over to chide him for soliciting business on church property.

Then, realizing it would be equally sacrilegious to provoke a fight, she quickly veered off in the opposite direction.

"Rita," called a man's voice. She turned and saw her cousin Alejandro, his wife and children standing off to the side talking to the priest. "You don't have time to say hi to family?" He smiled as he walked up and gave her a hug. Not until he stepped back did she see a flicker of sadness in his eyes.

"What's wrong?" she asked.

"Nothing, I just can't believe Dad's going to sell the back pasture."

"At least he's selling it to another rancher and not a developer."

"If only carpenters made more money. I'd buy the whole place and lease out the land for cattle grazing." He grinned, his good nature always surmounting any setbacks. "Be one of those gentleman farmers."

"Tía!" Tomás sauntered over with the slouching walk so popular among teenagers, his pants hanging low, threatening to slide off his hips any minute. "Can I bring a friend out to the yard this afternoon? He's got this awesome Buick he's priming. I told him you could help him out."

Rita wondered just how many teenage boys had come to her over the years with little money in their pockets and an avid desire to fix up their first cars. "Sure. Bring him by. I'll be home all afternoon."

"Tomás," said his mother, her voice that of a perpetual teacher, not stern, but forever guiding. "It's Sunday. Rita's day off."

"It's okay, Leticia. I'm there anyway. It's no problem."

Now Sandra, too, joined them, her hair recently cut short and spiky, her shoulders thrown back with a new confidence. "Tía, I've got something for you." She reached into her purse and pulled out a slim book, which she handed to Rita. "It's a collection of poems. The guy who wrote them used to be in prison. His words are really powerful."

"Great," said Alejandro. "We're sending our daughter to college to be educated by convicts."

"It's not like that, Dad, he . . ."

"Mi'jita, I was joking. I know how much you love to read. You and Rita here, the two of you with your noses buried in books."

"Fiction can be better than real life," Rita said.

Leticia reached over and wrapped her hand around Rita's. "We were sorry to hear Carlos is selling the far pasture."

Rita squeezed her hand in thanks before letting it go, appreciative of how Leticia had always understood her attachment to the land. "Like Tío told me, better to see cows out there than houses."

After promising to come over to their house for dinner that evening, Rita watched them leave, the two children walking in the middle, with their parents like bookends. It was the kind of tableau Parker had always longed for and she'd never provided. Rita turned in the direction of the plaza, pausing for a moment to look out over the town. The cathedral sat elevated, lending it an exalted air, and she liked that, the way it seemed to say there was something more important to life than everyday concerns.

She took the stairs down to the street, following the sidewalk behind La Fonda, bypassing most of the tourists shops, winding around the Loretto Chapel and over to the Alameda, where she walked along the river in the shade of the cottonwoods. Here she could pretend town hadn't changed that much, the dappled sunlight a welcome refuge from the mounting heat of the day. The state buildings above the river weren't particularly attractive, but they'd stood there long enough that Rita barely saw them as she moved along toward the railyard.

She passed by a former car dealership now converted into a nightclub. Once a run-down part of town, with warehouses and garages, the area had revitalized, the old buildings now housing restaurants and shops. A few abandoned trains covered with graffiti gave a defunct appearance to the railyard itself, but the station still functioned with a line that ran out to Lamy. Although the area had gentrified, Rita enjoyed it because it attracted more locals than it did tourists, especially on weekends when the farmers' market took place.

Sundays didn't draw the crowds Saturdays did, but it still surprised her how many people came—mostly Anglos, the women wearing straw hats to guard their complexions, the men frequently the ones to carry their children as they circulated among the vendors. Old hippies, and what Rita thought of as the new crop of hippies—young people with lifestyles similar to their sixties counterparts—sold produce that emphasized the word organic, along with a range of goods from corn husk angels to lavender sachets and soaps. The old-time farmers from the Española Valley tended to raise the foods they'd grown for years. Today they offered already ripened tomatoes, bell peppers, chiles, green beans, and apricots. A flourish of colors and fragrances.

"Qué bonita tu pareces esta mañana," said one elderly woman as Rita passed by.

"Muy bonita," echoed her husband, breaking into an appreciative grin that multiplied the wrinkles in his face.

"Gracias." Their praise made her feel inordinately young and pretty as she made her way to her uncle's booth with its yellow and purple awning that he'd painted so his customers could easily spot him from week to week. She already heard his laugh, dancing through the air with a heartiness that drew people to him.

Rita stood back, watching from the distance as he chatted with a mother and her little girl, the child gazing up at him in awe as he knotted a bandanna into the head of a rabbit with long floppy ears, a trick that had delighted Rita, too, when she was young. Then he turned to weigh the eggplants the woman had chosen, and a man, hidden inside the booth's shadows, took the eggplants from him and put them on the scale. After the woman and her daughter left, the man stepped forward to stand next to Carlos, the sun setting his red hair ablaze.

The morning's heat suddenly intensified, making Rita's dress clammy under her arms. Instinctively her hand went to her hair, lifting it momentarily off her neck, then fingering the strands around her face, rearranging them in what she hoped was an attractive frame. Wishing she'd reapplied her lipstick when she left the church, Rita ran her tongue over her lips, moistening them.

"There she is," Carlos said, nudging Miguel. "We've been waiting for you," he called out to her.

An abashed smile, wobbly with embarrassment, zigzagged across Miguel's face. The smile had promise, though, lingering rather than disappearing. A smile that spoke of gladness.

Encouraged, Rita moved toward them, these two men with their arms folded across their chests, watching her approach. Her uncle whistled and nudged Miguel again. "Qué guapa, no?"

Miguel blushed, like a boy caught flipping through the pages of *Playboy*, mortified by his eagerness to see her. "Sí, muy guapa."

"You're staring directly into the sun. It's blinded you both." She kissed her uncle's cheek and then awkwardly murmured hello to Miguel.

"Miguel's my new assistant," Carlos said.

"More of a hindrance than a help. Your tío's so popular, he's had people standing in line half the morning."

"Good thing somebody showed up first thing to lend me a hand." Carlos winked at her. "Miguel didn't want to take any chances on missing you."

Miguel's face went from a fading pink to a deep red. "I needed some salad makings and since you said you stopped by here on Sundays, I thought I might see you."

When Rita was in seventh grade, a boy had liked her so much he'd ridden his bike all the way out to the junkyard from town, saying he wanted a radio for his older brother, wandering through the cars for over an hour, nothing quite meeting his purported need, but happily keeping her alongside him.

"They have good cinnamon buns here," she said to Miguel. "Tío's not supposed to eat them, but maybe you'd like to join me in one and a cup of coffee."

"Just remember to bring back a small taste for me," Carlos said, shooing them off.

With her uncle watching them walk away, Rita felt almost as shy as she had back in seventh grade. Miguel walked close by her side, their hands within easy reach of each other, yet not touching. He cleared his throat. "Hot out today."

She laughed, relieved to hear Miguel, too, at a loss as to what to say. "It's a scorcher. Almost as warm as the dance hall last night."

They sat on two separate hay bales near a fiddler as they drank their coffee and ate cinnamon buns. "I had a good time last night," Miguel said.

"So did I. It was fun."

"The most fun I've had in months." He wiped his mouth with a paper napkin, as though preventing himself from saying more.

Rita watched him, now lifting his coffee cup, hiding behind it as he had earlier behind the napkin, his nervousness more apparent than her own. It gave her the courage to lay her hand next to his, the hay bale rough and prickly against her palm. Miguel looked down at her hand, near but not touching his, and he lifted his little finger as though saluting her, then lowered it so that his fingertip made contact with hers. Less than an inch of their skin pressed together, yet it quickened her breath.

"I need to return to California," he said.

Rita's hand jerked back from his and she clenched it in her lap, holding it pressed against her thigh. "I should get back to Tío. He could probably use some help." She stood up abruptly, then felt Miguel tugging at her hand, pulling her back down beside him.

"I'll only be gone a couple of weeks. I have to close out my practice there. Wrap up a few loose ends, so that I can feel like I'm really settled here."

A piece of hay poked her in the butt and she readjusted her position so that she was facing him, her knees turned toward his. "You're planning on staying in New Mexico, then?"

"Not only am I staying." He lifted his hand and brushed a strand of hair out of her eye, his fingertips lingering just long enough to send a ripple through her entire body. "I'm hoping to go dancing with you again."

Miguel's lips trembled with the invitation, and she leaned forward and kissed him as lightly as a butterfly fluttering above a flower.

|| **RITA** || Clouds hung over the mountains and the morning held an uncommon chill for summer. Rita sat on the front porch, nursing a cup of coffee. Miguel had been gone over two weeks, and it surprised her how much she missed him. They'd only seen each other a few times, but he already felt like part of her life. He'd called once from California, his voice strained, to tell her it was taking longer than he'd expected to wrap up everything. She knew it entailed more than closing his former practice. Although he had yet to talk about it, she sensed another woman still had a tight grip on his soul.

The sun failed to break through the bank of clouds. Sparrows clustered on the blue mist, the plant's slender stalks bowing under their weight. Their frenzied activity spoke of a pending storm. Rita's gaze drifted across the road. Not a single For Sale sign had appeared. Drew Stinson seemed to have changed his mind about developing the property. Or so she thought until she heard grinding gears, the churning of a bulldozer. But when she scanned the horizon, she saw nothing.

The noise stopped as abruptly as it had started, and Rita stilled herself by clasping the warm mug of coffee tightly in her hands. Then the grating sound started up again. It seemed to come from the hill to the north. The tears in her eyes surprised her. Rita had always prided herself on her strength, on the way she'd survived all kinds of setbacks. Surely she could withstand another encroachment on her land. Forcing herself to turn around, she looked at the houses to the south. Despite their varying shades of desert brown, they were too big to blend in with the landscape. They reminded her of an advancing army, immobile for the moment, but moving in closer and closer. All too soon, despite her wanting to believe otherwise, they would also approach from the east, for Drew Stinson was not a man to give up. If somebody built on the hilltop, too, she would be surrounded on three sides.

She couldn't let it happen. Walking out into the yard, she stood still, pinpointing the sound.

It definitely emerged from the ridgetop.

Enraged by the very thought of somebody building up there, Rita cut through the junkyard. Flojo and Loca tagged along as she headed toward the perimeter of old school buses, the furthest one painted in fading bold colors and psychedelic designs. Stepping beyond this border always felt to her like stepping into a fairyland. The land stood as it had for centuries, with no sign of people. Piñon and juniper trees reigned over the cactus-studded terrain.

A screeching noise ripped through the peaceful scenery, erasing her tears and raising her fighting spirit. Rita rushed through orange splashes of flowering globe mallow, their beauty obscured by her anger. It took her ten minutes to reach the arroyo that marked the edge of her property, the mechanical din accompanying her like a persistent headache. Finally she spotted the source—a bulldozer silhouetted against the gray sky.

Rita plunged down into the arroyo, slogging through the sand to cross it, and then scrambled up the opposite bank, the dogs racing ahead of her. It was a steep climb up the hill. She arrived short of breath at the top, where the bulldozer moved along, mowing down all the trees in its path.

Seeing her, the driver idled the engine and smoothed his mustache. It surprised her that even in her forties, she still caught men's attention. He took off his cap and ran his hands through his compressed hair, lessening the cap's mark. "What can I do for you?"

She skirted an uprooted piñon that had born its years proudly. "Why are you killing these trees?"

He shrugged, absolving himself from any responsibility. "Fellow told me to clear a road for a construction crew."

"A construction crew for what?"

"Gonna build a house down at the end."

Rita winced at the sudden pain in her chest. Telling herself not to vent her anger at this man, who was only doing what he'd been paid to do, she turned away from him. A rare fog had drifted in, blanketing everything within a few yards of her. She looked where she knew the Sangre de Cristos lay shrouded in the mist. Behind her would be the Jemez Mountains. A complete circle on a clear day, a view that had brought her up here many times over the years. The kind of view that prompted people to erect houses. All along the other side of the hill, people had built expensive homes, but nobody had perched one on top, for lack of space.

"This can't be legal," she said.

"He showed me his building permit."

"Where is it?"

The man again shrugged, clearly having lost his initial interest in her and ready to get back to work. "Contractor probably has it."

"Building permits are supposed to be posted."

"Look, lady, I just run this bulldozer. I don't know nothing about the laws."

The churning sound of a car struggling up the rough road caught their attention. The man resumed his bulldozing, and Rita walked over to see who was coming up the hill. She watched as an old Honda Civic carefully avoided the larger rocks in the bulldozer's tracks, slowly advancing up the slope until it got stuck, the tires spinning in the dirt. A silver-haired man emerged from the car and gave her a chagrined look before kneeling down to see what had grounded him. He tried to dig a rock out from under one of the front tires, but it proved futile, and he stood up, brushing off his hands. "Mind helping me out?"

As though he'd understood, Flojo charged down the hill, Loca following at his heels, their tails wagging. "Hey, pooches," the man said, bending over to rub both of them behind their ears. Even in the gray light, his silver head of hair shimmered, giving him a look of distinction. The hair initially made him appear older, until she got close enough to see that he was probably in his late thirties, with few lines in his face, except around his mouth, which curved into a sheepish smile. "I've always told myself one of these days I'd get into trouble for pretending my car was a truck." Although he was dressed in a tweed jacket and expensive boots, his faded jeans had a well-worn look. He wiped his right hand on his back pocket before holding it out to her. "Joe Oakes."

"Rita Vargas," she said, returning his warm handshake. Any man good with dogs and willing to dirty both his hands and his jeans instantly earned a measure of her trust. "Looks like between the two of us, we should be able to push your car clear."

"I'd appreciate it," he said. "Let me put a couple of rocks behind it to keep it from rolling down the hill."

Rita joined him in hefting some of the larger stones from among those shoved aside by the bulldozer, anchoring them in the road a few feet behind the back wheels. "That should keep her in place," he said, and they walked around to the front of the car.

"Here we go." Rita stood beside him, their hands on the hood. It only took one push for the two of them to ease the front end of the small car over the buried boulder and bring it to rest against the rocks braced behind it.

"Ah, the advantages of a lightweight car," Joe said.

"What is it, an eighty-one?"

"Amazing! How'd you know that?"

"I own the junkyard on the other side of the hill."

He patted the car and whispered, "It's okay, Nellie. Don't you worry. I'm not letting anybody haul you off to a junkyard." Then he grinned at Rita, as though all men spoke affectionately to their cars. "Nellie and I go way back. I'd hold onto her forever if I could. We've promised each other she'd stick with me for at least another two years, until our twentieth anniversary."

"I didn't mean to imply she was no good. Any car lucky enough to hang around that long wins my admiration."

Joe leaned against the side of the car. "Yeah, somewhere along the line we quit honoring the notion of making things last, didn't we?"

Despite her fear that Joe was somehow connected to the bulldozing of the ridgetop, she found herself liking him. "So what brings you up here?"

"Any other day, I'd say it was the view, but you can't see a darn thing today, can you?" He peered off in the direction of the Sangre de Cristos. "It's unbelievable that nobody's built up here."

"There's no way!"

His black eyebrows shot up, in dark contrast to his silver hair. "What do you mean?"

Turning away from the questioning intensity of his eyes, she pointed up the hill. "There isn't enough land."

"Not for a gargantuan house like everybody below has, but something modest will sit well."

Fighting to breathe evenly so that her words wouldn't come out too shaky, she forced herself to face him. "Are you the one who's clearing this land to build a house?"

It was as though the sun had burst through the overcast sky, so bright was the joy in his smile. "That's me. Usually I remodel old houses. This'll be the first time I've built anything new." He rubbed his hands together the way Parker used to as a kid when he sat down to play with his Tinker Toys.

"You can't!"

"What?" His mouth drooped, but his eyes hardened. She saw his hands clench before he shoved them into his jacket pockets.

If she told him he couldn't build up there because it was her private sanctuary, he'd smirk and remind her the land didn't belong to her. But once upon a time it had been hers, and she'd been told the hill would never support a house. Desperate to convince herself, she said, "It won't meet city codes."

Joe had one knee bent, a boot resting on the car as he leaned against it. Now he shoved himself off and stood up, his stance unyielding. "I've done everything necessary to get this project approved."

Rita's backbone tautened, stretching to her full height, as though metal lined her spine. She hardly stood as high as his chest, but she threw back her head and met his eyes. "Sometimes the city makes a mistake. Gives out a building permit when they shouldn't have."

He shrugged, as though tossing off any concern, but she could see the corner of his left eye twitching. "Even if that was true, it's too late to do anything about it. The construction crew will be here any minute." He nodded his head in the direction of the bulldozer. "They've promised to have the house done in time for me to celebrate the new year."

"Don't count on it." She would do everything she could to stop him. Hilltops were sacred; they should remain an homage to nature, not monuments to human egos.

His eye began to twitch frenetically, but he still managed an easy smile. "Yeah, I've been in this business long enough to know how many things can go wrong. Especially here in the land of mañana."

She didn't believe he'd misunderstood her threat, but she chose not to clarify it. "I need to get going."

"Thanks for your help." Joe held out his hand again, but she pretended not to see it and turned to walk back up the ridge. Flojo and Loca, ever loyal but frequently fickle, lagged behind, letting him tell them they were good dogs. They didn't rejoin her until after Joe started his car. He beeped his horn as he drove past, his hand out the window, waving.

Rita veered to the left and cut overland so she wouldn't have to watch him reach the top. It hurt too much to think of somebody claiming the hill. She and her father used to picnic up here. It had been their special place.

She started down the other side of the hill, hurrying, running to keep from falling, furious at the city for allowing anybody to build up there. When she'd sold the hill to Leroy, it had been with the understanding that the slope was too steep on her side and the top too narrow to support any houses. The hill was her last remaining buffer against the people who moved further and further out of town.

Her head filled with angry words, Rita swung her arms in keeping with her rapid pace and passed too close to a cholla, scraping against the needles. Cactus spines stuck in the back of her hand, stinging as she walked. Rushing across the junkyard, she practically knocked over Parker as he stepped out from behind an old VW van. He cradled several steering wheels in his arms. "Got any call for these?"

"Take them." She pushed past him, not noticing that he followed her.

"What's going on?" he asked, coming up behind her in the living room as she flipped through the phone book.

"Some guy's trying to build a house up on the ridge."

"How can he? There's no room."

She picked up the phone and punched in numbers. "Tell that to the city."

"As if anybody in the city would listen to us."

"Shit! Voice mail." She paused, listening to the message. "Oh, how convenient. He's out of town until next week." Impatiently, she waited for the recording to end. "Gilbert, it's Rita Vargas. You know why I'm calling. Get back to me first thing Monday morning."

She thrust the handset into the phone's cradle, only to have it fall to the floor. Parker shifted the steering wheels to one arm and bent down to retrieve it, calmly rehanging it on the wall. "Sounds like you've got a fight on your hands."

"I can't believe Gilbert allowed this."

"Doesn't surprise me. Look at the way his brother Leroy wheels and deals."

"What's happening to this town? I remember when people respected the land. Now all these rich folks are moving in, thinking they can do whatever they want."

"No point in getting all worked up when there's nothing you can do for now. Why don't you come see my latest sculpture."

Even before he learned to talk, Parker had had a knack for calming her. He used to climb up in her lap whenever she was upset, throwing his little arms around her neck, his head against her chest. She'd sometimes worried that being the only child of an unwed mother had forced him into an early maturity, cheating him out of a carefree childhood. Even after all these years, she kept bracing herself for him to take a bad turn.

They headed out behind her house, through the vegetable garden, out past the gnarled apple trees her grandparents had planted, down a path Parker had lined with some of his earliest sculptures, large figures made of everything from hot water tanks and mufflers to radiators and culverts. At night they looked like aliens patrolling the land, but in the light of day they reminded Rita of sentries, ever ready to protect her.

As she and Parker came around the hill, they saw a blonde woman in jogging clothes stroking one of the sculptures outside his trailer. Then the woman squatted down in front of the robotic figure, pushing on it, as though testing its stability.

"Go ahead, see if you can make it topple," Parker said.

Alarmed by his unexpected voice, the woman jumped up. She had long legs and the thinness of a serious runner. "I had no intention of knocking it over." Quickly recovering her composure, she held out her hand, her body rippling like quicksilver. "I'm Chloe Alexander."

Parker shook her hand, but Rita stood back. She had never trusted blondes. "You're trespassing."

"Come on, Rita," Parker said, "since when did you cater to property lines? You've walked over a lot of land owned by other people."

"Sorry," the blonde said. "I was running in the arroyo when I saw these sculptures, and I couldn't resist taking a closer look. I didn't mean to intrude."

"No problem. You can stop by here anytime you want. My name's Parker."

"Is this your work?"

"Or my folly, depending how you look at it." He grinned. Rita could tell the woman was charmed by him, as most women were. Parker only had to flash those white teeth of his or caress women with his brilliantly green eyes and they quivered. His easy smile, along with the emerald color of his eyes, were the only things he'd inherited from his father, a man who also had a way with women.

"This is the first time I've jogged out here, but you'll be seeing more of me." She pointed in the direction of the ridge. "We're building a house up on that hill."

Rita felt Parker's hand on her shoulder, turning her in the direction of his work shed before she could lash out at the woman. "It was nice meeting you, Chloe," he said, pressing Rita forward. "But if you'll excuse us, we have some work to do."

"Sure, don't let me interfere." She gave a wave and took off down the arroyo, running toward the ridgetop as the mist turned into rain.

|| **JOE** || Wondering what was taking her so long, Joe waited on the hill for Chloe to finish her jog. The construction crew had arrived half an hour ago and started staking out the foundation. Their steady progress helped to still his concern about Rita. Everything having to do with the house itself was legal. There was nothing she could do to stop him.

Even now, with the fog hiding the views, he understood why somebody would want to preserve this place. Yet all over Santa Fe, people had begun to build on the ridges. Why should he turn down this opportunity for a dream house? If he didn't build up here, somebody else would.

"Gonna be a beauty, Joe," Santiago said, walking up to him with the rolled plans in his hand. "You did a nice job on these drawings."

"It's the closest I'll ever get to being an architect." Hearing the bitterness in his voice, Joe hurried to cover over it, dismayed that after all these years he still resented his ex-wife for interfering with his career plans. "I had fun designing it."

"It's going to be a pleasure to build. You didn't cut any corners."

"Only the size. It's a pretty small lot."

"Won't be any adobe palaces up here, that's for sure. Can't believe how big some of my clients go."

"That last guy you built for. The CEO out in Las Campanas. He didn't go too big, did he?"

"Depends what you call big. Three thousand square feet."

"That's manageable."

"Sure it is, if it's where you live. But he's only going to be here a few weeks out of the year. He and his wife own three other homes." Santiago's tongue probed the inside of his cheek, as though looking for something. "I don't get it. Carlotta says it's all she can do to keep our one house clean. How can they handle four?"

"Believe me, that man's wife isn't the one who cleans their houses."

"True, but still . . ." Santiago shook his head. "Beats me why anybody would want more than one home. Not that I'm complaining. Keeps me and my men working."

"Shoot, you're working so much, I was afraid you wouldn't be available to do this. And I wouldn't have wanted anybody else."

"I've got a good crew, don't I?"

"The best." Joe might have drawn an acceptable design for the house, but it would be a trophy as a result of Santiago. "It's one thing to renovate an existing structure, and quite another to start from the ground up. This is a whole new ball game for me. I'm counting on your expertise to carry me through."

Santiago tapped the palm of his hand with the blueprints. "Hey, with these plans, nothing could go wrong."

Joe remembered how Rita had looked when she told him he couldn't build up here. With her rigid back, she'd come across as tall, though she stood no higher than his chest. When they'd pushed his car, he'd felt her strength, greater than his own.

Joe kicked a rock past Santiago's scuffed work boots. "You've been doing construction a long time, Santiago. You think there's a problem with this ridge not being big enough for my house?"

"Hell, no. You could put three more houses up here."

Three more houses, the exact number Joe was counting on. The knot in his stomach loosened. "A woman marched up to me this morning before you got here and said there was no way this hill would support my house."

"Be a little problem with erosion, but that's why the city has you putting in those containment ponds."

"I don't think that's what she was worried about. She acted like she owned the place."

He heard Santiago suck air between his teeth, filtering his words. "It's been hard for some of the old-timers to watch new people moving into town, buying up the land. Used to be you could come out here and there was nothing but old man Vargas's wrecking yard on the other side."

"That's who it was. Well, not a man, but a woman who said she owns the wrecking yard."

If Santiago's eyes hadn't crinkled, Joe wouldn't have known he fought a smile. "Rita, Rita." The trill of his voice revealed the affection behind the hidden smile. "She's been living out here so long, she thinks half the county belongs to her."

Again Joe pictured how on a clear day you could see both the Sangre de Cristo and the Jemez Mountains from up here. He didn't blame Rita for wanting to keep the place undeveloped, like a private park. But he owned the land now, fair and square.

"Problem is," Santiago said, his words immediately alarming Joe, "she used to own this hill. Her grandparents had a big ranch, but then her father got cancer, and she had to sell this hill to pay off some of the bills."

So she was the woman who had somehow scorned Leroy, resulting in his promoting the hilltop as buildable after promising he wouldn't. Joe had recognized a sense of betrayal underlying Rita's anger. It reminded him of his own feelings of having been cheated out of his entitlement in life. She was driven, as was he, to do all that was possible to regain what had been lost. "If she's from one of the old families, does it mean she has political ties that could keep me from building up here?"

This time, Santiago didn't try to contain his smile. "Rita? The woman could talk a man into doing lots of things, but she has fought city hall since the day they insisted she get a business license."

Joe felt the tightness in his stomach finally slacken. If Rita disliked bureaucracies, she wouldn't have the patience to find the loopholes in his plan. "So I guess the only thing that will slow us down is the weather."

The fog had turned into a drizzle. "Might have to call it quits early today," Santiago said, "but this storm should blow over soon." He opened the door of his truck and tossed the blueprints onto the front seat. "No point in you standing out here getting wet."

"Whatever you say, boss." Joe got into his car. "See you Monday morning."

He was fortunate to have Santiago as his contractor. It meant the house would be well-built and finished according to schedule. The sooner he and Chloe started living up here, the more secure he'd feel about everything else. The mere thought of Chloe living with him gave him a sense of optimism. At first it had been her physical beauty, her willowy body, that captivated him. Then, as he watched her fight to make her gallery a success, he'd regained his conviction that people could manifest their strongest wishes.

With his divorce, Joe had lost his belief in love, in the ability to forge a future with another person. Sharon had professed to love him the very first time they had sex on the tiny twin bed in his dorm room, and she'd risked her family's disapproval when they rented an apartment together. After they married, they bought a small bungalow, later moving up into a two-story Tudor. But as their living accommodations expanded, their love diminished. Sharon had an insatiable appetite for things he couldn't afford. Whereas Chloe was content to live on her own earnings, appreciating any additional means he provided as welcome, but unnecessary, extravagances. They would both pay for this house, working together to make it mutually theirs.

The passenger door opened, and Chloe got in, careful not to touch him with her wet body as she kissed his cheek. "You didn't even see me come up, did you?"

"Look at you! You're soaked. Aren't you freezing?"

"I ran fast enough to work up a good heat." She retrieved the towel she'd thrown into the backseat earlier and dried the water off her face. After a few vain dabs at the rest of her body, she wrapped the towel into a turban around her head. Anybody else, he thought, would have looked pathetic, legs splattered with mud and shoes squeaking with water, but she shimmered. "I came across some incredible sculptures while I was jogging. Work I might like to represent."

Joe pointed at the crew still working in the rain. "Before you know it, they'll be ready to pour the footings."

She gave a brief glance out the window. "Sorry, but I can't get too excited until there's something a little more three-dimensional. God, I wish you could have seen these sculptures, Joe. The work's so unusual, and I don't think anybody in town is showing it."

"I better take you home before you catch a cold," he said, starting the car and turning on the heater. He wouldn't show his disappointment in her lack of excitement about the construction process. Like she said, she needed to see something more substantial before it seemed real to her. For him, though, the very fact the work had begun made their house no longer a dream but a given.

|| **RITA** || By the time they reached Parker's work shed, the rain had swelled into a downpour and the temperature plummeted. Rita paced the concrete floor while he lit a fire in the woodstove. The corrugated steel room was slow to warm, but her rising anger quickly heated her. "Why wouldn't you let me say anything to that woman?"

"Want a cup of tea?" Parker held up an electric kettle. When she shook her head, he filled it with enough water for himself, then measured tea leaves into a brown earthenware pot, infuriating her with his slow, deliberate movements. Finally, he leaned back against the table and looked over at her, the kettle behind him sputtering. "I know how much that ridge means to you, Mom. But I . . ."

"No, Parker, you don't know how much that ridge means to me." She turned and gazed out the window that overlooked the arroyo. Through the clouded pane, she could see little but sodden chamisa, yet she knew the ridge lay on the other side of the arroyo. When she was a baby, her father used to carry her up there on his back. He claimed that her first word was not "Papa," but "cerro," the Spanish word for hill. After he died, she'd discovered that when she walked up there, it was as though he still accompanied her. Like there really was a heaven, and she'd come a few feet closer to it.

She turned back to face Parker. "You have no idea how much that hill means to me."

Parker kicked at a metal can, sending it clanking across the floor until it hit a roll of barbed wire. His lips pursed, like he'd just swallowed something bitter. "Look, we've been over this before. Call me dense, but you're right, I don't understand why a piece of dirt is so holy." He walked over, picked up the coil of barbed wire, and began to unroll it.

She wanted to rip the wire out of his hands, let the barbs rake across his palms. Instead, she watched as he bent the wire, shaping it into a bird with outspread wings. He could no more keep his hands still than she could her feet. Lifting the bird above his head, he made it swoop through the air, as though it were flying. Lost in what he was doing, he didn't notice her moving closer. When he brought the bird down to light on the back of a tattered armchair, she took it from him. She watched as his hands flopped about, wanting the bird, searching for something to hold. He crossed over to the table and poured a cup of tea, but she could see the tension straining his shoulders.

"You have your art," she said, returning the bird to him. "I have nothing but this land. It's what anchors me."

"You want to see my new sculpture or not?"

She fought the temptation to say "no." To hurt him, as he had her. It always surprised her that much as she loved Parker, she would some-times have flashes of incredible resentment toward him. Her own mother had abandoned her as a infant, and she had vowed she would never let Parker feel slighted, but sometimes she had these overwhelm-ing urges to be as self-centered and childish as he was.

"Where is it?"

"You're standing next to it."

Looking down, she saw a rocking chair that came up to her knees. Old tailpipes, polished to a high sheen, formed the chair, which rested on curved metal strips like the kind she used to edge her flower beds. Rita touched it with her toe and set it in motion. Rocking back and forth in the chair sat a metal child, presumably a girl, with wire shav-ings as curls and a mirror for her face. "Getting sentimental on me?"

He shrugged his shoulders. "Guess you could call it that. I'm going to make a whole family."

"Whole meaning with a mother and a father?"

"That's right. An idealized version of the family unit. Complete with a father. The ever more commonly missing element."

She chose to ignore his sarcasm. Parker had never met his father and she knew he faulted her for that. "So what spurred this? Don't tell me you're thinking about getting married and having kids."

She watched as his mouth opened wide in laughter. Parker had a no-holds-barred laugh, one that came from deep inside him. "Me married? That'll be the day. I'm worse than you are when it comes to insisting on my independence." He crouched down and tenderly lifted the child out of the rocker, setting her on his knee. "Doesn't keep me from liking kids, though. And this one's real low maintenance." He rearranged a wire curl on the girl's head, put her back in the chair, and stood up. "More importantly, I think it'll sell."

"Don't bank on it." She'd seen him get his hopes up too many times.

Her words angered him, cording the muscles in his neck. "I've got a far better chance of selling this baby than you do of stopping that house on the ridge."

III

Monday morning, Rita hovered near the phone, waiting for Gilbert's call. When eleven o'clock rolled around and she still hadn't heard from him, she changed from her tennies to cowboy boots and hopped in her truck.

She never went into town without regretting how much Santa Fe had changed. Not that long ago downtown had been the heart of the community. She'd made her first Communion at the cathedral, had her first date at the Woolworth's lunch counter in sixth grade, and got her first job at Big Joe's Hardware. Now tourists overran the place and locals rarely gathered there. Plus, parking had become a chore. Rita drove around for ten minutes before she found a space.

Getting out of the truck and pulling the cuffs of her jeans down over her boots, she eyed the meter, but refused to put money in it, remembering when none of the streets had meters. She resented the city charging for things that used to be free. If she was lucky and the right meter readers came by, they would recognize her truck and walk on past without giving her a ticket.

Outside city hall, Rita bowed her head at the statue of Saint Francis. She liked to think of him, with his love of animals, as her own special patron saint. Maybe he would help her. Environmentalists talked about a loss of habitat endangering species. She felt endangered by her loss of land. Would Saint Francis sympathize?

She entered the building through the side door and paused at the directory to locate Gilbert's department. Taking the elevator up to the second floor, she shrugged off the receptionist's questions and walked into his office. There he sat, leaning back in a chair, feet on his desk, reading the newspaper, not noticing Rita's entrance until the receptionist clattered up on her high heels. "Sorry, Gilbert, I tried to stop her."

Gilbert lowered the paper, but kept his feet on the desk. "It's okay, Becca." He nodded his head, dismissing the woman, who gave a little huff, and walked away as fast as her tight skirt would let her. Then he stood up, all smiles. "Rita, good to see you. I was just about to give you a call." Coming around the desk, his arms opening wide, he exuded the friendliness that had carried him further in life than she would have ever thought possible. Sensing she didn't want a hug, he let his arms drop, his hands open in supplication. "It's almost noon. Can I take you to lunch?"

"This isn't a social visit, Gilbert."

Not put off by her tone, Gilbert sat on the corner of his desk. He had gained weight, but it only deepened the dimples when he smiled. "Been what?" He paused, visibly doing the math in his head. "Almost a year since I've seen you. Not since last Fiestas. Qué pasa?"

Rita hated it when people who spoke very little Spanish would lapse into commonly known phrases in an attempt to establish an immediate kinship. This time, though, she opted to play the game. "Muchas cosas. Specifically the house on the ridge. It can't meet city codes."

Sitting on the desk, Gilbert only had one foot on the floor, and now the other began to swing back and forth. Whether the movement stemmed from nervousness or boredom, she couldn't tell. "Which house are you talking about? So many are being built, I can't keep track of all of them."

"The only one that concerns me is on that hill my family used to own." She waited for him to meet her eyes. "The one I sold to your brother."

"You mean the Oakes project?" Gilbert's foot swung harder, a counterforce to the lightness in his voice. "Piece of cake. Just the one house."

"One house is one too many!" She started to launch into a lecture about how the city was getting overrun, but then noticed the enormous street map on the wall behind his desk and reminded herself that most people espoused growth as good for the economy. Forcing herself to calm down, she looked across his office and out the window, garnering strength from the outdoors. A cottonwood rose above the building, its upper branches swaying in the wind. "This last storm didn't bring much rain, but if somebody builds up there, the first gully washer that comes along is going to dump a ton of mud on my land."

"Come on, Rita. That ridge has been there forever. Anybody can take a look at the arroyo below it and see where all the runoff goes. Your property won't suffer."

"What about the escarpment ordinances?" Surely some rule had been violated, some corner cut, to allow Joe to build on a hill she'd been told would never support a house.

This time Gilbert rolled his eyes, showing he routinely had to deal with such questions. "He's in compliance with all the codes." Gilbert stood up and briefly laid a hand on her shoulder. "You should meet the guy. Nice fellow. He's not doing anything outlandish up there. Just a small house, not much bigger than yours really."

Rita thought back to Joe's old car and how he prided himself on keeping it for a long time. A simple car, nothing fancy. Maybe he would keep his house unpretentious too. "Show me the plans."

Gilbert walked back around to the other side of his desk. "The house plans? Sure, I can get those for you." He shuffled through a messy pile of papers on his desk and then looked at his watch. "I have a meeting right after lunch. Might last most of the afternoon. Can you come back tomorrow?"

"Can't somebody else get me the plans?"

"No telling whose desk they're on. Let me handle it and I'll have them for you first thing tomorrow morning."

Rita hated to drive back into town again, but she also didn't want to hang around waiting for somebody to find the plans. "I'll come by at eight tomorrow."

Gilbert scratched behind his ear, a habit she remembered him resorting to whenever he was embarrassed. "I don't usually make it in until eight-thirty. You know how it is. Have to get the kids to school in the morning."

Rita had never met his second wife, but she'd seen him with his second set of children, a boy and a girl not much older than his grandson. No wonder he had rings under his eyes. "Just leave the papers with your receptionist."

Gilbert switched to scratching his other ear. "She might misplace them."

Rita sighed. "I'll meet you at eight-thirty tomorrow."

|| JOE || Joe never entered Chloe's gallery without a glow of accomplishment. He considered it the best of all his renovations. He loved the way the sunlight came through the expanded front window and played on the warmth of the refurbished hardwood floors. By knocking down the wall between the living room and the dining room, he'd created an inviting, open area where she displayed large artworks.

When he passed into one of the side rooms that housed smaller pieces, he saw a man standing too close to Chloe as they examined an alabaster sculpture. The man had a vague familiarity, like somebody Joe had seen in a movie. It wouldn't be the first time an actor had bought a piece from Chloe, but it made him particularly uneasy to watch good-looking men flirt with her. This one ran his hands suggestively over the sculpture, murmuring, "I love the smoothness."

"Her work beckons to be touched, doesn't it?" Chloe trailed her fingers across a rounded curve.

Much as it upset Joe to hear her play along with the man, he had to admire her finesse, the way she knew to echo and enhance a customer's sentiments. Aware he might hinder a possible sale by hovering too close, he scooted out of the room, trying to look as inconspicuous as possible with his picnic basket and folding table.

He went into Chloe's office, where art books filled the built-in shelves of a former pantry. The rooms suited her needs so well, it was as though he'd remodeled the house specifically for her. He would never forget the first time she saw the place and exclaimed that fate had intended for them to meet.

The man in the other room asked how late the gallery was open and Chloe murmured a reply. Shortly afterward, the bell over the front door chimed and she came back to her office, disappointment slouching her shoulders. "Another 'let me think about it.'" She kicked off her shoes and slumped against the wall. "I must be losing my touch."

"He obviously liked the piece. I bet he'll be back."

"I hope so." Chloe sighed, digging her fingers through her hair and pulling it away from her face like some form of penance. "I've got to make more sales if we're going to build our house."

"We'll build our house, don't you worry." Joe unfolded the teak table he'd brought. Then, opening the picnic basket, he whisked out a linen tablecloth, unfurled it with a snap of his wrists, and covered the round table. Next he brought forth a small bottle of champagne and crystal flutes.

"What's all this?" Chloe asked, as he handed her the two glasses.

"It's a special occasion," he said, uncorking the champagne.

Chloe quickly slipped the glasses under the bottle to catch the bubbly flow. She gave him one and raised her own. "What are we toasting?"

Joe lightly clinked his glass against hers. "Here's to breaking ground on our new house."

"That was last Friday, silly." Taking a sip of her champagne, Chloe began rummaging in the picnic basket. "What other goodies did you bring? Oh, yum, a baguette." She pulled out the bread and set it on the table.

He told himself her nonchalance about the ground breaking was really a good thing, a sign she took their house for granted. "Sit," he commanded, "and let me wait on you."

With a sigh of pleasure, Chloe pulled a chair up to the table and sat down, watching as he put three imported cheeses on a plate. When he placed a container of olives on the table, she began nibbling them. "I'm starved."

Joe's ex-wife had dieted constantly, taking the fun out of their meals. He loved that Chloe had a big appetite and relished food without a thought about calories. He sat down and leaned across the table to kiss her again. "Save room for dessert."

"When have you ever known me not to have room for dessert?" She spread some Brie on a slice of baguette and passed it to him.

Before he could take a bite, his cell phone rang. Chloe's lips crumpled and then pressed together in an obvious effort not to complain. She'd once commented that his phone felt like a peeping Tom, intruding on their most private moments.

"Hello."

"Joe? Gilbert Sena here. We've got trouble. Somebody insisting on seeing the plans for your house."

"According to what you and your brother told me, there shouldn't be any problem." Joe nodded his head at Chloe, encouraging her to eat, as though everything were normal, while tension twisted his own stomach.

"What if she starts snooping around?"

If Chloe hadn't been sitting there, Joe would have lambasted him. Gilbert and Leroy had insisted that once his house was approved, everything would proceed smoothly.

"Who is it? Rita Vargas?" He saw Chloe tilt her head, listening to what he said, a glass suspended halfway between the table and her lips.

"How'd you know?" Gilbert asked.

"I ran into her snooping around the site." Joe stroked Chloe's hand, urging her to drink her champagne. "She helped me get my car out of a rut and then tried to tell me nobody could build up there."

"If she had her way, nobody would."

"But I am."

Momentary silence on the other end. "So you think if I show her the house plans, that'll satisfy her?"

Joe wondered what had happened to Gilbert's self-assurance. Did Rita wield such influence that she could bring him to the point of confessing what they'd done? Joe pointed at the Stilton, motioning for Chloe to cut him a piece, trying to act as though nothing were wrong. "When is she coming to look at the plans?"

"Tomorrow at eight-thirty."

"I'll meet you then." He didn't trust Gilbert to be discreet. They had to make sure Rita thought only one house was being built. Wait until after the city approved the plat division for her to find out about the other three.

Joe put the phone back in his jacket, dipped a knife into the goat cheese, spread some on a piece of bread, and handed it to Chloe as a token of apology. "Sorry about that."

She bit into the bread, searching his face for the answer to some unvoiced question. "May I have more champagne?" She held her glass out to him, and he refilled it, waiting for the real question. "Is Rita Vargas the woman who lives down by that junkyard?"

It wasn't the question he'd feared. He'd assumed she would ask why Gilbert had called, and he'd have to frame his answers carefully, concealing the manipulations necessary to guarantee the subdivision's eventual approval. "How do you know Rita?"

"I met her and that sculptor last Friday when I was out jogging."

"What sculptor?" He recalled how she'd returned late from her run that rainy day, talking about somebody's artwork, but he hadn't paid much attention.

"The guy I told you about who uses scrap metal. Young fellow."

"How young?"

Chloe paused, wiping at the corner of her mouth as though it were dirty. "My age. With a real surety to his work."

She said it curtly, with a crispness cold as winter, and Joe hurried to cover his jealousy. "So what's his stuff look like?"

Instantly, her eyes brightened. "You should see it, Joe. He had this woman, made out of a car bumper, stretched out on old rusty bedsprings, with a truck grill as the headboard." She moved her hands as she talked, trying to duplicate the sculpture in the air. "The amazing thing about it was, there's all this hard metal, yet somehow he'd made it sensuous."

Joe poured himself more champagne, remembering some ugly things made out of old tires and trashed metal that he'd seen between Berkeley and San Francisco, rising out of the mud flats like creatures from the deep lagoon. "So you liked this guy's stuff?"

"I liked the couple of pieces I saw, but I need to look at more of it to know whether I want to carry him."

"And you say he works down by the junkyard?"

"Lives there, from what I could tell."

Joe wondered whether this man, too, would try to intervene in his subdivision on the ridgetop. "You think he's the junkyard woman's husband?"

Chloe laughed. "I hope not. He's almost young enough to be her son."

Joe had seen plenty of men with wives young enough to be their daughters. The eleven years between him and Chloe wasn't that big of a divide, but he worried she would one day seek a lover more her age, somebody artsy.

"On the other hand," she added, "they're obviously close."

"Maybe they have some kind of deal where he helps her in exchange for spare parts."

"Could be. Although he sure didn't talk to her like an employee. Chewed her out when she accused me of trespassing."

"Trespassing! You should have seen her charge across the ridgetop like she still owned it."

"She used to own the land where we're building?" Chloe's voice quavered. He could tell she was thinking about her parents who'd been forced to sell part of their farm after a prolonged drought.

"You know how the Hispanics are in this town. Tracing their families back to the Spaniards' arrival. They act like they have a divine right to the land."

Chloe spun the knife that lay between them, its cheese-coated blade blending with the linen tablecloth as it turned around and around. "We're displacing them, just like they did the Indians."

"Nobody forced her to sell that hill."

Chloe leaned back, her body ever supple, like clay molding itself to the curved back of the chair. "Why does she want to see the house plans?"

"Dessert?" Joe reached into the picnic basket, and presented two chocolate brownies. "I got your favorite."

Chloe unwrapped the plastic from her brownie and licked the gooey icing off her fingers. "Is she trying to stop us from building up there?"

"There's no way she can."

"I don't know. The way she treated me, I gather she doesn't much care for people and would do whatever it takes to maintain her privacy."

Joe took a bite of his brownie, the richness almost too much for him. Wishing he had a cup of coffee to wash it down, he rubbed his tongue over the roof of his mouth, loosening the cloying stickiness. "When I bought that land, Leroy said some people would resent me building on it because they were used to hiking up there for the view. But that's what happens when a town becomes a popular place to live. Unless you can afford to buy up all the land around you, you have to get used to the idea of having neighbors."

III

Joe showed up at city hall early, anxious to meet with Gilbert before Rita arrived. When he approached the receptionist, she sat applying polish to her nails, barely acknowledging him with an upward glance of her eyes. He wondered if the fumes had rendered her speechless.

"I have an appointment with Gilbert."

"You Joe Oates?"

"Oakes," he corrected her.

She shrugged and started painting another nail. "Gilbert just called. He's going to be a few minutes late. Said you can wait in his office with that woman who has an appointment too."

Joe's hands instinctively contracted into fists. He hid them in his pockets, debating whether to face Rita alone. Maybe he could disarm her, chat about something else while they waited. Keeping his hands in his pockets, affecting a carefree look, he sauntered into Gilbert's office.

Her back to him, Rita stood behind the desk, looking at the large street map on the wall. The sun coming through the window bounced off the long black hair that shielded her like armor. "Good morning, neighbor."

Her shoulders stiffened at the words, and it seemed to take her a long time to turn around. When she did, her eyes stabbed him. "I'm not your neighbor. You're not living next to me."

Obviously she wasn't going to respond to any attempted pleasantries. He might as well get their business out in the open and act as though everything was hunky-dory. "I hear you want to see my house plans."

He fingered some loose coins in his pockets as she looked at him, her head tilted to one side, like a bird, assessing him. "I'm curious," she said. "The way you love your old car, can you understand how I love that hill?"

It was so far removed from anything he'd anticipated her saying that he couldn't think of a response. The sound of the money in his pocket filled the room. He let go of the coins, the metal jangling, then falling silent. Placing his hands on the desk, he leaned toward her. "Who wouldn't love that hill? It's an amazing place. That's why I'm doing all I can to preserve its beauty."

"By tearing down trees and erecting a house that'll stand out like a sore thumb?"

"I'm cutting no more trees than absolutely necessary, and my house is meant to blend in with the hill as much as possible."

"But it's still a house. A house on a hill that was never meant to hold a house." She walked out from behind the desk, her hair swinging back and forth angrily. "I never would've sold that land if I'd known somebody would build up there."

Joe backed away from her, shoving his hands into his pockets again. "I never would have bought that land if I couldn't live up there."

Rita had a fine featured nose, but now her nostrils flared in open contempt. "Leroy sold it to you, didn't he? Probably said he'd only bought it to help out a friend, and that he was giving you a great deal."

Chagrined to think Leroy had made a fool of him, Joe did no more than nod.

Rita gave a snort of shared indignation. "Leroy's real good at that kind of thing. Making it seem like he's doing everybody involved a big favor."

"Sorry I'm late." Gilbert trundled into the room. "Got halfway to the school before my daughter remembered she'd left her homework on the kitchen table." His cheeks puffed up and he let out a sigh of feigned exasperation. "Kids! Can't count on them to be responsible."

"All depends what their parents teach them," Rita said.

"Yeah, we try our best," Gilbert said, as though she'd handed him a bar of soap to wash himself clean of any fault.

"I've been explaining to Rita that your brother sold me that hill."

Joe had meant the words as a warning, but Gilbert only beamed. "Yeah, Leroy knows the best buys." He turned to Rita. "He says you sold it to him for practically nothing."

"Enough to help pay my father's medical bills."

"You should have asked for more."

Rita took a step toward Gilbert, red cowboy boots flashing under her jeans. "A hill with only one buildable slope isn't worth much money."

Before Joe could jump in with an explanation, Gilbert repeated what Leroy had told him. "Construction techniques have changed a lot in the past ten years. We've learned ways to stabilize a hillside so people can build on top."

Rita rocked back and forth on her red boots, rising up to her toes as she addressed Gilbert. "Ten years ago nobody would have paid your brother's price."

Joe still winced to think how much the hill had cost him. If the subdivision didn't go through, he'd have to declare bankruptcy. "I paid a lot, but I worked hard to earn the money."

"And now you're going to stick some ridiculously large house up there to prove to the world what you're worth."

Joe felt like she'd taken aim with those pointy toed boots of hers and kicked him in the balls. He might have some insecurities about not being as rich as his ex-wife would have liked, but he'd never had a need to display his wealth. "I don't have the slightest interest in a big house. What I do want is a beautiful piece of property. And that's exactly what I bought."

Gilbert opened his arms and put one around each of them, like a boxing referee intervening before they could beat up each other. "Let's take a look at those house plans and see just how small Joe's place is." He nudged them both over to a table under the window, where several rolled papers lay.

Joe quickly scanned the names printed on the rolls, hoping Gilbert hadn't inadvertently included the drawings for the proposed plat division. Rita snatched a roll labeled "Oakes," stripping the rubber band off and flattening it on the desk with the quickness of an eagle swooping down on a rodent.

Gilbert pressed in beside her, his pudgy hands holding down the curled edges. "I'm just guessing, but I'd say your house, Rita, is about twelve hundred square feet. Joe's will be two thousand, not much bigger really. Very similar when it comes down to it. A great room, a . . ."

"What in the hell is a great room?" she asked.

Joe chuckled, relieved to add some levity to the situation. "It's an ostentatious name for a combination living, family, and dining room. The idea is to create a more open space."

Rita didn't grant the respect of turning to look at him when he spoke. If anything, her back became more rigid, and a craggy silence rose between them.

Then Gilbert patted the plans, a reassuring thumping sound like a heart resuming its beat. "He's going to have three bedrooms, one more than you have. A kitchen big enough to be functional without being huge. And a second bathroom, which just about everybody has these days. Only thing different really is he has a garage and a couple of patios."

Joe stood behind Gilbert and Rita, watching them as they hunched over the drawing. Rita traced lines with her finger, verifying the displayed dimensions. "The master bedroom is twice the size of the other bedrooms?"

"That's the style these days. Me and Valerie have one big enough for a loveseat. We like to watch TV in there after the kids go to bed."

Rita's head bobbed, barely afloat with the concept. "And the patios?" Finally she turned around to look at Joe. "Going to enclose them with high walls?"

"And block out the view I paid all that money for? You've got to be kidding!"

Her front teeth worked her lower lip, scraping over it for a minute before she turned back to Gilbert. "And all this is legal?"

"Hundred percent."

She began marching back and forth in front of the window, the sun flashing off her hair when she crossed its path. "What about the road coming up from the other side? It looks like it'll cause some serious erosion problems."

The dimples in Gilbert's face wobbled as he tried to restrain a smile. "Since when have you worried about the rich people on the other side of the hill?"

Rita stamped her foot, like a petulant diva accustomed to getting her way. Joe could see what Santiago meant about her ability to entice a man. She had a mixture of regal beauty and feistiness that gave off a strong sexual spark. "I don't trust you, Gilbert. You or your brother. This wouldn't be the first time you got city approval for a shady deal."

"There's nothing shady about my house," Joe said. "We went over the city building codes very carefully. The site conforms to all the slope restrictions and there'll be drainage ponds to prevent erosion on either side of the hill."

Rita's mouth pursed with skepticism. "I think I better take a look at those building codes myself. See what's really going on."

Behind her, Gilbert raised his eyebrows, waiting for him to respond. Joe thought of the numerous manuals he and Leroy had paged through to make sure everything, with the exception of the road, was in order. Since Rita didn't know about the plan to build more houses, she'd never uncover their one and only infringement of the rules.

"You might want to bring a magnifying glass," Joe told her, "to read the fine print."

|| **RITA** || When walking the land failed to calm her, Rita headed over to her uncle's. Even before her father died, she had turned to Carlos for consolation. Different though the two brothers were, they shared a solidity that kept her rooted when she felt she might dissolve in a storm of emotions. Although she'd never known her mother, people told Rita she had Loretta Salazar's temperament, quick to inflame and slow to soothe. Incidents like this morning's meeting at city hall fanned an anger in her that she could not control.

She felt as crowded as the cows in the cattle truck sitting in her uncle's driveway. Fear widened their eyes and Rita winced at the sound of their misery. They moaned and bellowed as Pat Archuleta coaxed them out one by one, down the ramp to where Carlos shepherded them from atop his horse, moving them toward what had once been the front pasture. Caught up in their work, neither man could do more than nod at her. Carlos circled around the cows, his gravelly voice nudging them along with a gentle prod, only yelling if a startled one bolted. Although he mocked cows for their dumbness, she had seen him cry whenever one died. At birthings, he had the patience of a midwife, softly reassuring the mothers as they labored, welcoming the calves into the world. Nowadays he spoke to his vegetables, but she knew he missed the reciprocity of animals and couldn't resist this opportunity to participate in one last cattle drive. The frightened cows churned the dirt, raising skirts of dust and filling the air with their laments, as he moved among them with his dogs, working to keep them herded together.

From around the front of the cattle truck, Miguel emerged astride a bay mare. Seeing him so unexpectedly brought her a rush of pleasure. His shoulders had the relaxed curve of a man at ease on a horse. Although he'd forsaken ranching, he had obviously not lost his familiarity with it. He whistled and called to the cows, helping to round them up for the move to the far pasture.

When he saw Rita, he gave her a familiar grin as though weeks didn't lie between them. "I just got back into town last night. Why don't you grab a horse and join us?"

"Your saddle's in the tack room," her uncle added unnecessarily.

"Okay if I take Gordo?"

"He's whinnying for you already," Carlos said. Indeed, Gordo had come up to the corral fence and stood eyeing her.

"Looks like he could use the exercise," Miguel said, noting the horse's wide girth.

"Doesn't do any good. He eats everything in his path." Sure enough, as she entered the corral, Gordo began leading her to the bushel basket of apples in the stable. "I'll be back in a couple of minutes."

Joining the cattle drive would help take her mind off the house on the ridgetop. And it would serve to remind her that even with people building to the south, east, and north of her, at least for now the western side would stay open. Pat's owning the far pasture provided a semblance of things remaining the same, with cattle grazing in the setting sun.

By the time she saddled Gordo, the men had gotten all the cows out of the truck, and Pat mounted his horse too. He and Miguel channeled the herd toward the back gate, moving them across the first pasture, where her uncle planned to raise corn next year.

"Something the matter?" Carlos asked, bringing up the rear with her.

"I'm better now," she said, laughing at Flojo and Loca, who were pretending to be cattle dogs, yapping at the heels of a yearling who ignored them and trailed far behind the rest of the herd.

Carlos whistled for one of his own dogs who successfully pressed the young cow to rejoin the others. Then he directed his attention back to Rita. "Why didn't you tell me there's a man threatening to close the junkyard?"

"Because it upsets me to talk about it." The cattle's hooves beat into the dirt like hands on a drum, pounding out a rhythm of dust. Rita sneezed as the dust filled her nose, her eyes tearing. "Everything I have that reminds me of Papa is being erased."

"Miguel says he spent all this morning at the law library, trying to find a way to keep you in business."

"He did?"

Her uncle tugged at his mouth like he was trying to pull a smile off his face. "He also told me you're a damn fine dancer." Carlos gave way to the smile, shaking his head. "You and your mother. Always charming the men."

Rita knew her mother had dated Carlos first, playing the two brothers against each other, before finally marrying Ernie. And when Loretta fled New Mexico, she had done so with a would-be actor, escaping to Los Angeles where, the last anybody heard, she'd taken up with a yacht salesman. That she looked like her mother, Rita couldn't deny—photographs confirmed the resemblance—but she preferred to believe she had none of her mother's wiles.

"You gave Pat such a good deal on the pasture," she told her uncle, "that Miguel felt he owed our family a favor."

"I can't argue with that." He winked at her. "But it don't hurt none that you're pretty."

She remembered how Joe Oakes's eyes had appraised her that morning in Gilbert's office, staring at her boots as though calculating their cost before writing her off as too poor to fight him. "Nothing seems to be helping me right now. Everywhere I turn, I'm losing some battle. I thought I could stop the guy from building on the ridgetop, but I was down at city hall today, and it looks like there's nothing I can do."

Her uncle scanned the horizon, gazing past the cattle on toward the Jemez Mountains. "Santa Fe has gotten like the Tower of Babel." He rarely went to Mass, but from time to time he would refer to some Biblical incident that embodied his take on the world. "People acting like they're gods. Eventually it'll all come tumbling down."

Rita wished she shared her uncle's belief, but as far as she could tell, Joe Oakes would reign on that ridgetop until the day he sold his house to somebody else who, in turn, would lord it over her.

When they reached the far pasture, Pat got off his horse, unlatched the gate and, on foot, urged the cows to enter. Some still skittered and Carlos took off after them on his horse, his dogs joining him in bringing the stray cows back to the herd. Gradually the lowing sound decreased as the cows began to settle into the pasture, where Carlos got off his horse and walked among them, he and Pat, here and there, petting a distraught cow as though it were an overgrown dog.

Miguel dismounted, too, and leaned on the fence, beckoning Rita to stand alongside him. He smelled of horses and leather, and she longed to breathe deeply of him but forced herself to keep several inches between them.

"You look almost as good sitting on a horse," he said, "as you do moving across the dance floor."

She didn't know if it was because she still had on her red boots and black jeans from the meeting at city hall that he thought it necessary to compliment her or whether he was flirting. His eyes trailed through her hair and she wanted to again feel his fingers there, but she couldn't get a good read on this man. One minute he'd show what she interpreted as a strong sexual attraction, and then he'd abruptly turn away from her as he did now, leaning across the fence and looking out at the pasture. "Pat's never happier," he said, "than when he's stepping in cow shit."

"And you?" she asked. "What makes you happy?"

She noted how his hands gripped the top fence rail, his knuckles straining to hold on tight, as though afraid the ground might slip out from under his feet. "I may have lost the capacity for happiness."

His trip to California had intensified the weight of his sorrow. She could see it in the way his back bowed, his shoulders caving in on themselves. But she'd known him to give in to joy, had felt it when they danced together, enough so to believe he would eventually shake the grief that hobbled him. "You looked happy enough while we were driving the cows back here."

He tossed her a grin, while shaking his head as though to deny it. "I could never be a rancher," he said. "But I love being back in New Mexico, having a law practice in town, and playing cowboy when Pat needs me."

"It's a delicate balance, isn't it? I like living out in the middle of nowhere, but I need my welding work to keep me sane."

Turning around to face her, Miguel shaded his eyes with a hand to block the midday sun. "That low-rider guy, Ramón, mentioned your welding." Miguel paused, as though debating whether to continue.

"Is it something that could support you if you didn't have the junkyard?"

"That's like a doctor asking me if I could get by with only one hand." To illustrate the comparison, she put her right arm behind her back, held out her left, and awkwardly shook Miguel's hand. "Yeah, I could still function, but not with the grace I once had."

Miguel held onto her hand. "Sometimes," he said, his thumb stroking hers, "we end up seriously handicapped, but we still manage to survive." She didn't know whether he was speaking about her or himself, but as he continued to clasp her hand, she wondered how much strength two people could give each other. A drowning person could not save another drowning person, but perhaps two crippled people could join forces and function better together than apart.

When he let go of her hand, she put it on her hip, hoping it gave her a defiant look. "In other words," she said, "you're telling me I'm going to lose the junkyard."

She watched as Miguel took a deep breath, like what he had to say hurt him too. "Drew Stinson forced a silver mine outside of Scottsdale to close so that his adjacent property would be worth more money. The man's a pro. He won't let your junkyard stand in the way of his making a big profit."

It was too much to hear in one day. First the ridgetop gone, now the junkyard. She thought of women who'd experienced wars, who'd lost so much more than she, yet kept on going. Nobody had been killed, and the land remained hers, though it felt tremendously diminished. "The junkyard was my father's second child, almost as loved as I was. I promised him I would take care of it."

The tears ran before she could stop them, dissolving her attempts to appear strong. She stomped her foot. "It isn't fair. We were here first."

"Try telling that to the Indians."

"Don't give me that politically correct bullshit. You're a lawyer. How can I fight this guy?"

Miguel shook his head. Behind him, Carlos and Pat continued to move among the cows, calming them. Miguel looked over his shoulder and watched for a moment before again facing her. "You'd be wasting your money. Legal precedent is on his side."

The words were blunt, but he said them gently, in a steady, even tone similar to that which Pat and her uncle used with the cattle.

"In other words," she said, "I might as well give up."

Miguel leaned forward, enveloping her with the scent of leather and horses, gently placing a fingertip on her cheek, following the tears down to her chin. "Don't give up, but surrender with dignity."

"Hard to do when your nose is running." She dug in her pocket for a tissue, her face afire from the touch of his hand.

"Drew Stinson doesn't strike me as a man who'd be moved by tears," he said, "but he'd hate to see you in court."

"I thought you said I didn't stand a chance against him."

"I said you'd be wasting your money to fight him, but he's not any more eager than you are to pay big attorney fees. He'll be willing to settle out of court, and while it won't save the junkyard, it will buy back what your father invested."

Although she'd known Miguel was a lawyer, this was her first glimpse of the way the profession shaped his thinking. Much as she detested legal manipulations, she saw that he knew how to use them to bring her more of what she wanted.

Drew Stinson might be a pro, but Leroy and Gilbert were amateurs. She was convinced they'd done something illegal to get approval for Joe Oakes's house, otherwise somebody would have built up there long ago. The ridge bordering her property was barely discernible from this distance, but she pointed it out to Miguel. "How many Chevy truck parts would it cost me for you to look over the city ordinances involved in building on that ridgetop?"

"I'd rather get paid," Miguel said, "with a home cooked meal."

|| **JOE** || A dentist had rented the house with its suite of offices for seven years, and Joe needed to fix up the place before he could rent it again. The incessant hammering pounded on his brain, aggravating an already intense headache. He winced as he finished cleaning the last window, Windex fumes burning his nose and eyes. He'd been up since five, and the afternoon heat that bore down on him seared his nerves. The past few nights, he'd slept poorly, the ceiling fan's drone cutting into his dreams.

"Wes!" he yelled. The hammering continued. Joe tossed the Windex into a plastic tray, flinched at the clatter, and walked outside. A man in a ponytail and a tie-dyed T-shirt, his neck creased in wrinkles, knelt by the porch railing, hammering the lower framework into the floorboards. He wore a headset and was unaware of Joe standing next to him and calling out his name. When Joe tapped him on the shoulder, he dropped his hammer.

"Scared the shit out of me, man!" Grinning, he removed the headset. "Can't hear a damn thing with this on." He stood up, and before Joe could say anything, bounded down the steps to pick up the hammer that had fallen through the railing to the ground below.

"Why don't you call it a day? I've got folks coming to look at the place in a few minutes, and the noise will drive them away."

"Let me reinforce this last strip, and I'm done." He took the steps in two strides and pounded in half a dozen more nails. "There, that should hold it." Wes gripped the banister, gave it a shake, but it remained firmly in place. "Won't have to worry about anybody tumbling off this porch now."

Joe paid him in cash, knowing he kept most of his income off the books. He envied Wes the simplicity of his life, unburdened by heavy loans or a guilty conscience. Ever since his divorce, Joe, too, had prided himself on living within his means, unhampered by debts or questionable ethics. But buying the ridgetop had changed everything, the liability huge as a rhinoceros, pressing up against him, digging its horn deep into his back.

He watched Wes drive away in a VW van faded from red to pink, covered with bumper stickers that promoted everything from freeing Tibet to visualizing whirled peas. The puttering engine echoed in the still air, gradually dissolving in the distance, giving way to the whirring keen of insects. Joe leaned against one of the porch posts, succumbing to his exhaustion. That morning Santiago had called with another unforeseen expense. The picture window looking west from the living room would let in a blinding amount of light, and he'd recommended adding a portal. Chloe immediately agreed, loving the idea of them sitting outside in the shade on hot evenings like this. Indeed, it would add a nice feature to the house, but it would also add another few thousand to the projected costs.

A car pulled into the parking lot on the side of the house, gravel crunching under the wheels. The skin on Joe's face tightened as he stretched his lips into a smile and walked down the steps to meet his prospective renters, two massage therapists.

"It's absolutely charming," the woman said as she got out of the car. He couldn't quite remember her name. "C" something. Clarissa? Claudine? It was written on a notepad in his office, scribbled down when she dropped by yesterday saying she'd seen the dental practice moving out of the house and wondered if it was available. Her mouth opened in a big smile that conveyed a wide acceptance of the world. She had the sagging breasts and padded hips of a peasant woman clothed in batik pants and a terra-cotta shirt. The amplitude of her body made Joe long for an all encompassing hug like his grandmother used to give him as a boy, cushioning his head in the softness of her bosom.

"The paint's peeling off the porch," said the driver, a man whose thin wiriness and long face should have made him the perfect partner for a comedy act.

"The painters are coming tomorrow. I'm only showing the place to you now because you asked to have first option." Joe tried to give the impression he had a waiting list of people eager to rent. In truth, it never took him long to turn over a unit, but he usually lost a couple of weeks in the transaction. This time, he needed immediate revenue. Not that it would go far toward covering his expenses, but like a homeless man sifting through trash cans looking for food, he grabbed at any money he could find.

"I'm sure we can see beyond the surface details," the woman said. "And I absolutely love the front porch."

"It adds a nice contrast to the brick, doesn't it?" In a town of mostly adobe and stucco buildings, the brick house was distinctive. As he led them inside, Joe caught the man eyeing the worn tread in the entryway. "The carpet layers are coming tomorrow too."

"At least the windows are clean." The man's thin lips squiggled like a worm, moving somewhere between a smirk and a sneer.

"I guarantee you, everything will be flawless before anybody moves in." Joe briskly walked over to the plastic tray with his cleaning supplies and tucked them out of sight in the window seat, his aching head reprimanding him for the quickness of his anger.

"That bay window makes the room." The woman came and stood near him, both of them gazing out at the front yard with its gnarled apricot tree. She placed a hand atop the tightness in his upper back. "You carry a lot of stress in your neck and shoulders." A soothing heat radiated out from her palm.

The man pounced. "Maybe we can make a deal. We'll give you weekly massages in exchange for a reduction in the rent."

An involuntary shudder ran down Joe's spine at the thought of the man's bony fingers boring into his naked skin. "I prefer to keep my business transactions separate from personal matters."

The woman kneaded his shoulders, dissipating the knots. "I understand." When she removed her hand, he felt like a baby yanked away from the breast, hungering for more.

"This place is probably too expensive for us anyway," the man said.

"It's no higher than anything else you'll find in this neighborhood." A whine wove its way through Joe's words, embarrassing him with his neediness. "If you compare prices, you'll find this a good deal."

"He's right, Forest. I've checked out a couple of other places, and this is the best I've found so far."

Joe had to nab them now, before they looked elsewhere. "Come see the other rooms. You'll find the place very cozy." He started to lead them down the hall, but Forest paused as they walked by the kitchen.

"If you're charging by the square foot, this is an absolute waste of space for us."

The woman squeezed past Forest. "Oh, look! It has a washer and dryer. Perfect for all the sheets we go through. And we won't have to clutter up the reception area with our tea makings. We can do it all in here. I don't know about you, Forest, but I'm tired of eating takeout. I'd love to be able to have a cold pasta salad on a day like this, or heat up a bowl of homemade soup in the winter."

"I suppose." Forest obviously wasn't one to admit somebody else had more insight than he. He passed down the hallway ahead of Joe, barely glancing into the first room, and snorting when he saw the second, which had once been renovated as a master bedroom, complete with a fireplace and a skylight. "This is far bigger than anything we need."

Joe debated whether it would be worth offering to divide the room into two. But before he could calculate the cost of building a wall he might have to tear down for any future tenants, the woman waltzed into the room. "I'll take it. I never mind extra space."

"Crystal! How do you expect us to afford this?"

"I have more clients than you do. I'll pay a larger portion of the rent to compensate for my taking the largest room."

Miffed, the man stormed down the hallway, coming to an abrupt halt at the last room. "Talk about extremes. This room is too tiny to be of any use whatsoever."

Fed up with the man's constant faultfinding, Joe wanted to tell him to look elsewhere, but he fought against the impulse. "The previous tenants used that room to store their files, I thought you might . . ."

"A storage space!" Crystal's voice again rose in enthusiasm. "How perfect. We can keep all the linens and lotions in there." She actually clapped her hands.

As though responding to applause, Leroy Sena entered the front door. "Hey!" he said. "Don't mind me. I'll wait out back."

"Is he looking at the place, too?" Competition edged Forest's voice.

The man might have renamed himself in favor of nature, but he had the pettiness of a corporate executive who couldn't see beauty for the bottom line.

"Leroy's a realtor who's always on the lookout for a steal." It was close enough to the truth.

"We need to make a decision, Forest."

Joe's cell phone rang. "Excuse me." He walked into the kitchen to take the call.

"Joe, I just had a marvelous idea! Let's go up to the building site, check out where the portal's going to be, and watch the sunset." The high pitch of Chloe's excitement jangled in his ear.

"I'm tied up right now with prospective tenants."

"Sunset's almost two hours away. Come on. I'll bring a bottle of Chardonnay and we'll toast our soon-to-be portal. God, I'm so glad Santiago thought of it. It's going to be heaven on nights like this. Let's meet around eight." She hung up before he could tell her he might not be finished in time.

Joe glanced out the kitchen window and saw Leroy paging through his day planner. What deal was he cooking up now? Surely he didn't expect Joe to buy yet another property.

He heard a polite cough in the other room. Dust motes danced around Crystal, who again stood by the bay window. An aura of quiet satisfaction surrounded her like a subtle perfume.

"Well, what'd you folks decide?"

"We'll take it," Forest said, clearly needing to appear in charge.

The kitchen door opened and closed as Leroy reentered the house. Though he remained in the other room, Joe could hear his gum snapping, like a cap gun, one shot following another.

Crystal seemed oblivious to the interruption. "We'd like to go over the lease at your office, where we can sit down and talk about it."

"No problem." He escorted them out the door, motioning with his head toward where Leroy awaited him. "Give me a few minutes to finish up here, and I'll meet you there."

They hadn't even cleared the yard before Leroy shook the porch with his heavy tread, bellowing, "They gonna take the place?"

Joe waited until they got into the car, out of earshot, before responding. "The guy's a jerk. He'll find all kinds of things to quibble over in the lease, but, yeah, ultimately, they'll sign."

"Even with the place looking like this?" Leroy ran his palm over the peeling paint on the porch banister, then brushed his hands together. "Man, you got the Midas touch. Everything you own turns to gold."

"Be a long time before that ridgetop you conned me into turns a profit."

"Patience, my man. That's all it takes. You're sitting on a true gold mine out there."

"Right now I'm sitting in a shithouse with the money leaking out of me so fast I'm about to keel over."

Leroy pulled out a packet of gum and removed a piece. With an irritating slowness, he slipped off the outer paper, unwrapped the foil, popped the stick into his mouth, and chewed it before finally speaking. "In the end it'll be okay, but you might run into trouble with that driveway."

Joe jammed his hands deep into his pockets so Leroy couldn't see them knotted into fists. "What in the hell are you saying?" He shifted from one foot to the other, the wood creaking under the weight of his anger. "Nobody even knows it's a road. How can there be trouble?"

Leroy shrugged his shoulders, snapping his gum like some smart-ass punk. "I didn't say there was trouble. I said you might run into it further down the line."

"It's Rita, isn't it? That woman's nothing but trouble."

Leroy leered. "Rita's a handful all right." His leer turned into a frown. "But she's not the one to worry about. It's her new boyfriend. Used to be a big environmental lawyer out in California. She's got him looking over the plans."

Joe forced himself to take a deep breath, drawing from low in his belly and slowly blowing it out through his nose. "There's nothing wrong with my house plans. I drew them strictly to code."

"Yeah, but if this guy has a head for rules. He might remember the difference between the width of a road and a driveway when the time comes for approval of your subdivision."

In the past, Leroy had always referred to the subdivision as "ours," talking about what they'd do to get "our" plans approved. Now he shifted it all over to Joe. He had a sudden urge to push Leroy through the newly grounded banister, busting up the whole front porch with his sledgehammer body. Instead, he locked the front door. "I've got clients waiting for me."

"What're you going to do?"

"Get them to sign a lease that takes effect immediately, and deposit their check for the first and last month's rent."

"I mean about this guy prying into your plans."

"The thing I can least afford." For every day Joe delayed the further development of the ridgetop, he paid. But he saw no other choice. "I'll postpone filing for the plat division. Wait until his memory weakens."

"Or until Rita trades him in for a new boyfriend." Leroy grinned again, his head bouncing up and down in time to the snapping of his gum.

Joe resisted the urge to cuff him, settling instead for a mere vision of his wobbly head toppling off his thick neck and rolling across the yard. "Maybe you should ask her out on a date, Leroy. I hear you're quite the two-timer."

He turned and walked away, Leroy's laughter encasing him, as though Joe had paid him a compliment.

|| **RITA** || The flowers along the porch looked droopy, so Rita watered them as she waited for Miguel to pick her up. Careful not to get her feet wet, she glanced toward the rear of the house and saw Parker loping in her direction. She felt badly about asking him to watch the junkyard after he'd worked late the night before.

Parker carried his customary mug of tea, and although he hadn't bothered to shave, he resonated a high volume of energy. "Lipstick," he observed.

She turned off the hose and rewound it, hoping he wouldn't notice her new shirt too. "I usually wear lipstick when I go into town."

"Do you?" He pursed his lips like she used to when he came home late from school with some far-fetched tale about where he'd been.

Rita wanted to wipe the prissy expression off his mouth, but had to laugh at his imitation of her. "I wear it when I remember to put it on, okay?"

"And you had no trouble remembering this morning." His grin hinted at sexual implications. "I'd like to meet this Miguel fellow. Tío tells me he's . . ." Parker paused. "Muy amable."

"Miguel's very nice, but this is strictly business. Like I told you, we have a meeting at city hall." She wasn't ready to admit Miguel intrigued her. Parker had seen her various infatuations, men who had excited her initially, some enough to hold her attention for a year or two, but all of whom eventually bored her. Miguel, however, seemed different, like he had more depth, with the potential to retain her interest.

"I don't know, Mom. You've got that dreamy look."

"Yeah, well you've got sleepy dirt in your eyes."

"Do I?" He lifted his cup, and peered over the rim at her as he sipped his tea.

"I thought you were eager to get some welding done today."

"Trying to get rid of me?"

"I could care less what you do." She plopped down on the porch steps in what she hoped was a casual pose. If her truck hadn't been in the shop, she could have driven into town herself instead of just sitting there, waiting for Miguel.

"Where are the dogs?"

"I left them in the house so they wouldn't be in your way."

Parker looked down the road. "That's probably your friend now, raising all that dust." He took another sip of his tea, purposely idling. Then he bent over and kissed her cheek. "My cue to disappear."

"You don't need to disappear."

"I'll meet him when you're ready for me to meet him." He winked, needling her with his insolence.

She didn't stop him from leaving. Her relationship with Miguel was too new to expose to Parker's scrutiny. She waited until he disappeared, then glanced down the road. The dust he'd seen was still quite a ways in the distance. She reached down to pull a couple of weeds from the flower bed. From inside the metal shed came the sound of Parker welding. It was a familiar noise, one she found surprisingly comforting. Usually she preferred silence, but it had always made her happy to have Parker working on his sculptures.

Miguel pulled into the yard, his Toyota 4-Runner rumbling. He had the window rolled down and his hair was windblown, giving him a carefree look.

"You call that a truck?"

Grinning, he got out and measured himself against the cab. "A small truck for a short man."

Rarely had she met a man so at ease with who he was. Miguel had no obvious insecurities, no complexes that incited ugly behaviors.

He turned his head toward the noise coming from the welding shed. "What's all the ruckus?"

"My son's doing some work while he keeps an eye on the junkyard." She opened the passenger door of the truck.

"Aren't you going to introduce me?" Miguel wore a quizzical smile, one that resembled a challenge.

One foot already on the floorboard, she hesitated. "If you'd like."

When Parker was little, any man she brought home he welcomed as a potential father; but since he was about eleven, he'd grown critical of everybody she dated. That tendency had only gotten worse as he got older, to the point that he'd make derogatory comments about something as minor as a man constantly wearing a baseball cap to hide early signs of balding. Ironically enough, the more outspoken he became, the more she trusted his opinion. She might as well find out what he thought of Miguel.

Parker was using the TIG torch when they entered the welding shed and didn't notice them until he lifted the face shield on his helmet to check the weld.

"Whoa," Miguel said, not waiting for an introduction. He walked over to Parker's sculpture of a woman made out of carburetors. "I thought Tony Price was the only one in New Mexico doing anything this awesome."

"You know Tony's work?"

"Atomic art? You bet. I'm even lucky enough to have a small piece. I'd fill my house with sculptures if I could afford it. As it is, I've only got one of Tony's masks and this incredible work by a woman back in California who does metal montages."

Feeling left out of the conversation, Rita stepped over to the sculpture and ran a hand over it before asking, "Is this Rocker Girl's mother?"

"You mean the family resemblance is that obvious?" Parker said. He reached out to shake Miguel's hand. "I'm Rita's son, Parker."

"And I'm Miguel, the man she's reluctantly accepted as her attorney."

The two men exchanged knowing grins, as though they shared secrets. "If Mom agreed to let you represent her, I'd say you're either a very smooth talker, which she's been susceptible to in the past, or she's decided you're more scrupulous than the average lawyer."

Miguel laughed, the sound cartwheeling through the room. "She hasn't let me smooth talk her into anything, but thanks for letting me know there's a possibility."

At that point, Parker caught her eye and gave a wink of approval. "Careful, Mom, this guy might take you for all you're worth."

"Yeah, well, anybody can see that's not much," she said.

Miguel's mouth closed into a grim line. "Truth of the matter is, you're a relatively wealthy woman, Rita. Cash poor and land rich, like so many of our people. That Leroy fellow would sell this place out from under you in a heartbeat."

"Leroy doesn't stand a chance. No man comes between Mom and her land."

"Nobody's going to steal my land from me, that's for sure. But I also don't want to be fenced in by a bunch of rich gringos."

"My mom, the bigot!" Parker raised a hand to his helmet, lowering the face shield and waving the torch at them to step back. Miguel watched him weld for a moment before following her outside.

"Sorry you had to drive all the way out here to get me, I would have . . ."

"My pleasure," he said, reopening the truck door for her with an exaggerated flourish.

His gallantry sometimes caught her off guard. She slid onto the seat, mortified to find dirt under her fingernails.

"My small chariot and I are happy to be of service," Miguel said, backing the truck out of the driveway and onto the road.

"What's this meeting all about?" She couldn't keep the agitation out of her voice. When he'd called last week, he'd disappointed her with the news that it appeared Joe Oakes had followed all the rules. Then he'd gone on to say one thing bothered him, refusing to tell her what it was but insisting they look at the drawings she'd originally seen, the ones that showed the house's placement relative to the entire hill.

"Like I said, it's probably nothing."

"I'd hate to drive all this way into town for nothing."

"I'll take you out for coffee afterward, how's that?"

Before she could answer, he began asking a string of questions about his father's truck. Reluctantly, she went along with the subterfuge, telling herself she would find out all too soon what it was about Joe's house that had aroused Miguel's suspicions.

When they arrived at Gilbert's office, he was pacing by the window like a pigeon, his rounded belly leading the way. "Como estás?" Bustling across the room, he clasped Rita's hand in both of his. "Why don't you tell your friend here that we've already been over Joe Oakes' drawings and everything is fine?"

"You've got a little bit of sugar on your chin, Gilbert." She politely looked away as he rubbed the telltale sign of powdered doughnuts off his face.

Miguel made a beeline for the window, sat down, and sifted through the plans that lay on the table. "Come take a look at this," he called over his shoulder.

"What?" Gilbert demanded, stepping in front of Rita to look where Miguel had his finger on the plans.

Miguel rolled the chair, scooting Gilbert to one side to make room for her on the other. He tapped the spot where Joe was putting his house. "Why do you think he's building here, when these other three sites are bigger?" His finger arched across the paper, pinpointing three areas where the land curved away from the road.

Before she could decipher the significance of what he was asking, Gilbert butted in. "Joe only wants a small house and the views at the end are the best."

Miguel swiveled the chair around, away from the desk, his elbows draped over the armrests, looking very casual, the way she'd noticed he often did just before he had something important to say. "What's to stop Oakes from selling those other lots to people who also want a view, but bigger houses?"

Rita's mind sped ahead, like a video on fast-forward, flashing images of not one but four houses on the ridge.

"You obviously don't know my client." Leroy's voice startled them all. He stood in the doorway, his broad chest and massive biceps filling the space. His neck almost disappeared into the bulk of his shoulders and he swaggered as he walked into the room. "I didn't know any of Rita's dance partners liked to play detective."

Notably smaller than Leroy, Miguel folded his arms across his chest. "Sherlock Holmes was my childhood hero." He rose out of the chair, retucking his sky-blue shirt into his jeans. "Sherlock Holmes and Don Quixote."

Gilbert edged himself between the two men, addressing his brother. "I already showed him how Oakes did everything according to the books."

Leroy snapped his gum, a habit he'd picked up several years ago when he quit smoking. Rita kept hoping one of these days he'd give up gum too. His jaw mashed even as he talked, setting her nerves on edge.

"Joe does everything aboveboard." He gave his gum another snap. "One look at his commercial properties will tell you that. The man's worked hard to earn himself a nice home. He's not about to share that hill with anybody."

"Six hundred twenty-five thousand," Miguel said, pronouncing each word very distinctly. "That's a lot of money for a man with only thirteen small rental units."

Rita could see that Leroy was as surprised as she at the thoroughness of Miguel's research. Leroy walked over to the trash can beside Gilbert's desk and spat out his gum, immediately reaching into his pocket to replace it with a fresh piece before replying. "He's not buying the place by himself. His girlfriend is a successful gallery owner."

"How successful?" Miguel asked. "She's had the business a little over a year, and lives behind the gallery, which would seem to indicate a shortage of funds."

"The bank had no problem approving their credit." Leroy gave his gum an extra loud snap.

"Banks often have to foreclose."

"Three more houses!" Spit sprayed out of Rita's mouth as she confronted Leroy. "He's going to put three more houses up there?"

"Rita, Rita," he said. "Relax. Everything's going to be fine."

She wanted to punch him, send that piece of gum hurtling down his throat, choking him.

"Let's go," Miguel said so softly it was like a whisper in her ear, coaxing her to trust him. Gently he cupped her elbow and moved her past Leroy. "Thanks gentlemen. You've given us all the information we need."

Too demoralized to argue, Rita let him steer her out of the room. Their feet echoed on the linoleum floor as they walked down the hallway. Neither of them said anything as they got into the elevator, where she collapsed against the wall.

"Are you okay?" he asked.

"Why didn't you tell me?" The tears welled before she could squelch them.

"Don't give up, Rita. I think . . ."

The elevator door opened on the ground floor, where Joe Oakes stood waiting to step inside.

"Rita!" Joe extended his hand as she got out of the elevator.

"Developer!" She hurled the word at him, like the obscenity it was. "How can you call yourself a renovator when you're demolishing an entire hill?"

Joe's face turned as gray as his hair. "I don't know what you're talking about." He quickly entered the elevator and punched the button for the next floor. The doors closed between them.

|| JOE || Joe regretted not taking the stairs. The elevator didn't move quickly enough. Finally the doors opened onto the second floor. Bursting into Gilbert's office, he found him with his feet propped on the desk, Leroy sitting across from him laughing.

Gilbert immediately stood up, his face full of good humor. "Joe, come on in. We were just talking about you."

"Laughing at me, you mean, for having bought that ridgetop."

Now Leroy stood too, motioning at his chair as he walked across the room to get another. "Have a seat, Joe." He rolled a chair toward the desk and patted the one he'd vacated. "Take that one, it's more comfortable."

"Comfortable?" Joe remained standing. "How can I be comfortable when Rita knows about the subdivision?"

Gilbert came out from behind his desk. "Sit," he said, clasping Joe's shoulder, guiding him into the chair. Then he propped himself on his desk, between Joe and Leroy, facing them both. "Rita knows nothing about the subdivision. Her attorney realized you could put three more houses up there, but we told them you weren't."

"Terrific! And then what's he going to think when we apply for the plat approval? He'll know something fishy is going on."

Neither of the brothers answered. Then Leroy snapped his gum, breaking the silence. "The guy's very thorough. Gotta hand him that. He knows what you paid for the land, how many pieces of rental property you own, and, probably, the exact amount of income you make off them. He put two and two together and knows you need more revenue. When you apply for the plat approval, he won't be surprised. Matter-of-fact, he'll probably tell Rita how smart he is for having figured it out ahead of time."

Leroy's jaw churned a couple of times before he resumed talking. "The guy spent hours looking over city codes." Tilting his chair, he spat his gum into a nearby trash can. Then he displayed his bucktoothed grin. "Thing is, he couldn't find nothing. Rita won't like it, but they're going to have to accept your subdivision. That's all there is to it."

"She was pissed when I saw her. Too pissed to give up fighting. What's to stop them from finding out about the road?"

Gilbert still sat on the edge of his desk. One leg began swinging back and forth, an almost hypnotic movement, in keeping with his calm, even tone. "Like Leroy said, her boyfriend's gone over all the regulations and couldn't see anything you did wrong. It's smooth sailing from here out."

Sailing seemed a strange metaphor for a man born and raised in the desert. Yet Gilbert said it so convincingly, his voice lulling, carrying Joe along with the image, floating off into the sunset, not a care in the world.

Then his cell phone rang, jerking him back into reality. Joe fumbled to get the phone out of his pocket, dropping it onto the floor. Leroy reached down, picked it up, and handed it to him in one, fluid movement.

"Hello."

"Joe?" Chloe seemed to be questioning whether it was really him. "Where are you?"

Wednesday! It was Wednesday, her day off. They were supposed to go horseback riding together; he'd forgotten all about it. "Sorry, Chloe. I completely lost track of time." Hell, he hadn't even remembered what day of the week it was. He searched desperately for a believable excuse. "Got tied up with a client. It's those new renters I told you about. The masseuses. I knew that guy would be trouble from day one. He insisted on . . ."

"Why didn't you call me?" She sounded hurt.

"I had no idea it was this late. He's had me over here, badgering me nonstop about this and that. I haven't had a moment to myself. Give me five more minutes to wrap things up."

Silence. Then a sigh. "Speedo's restless. I'm going to take him for a short run. Meet me at the stables around ten?"

"Sounds good." Then, despite Leroy and Gilbert's presence, he added, "I love you."

"I love you, too. But don't ever forget me again." She hung up before he could say anything more.

His wife, when she began an affair, had started lying to him, making up stories about how she'd spent the day. He hadn't found out about it until much later, but he'd noticed the way her eyes often failed to meet his. The phone had eliminated the need to look Chloe in the face, and for that he was grateful.

"Lying to the girlfriend, huh?" Leroy winked.

Joe knew he meant the wink to be a sign of a shared brotherhood, the fellowship of men who took pride in their ability to deceive women. But Joe was ashamed for lying to Chloe. It demeaned his love of her, marred what had once been honest and open. "I need to leave."

Gilbert nodded. "No problem. We've got everything under control." He walked over to the table by the window and rolled up the plans lying there.

"I need to get going, too," Leroy said. "Got a client looking at some property off Bishop's Lodge Road. Talk about expensive! You don't know what a steal you got on that ridgetop."

"A steal? What's been stolen is my peace of mind. I'll sleep a lot better once that subdivision is approved and all the lots are sold."

"Relax. It'll happen soon enough." Leroy clapped him on the back, following him out to the hallway.

The thought of being cramped in the elevator with Leroy was too much for Joe. "I'm going to take the stairs."

"I'll join you. I could use the exercise." Leroy trotted alongside him like an obedient dog.

Even outside the building Joe couldn't shake him. "See you later."

"Where you parked?"

"Over on Otero."

"Same direction as me. I'll walk with you." Leroy whistled a bouncy melody. "Beautiful day," he said. "Perfect for selling real estate."

"Don't remind me." Autumn was a season that tempted many people to move to Santa Fe. The sun had lost its harshness, and the land had softened in washes of gold and lavender. Joe knew he could easily sell his lots on a day like this. "You really think that attorney won't figure out what we're doing with the driveway?"

"Guy's an environmentalist. He's looking for more serious violations. Doesn't have a clue about little things like road width specifications."

Joe thought about Chloe out on her horse. He pictured her galloping, giving vent to her anger at him for not showing up when he'd promised. He'd never before forgotten a date with anybody, much less her. "I can't afford to wait until next year to file for approval of the subdivision."

"That's up to you." Leroy paused at the street corner, waiting for the walk light. "Thing you need to keep in mind is Rita can get pretty crazy when she's riled up. She could make it very ugly for you. If you let her calm down a little longer, get used to the idea of you living up there, it'll be easier."

Joe remembered her anger the day she learned he was building on the ridgetop. Her face had darkened and her body tightened like the funnel of a tornado. He didn't want to be in the path of her rage any more than he did that of a tornado, but he had to find a way to work around her before he lost everything.

|| **RITA** || It was one thing to have a man open a door for you because your hands were full or you were going out on a date and he was being chivalrous, but when Miguel stood outside city hall holding his truck door open for her, Rita felt like a frail old woman. She couldn't rid her mind of the picture of a row of houses lining the ridgetop. And the image made her weak, too weak even to speak.

They rode in silence past the outskirts of town before she recovered enough to ask, "What makes you think he's going to put more houses up there?"

"That hill cost too much for a man of his means. The obvious way for him to afford it is to develop it."

"Then why won't he admit that's what he's doing?"

"I suspect there's some illegality involved. And we need to figure out what it is so we can stop him." Miguel hesitated, taking his eyes off the road to look at her. "Can you handle going up there with me and checking it over?"

Her breath came out in a puff, whistling through her compressed lips. "It's hard for me to see it under construction, but if that's what we need to do . . ." No more words came to her.

"I could go by myself, but you know the place better than anybody. You might see what I've overlooked."

"Like what?"

"I don't know, but I'm convinced he isn't putting only one house up there."

"Isn't one enough?" The question shot out like an arrow, zinging through the small cab of the truck and making Miguel wince.

"I'm not condoning what he's done, Rita. I'm trying to keep him from doing yet more damage."

She needed out, out of the truck, out in the fresh air where she could breathe freely. "Park here by the house. The further we have to walk, the better I'll be able to deal with all this."

"I know the feeling." He turned off the ignition, but made no move to get out of the truck. "I used to jog like a maniac, running because the world felt like it was coming to an end. Then my knees gave out." He put his hands on both knees, rubbing them, as though trying to rub away the memory of whatever had once upset him so much that he ran until the physical pain surpassed the emotional one. He gave her a faint smile. "A walk sounds good."

She returned his attempt at a smile, feeling closer to him in the knowledge that they both had demons to exorcise. And though he still hadn't told her what past experience had wounded him so deeply, she appreciated that he could admit to the pain. Too many men hid their hurt, denying any injury, as though to acknowledge it would make them weak. Miguel struck her as plenty strong, perhaps even stronger as a result of his suffering.

When they got out of the truck, Flojo and Loca came running up to greet them. "Who've we got here?" Miguel bent down to scratch the white star on Flojo's chest. Loca rolled over and lay waiting for him to pet her too. "What a floozy you are." He vigorously rubbed her stomach.

"I'll have you know, she doesn't do that for just anybody."

"Got to have a feel for a girl's magic spot." Miguel stood up, both the dogs hanging close by his legs. "Only time I've been without a dog was my first year in college. Most guys move out of the dorm so they can party or live with a girlfriend, but I rented a house with a yard so I could have a dog."

"And the girlfriend came next?"

Miguel looked off across the junkyard. "How do we get to that hilltop of yours?"

She didn't blame him for not answering. She didn't like it either when men inquired about her past love affairs. "This way," she said, leading him through the junkyard. Off to the left, she saw Parker talking to an old hippie by one of the VW vans. She gave him a wave and pointed toward the hill. Parker nodded to indicate he'd take care of any necessary business. Meanwhile, the dogs raced ahead of her and Miguel.

"Your dogs look ready for a walk."

"They're always ready for a walk, even though I usually take them twice a day."

"Dawn and dusk? When the light's prettiest?"

"Sunrise and sunset." She told herself it was silly, but it pleased her that he'd guessed when she most liked to walk. "Except in the winter. Then I put up an 'out to lunch' sign and we go around noon."

"When it's warmer."

Rita nodded, not needing to say anything, knowing he understood. They walked in silence. No compulsion to force a conversation to fill the space between them with useless words, as she had so often felt with other men.

The September morning hummed with heat. Asters and chamisa danced across the land in splashes of purple and yellow, a wild tango of summer's final colors. The ridge rose before them, reaching for the sky. Miguel paused, pointing to the foot worn trail that wound up through the junipers and piñons. "Is that just from you?"

"Me and my father. We used to go up there every Sunday until he got sick. Then I started going practically every day by myself. At first it was kind of like a pilgrimage, a way of praying that he'd beat the cancer. Then, after he died, it became a way of paying homage."

"Like scattering ashes over the ocean."

"What?"

"Nothing. I mean . . ." He brushed his fingers across the top of a nearby chamisa. "We all have personal rituals. Things we consider sacred. Our own ways of healing." Seeds fell to the ground, some clinging to his jeans as he let go of the chamisa. "I used to be an altar boy, but the church never did as much for me as nature." He tilted his head to look up the hill, the dogs already halfway to the top. Then, without checking to see if she was following, he started up the dirt path.

A burst of hammering shattered the quiet. The noise seemed to hasten Miguel's stride, and she worked to keep up with him. At the top of the path, peering down at them, stood Santiago, his hands on his hips in a proprietary stance. When she'd first found out he was the contractor, Rita had felt doubly betrayed, an old friend doing the very work she hated. Behind him, his crew raised the house beams. Rita's breath snagged in her chest, just as it had the day she first saw the bulldozer.

She'd deliberately avoided climbing the ridge since then, knowing the construction would bring her to tears, but she had not expected it to have advanced this far. The wooden framework made the house an inevitability, a stark outline against the blue sky.

"Morning, Rita. Out for a hike?"

Santiago's smile told her he meant it as a friendly question. Nonetheless, his naiveté exasperated her. "I used to hike up here all the time, but not anymore. It hurts too much to see the place destroyed."

The sparkle dimmed in his eyes. "We're doing our best to build a nice house."

"That's her point," Miguel said, his voice subdued but persistent. "Nothing against the house itself, but you're putting it where no house belongs."

Santiago rubbed his jaw, as though Miguel had punched him.

"These hills weren't meant to hold houses," Miguel continued. "That's why nobody built on them before."

"Nobody built on these hills before because we didn't know how." Santiago said it as patiently as Rita imagined him explaining a complicated procedure to a new employee. "And we didn't do it because our grandparents preferred the flatlands to raise their crops and graze their cows."

"True enough," Miguel said, raking a hand through his hair, causing it to stand on end, "but there's a . . ."

"Did you run track in high school?" Santiago asked, staring at Miguel's mussed up hair.

In anybody else, Rita would have ranked the question as a blatant attempt to change the subject, but she knew Santiago to be guileless.

Miguel glanced over at Santiago's truck, which had the company logo and name printed on the door. "Ulibarri Construction," Miguel read. "I competed in the regional championships against a Salvador Ulibarri."

"That was my brother. They couldn't decide which of you came in first so they called it a tie. I don't remember your name, though. Just the red hair and how fast you were."

"Yeah, coach used to call me Mercury."

"Like the red stuff in the thermometer," Santiago said.

Rita watched to see how Miguel would correct the error. He guffawed, and she winced, hating for him to make fun of Santiago's ignorance. "Yeah, all the guys on the team used to tease me on my off days, telling me I was slow as mercury."

In that instant, Rita loved Miguel for not needing to parade his intelligence and make somebody else feel inferior for knowing less than he did. The winter her father was dying, Santiago had shown up with a cord of firewood, claiming he'd chopped more than his family needed. She couldn't have tolerated it if Miguel had demeaned him.

"Did your brother go into construction too?" Miguel asked.

"Salvador? Nah, he's too lazy. Dad said the only reason Sal ran track was to get out of doing chores. Now he's got a cushy job with the state."

"What about this guy you're building for, is . . ."

"Oakes? What about him?"

"Is he the kind of guy who'd try to get away with a fast one?"

"Nah, just the opposite. I've done a couple of remodels for him. The man never cuts any corners. Always goes for the best. Even more so with this place. It's for him and his girlfriend, and he's doing all he can to please her."

"I met her once," Rita said, remembering the woman who'd admired Parker's sculptures. "One of those blondes who can get men to do whatever she wants."

Santiago grinned. "Y tú? How many men have done what you wanted? I've lost count."

Miguel looked at her with a raised eyebrow and she felt an unfamiliar shame heat her face. "I admit I've had a few boyfriends over the years, but I never made any of them do anything for me."

"What about Julian?" Santiago reminded her. "Didn't he build that welding shed for you?"

"That was different. He was living at my house rent free and wanted to do something to repay me."

Now Miguel joined Santiago in grinning at her. "I bet Joe Oakes's girlfriend does things for him too."

Rita's face heated even more, recalling the sexual intensity she'd had with Julian. "Let's do what we came up here for and check out those other building sites."

"What other building sites?" Santiago clearly had no idea what she was talking about.

"See the way the land curves away from the road in three spots to the east of us?" Miguel said.

"Yeah, Rita tried to tell Joe there wasn't enough room for his house, but the thing is, he could easily put three more houses up here. Possibly even a fourth, if he wanted to stretch it."

"But he's not?" She meant to make it a declaration, but it came out as a plea.

"Nope. Just him and Chloe going to be living up here."

"He's never talked about building more houses later, or selling lots?" Miguel asked.

"You kidding? The man's in love. He wants this place to be his castle. A small castle, on a big hill."

"And if he could, he'd build a moat and fill it with alligators. Anything he could to protect them." Miguel's eyes clouded, and she wondered what he'd been unable to protect.

"I wish I could build a moat too," she said.

"Shoot," Santiago said, "at least you still got most of your family's property. Taxes got so bad, mi abuelo had to sell ours years ago. The old ways are gone, Rita."

"The old ways may be disappearing," Miguel said, "but that doesn't mean we have to let people cheat us."

A drill started up in the background and Santiago looked at his watch. "Me and my men have work to do. Nobody's cheating us."

Before Rita could tell him he'd been robbed of the very land that once nurtured his family, Miguel shook Santiago's hand. "Great to meet you. Tell Salvador hello for me."

Then he took Rita's hand and gave a gentle tug, pulling her down the hill with him. She yanked her hand out of his. "I thought you wanted us to investigate. Look the place over."

"We'll come back later, after they quit working. It'll be smarter to wait and . . ."

"Wait for what?"

"Until nobody's around."

"But that's how this whole thing happened. Nobody was around to stop it."

"Rita, please, if we're patient and wait, we can . . ."

"I'm tired of sitting around waiting while everything falls apart."

"Look, we'll come back this very evening, before anything more can happen. We just need to wait a few hours, that's all."

His caution enraged her. "Is that why you came back to New Mexico? To wait out whatever hurt you in California?"

She hadn't known freckles could stand out so lividly on somebody's face, but as Miguel's skin blanched, the dark spots intensified. "If you're not careful," he said, "bitterness will poison everything you touch."

"What's that supposed to mean?" She'd had it with his vague references, his philosophical remarks that obscured the facts.

Abruptly Miguel sat down on the ground. His back to her, he pulled flowers off a ragweed, scattering the yellow petals on the ground. "I didn't come back to New Mexico to wait for anything. There's nothing left to wait for. I lost it all." When he turned to look up at her, a fury she wouldn't have thought him capable of burned in his eyes. "A drunk driver killed my wife and our ten-year-old son. You can't outwait death." He reached for another ragweed, yanking the entire plant out of the ground and throwing it down the hill.

Too stunned at first to say anything, she sat down a few feet away from him. "I'm sorry. I didn't know."

"After it happened, a friend, an attorney who specializes in personal injuries, wanted me to sue the man for damages." Miguel stared down at his empty hands. "How do you buy back what can never be replaced?"

Rita gazed at the land that spread out below them, the land her grandparents had settled and bequeathed to their sons with the intention that it remain in the family forever. Try as people might, nothing lasted forever. She knew that, yet she struggled to hold onto some sense of continuity, of life having meaning.

Flojo, ever sensitive to misery, came over and started licking Miguel's hands. He buried his face in the Lab's neck, his hands going back and forth along the dog's sides. A few moments passed before he lifted his head and cleared his throat. "I want us to pretend we've accepted what everybody has said about Joe only building one house up there. We'll wait for him to make the next move. Then we'll trap him. Find out what rules he's breaking and stop him from going any further."

Rita wanted to believe Miguel, wanted him able to do all he said he could do. This man who somehow got out of bed each and every day and went on with his life after all meaning had been ripped out of it. She knew he would go on fighting, but she feared he would lose. He looked too vulnerable, sitting there on the hillside with his empty hands. And his emptiness scared her for all the demands it could place upon her own life if she let him too near. Yet intermixed with her fear was a yearning, a curiosity to know whether two people could take the bits and pieces of their separate lives and build something strong enough to withstand the onslaught of time.

|| PARKER || The next time she showed up, Parker was in the studio, experimenting with different glues, testing which bonded best with steering wheels. Not having worked much with plastics, he sought a strong but flexible adhesive. Vaguely aware of foot-steps behind him, he didn't turn around, too intent on pressing one steering wheel atop a tilted coil of seven, waiting for the epoxy to harden.

"They look like miniature hula hoops, ready to take off on a roll." She walked up to the bench, close enough that he caught the scent of lavender along with a whiff of hay, reminiscent of a horse who had just finished a long run. Indeed, she again wore jogging clothes and a fine sheen coated her skin.

"Come on in, why don't you?"

"The door was wide open." She showed no embarrassment over her boldness. He liked that. Too many women feigned shyness, manipulating to get what they wanted.

When he was sure the canted steering wheel would stay in place, he released his hold, stepping back to appraise the overall effect. "Hula hoops, huh?" Instead of the yellow he first envisioned, he now considered painting each steering wheel a different color. "I'll have to keep that in mind."

He turned to look at her more closely. Strands of hair had escaped a ponytail and clung damply to her long neck, where he could see her pulse still beating rapidly. Damp crescent moons on her halter top underlined her small breasts. Electric blue shorts rode low on her long hips and dust encased her shoes.

"Inspection done?" she asked.

He hadn't meant to survey her so minutely, and it embarrassed him to have been caught. "Did you have a good run?"

"I always have a good run." She came closer, this blonde whose name he couldn't remember, and carefully touched the top steering wheel, the one tilted at such a precarious angle that he didn't trust the glue to hold it in place. "You're trying something new here."

He hadn't expected anybody to notice the digression. "Pretty much the same thing, really."

"No, it isn't. All your other sculptures have been metal. Even the ones where you didn't use car parts. Like that robot guy made out of a hot water heater. You left it rusty and corroded along with what I assume are your other early pieces, and the later work you've tended to polish. But everything's been made out of metal. Plastic is a whole different medium for you."

"Very observant." She either had a strong intuitive sense of his work or she'd come by more than the one time he'd seen her. "You'll have to excuse me," he said. "I'm terrible with names."

"Chloe. Chloe Alexander." She said it like it was a name he should recognize.

"Chloe." He paused, letting her name imprint itself on his tongue. "You're right. Plastic is foreign territory for me. I don't know where I'm going with it. Might prove a complete dead end, but I wanted to play with color and different textures."

"Easy to get stuck doing the same thing over and over. It's good to risk something new now and then."

"Might turn out an abysmal failure."

She pressed her fingertip against the top steering wheel, as though testing its balance, causing the entire assemblage to totter. She lifted her hand and let the piece settle back into place. "Then again, it might take you places you never imagined."

Her smile mirrored the challenge of her words, beckoning him to dare more.

"So what can I do for you?" Parker picked up a rag and swept plastic chips off the workbench into the adjacent trash can.

Rather than answer, she walked over to his latest family piece, the woman made out of carburetors. He noticed Chloe was never content with merely looking at his sculptures. She had to touch them, as she had that first time he saw her, and as she did now, tracing the way the woman's arms folded across her stomach. "You going to leave her like this or buff her?"

He crumpled the rag and tossed it into a back corner of his workbench. "Since you asked, would you mind giving me a hand? I need to carry her outside, where the ventilation is better, and I can give her a sandblast."

"I'd be glad to help," she said, squatting down and grabbing hold of the base of the sculpture before he even got there.

"Careful!"

"Don't worry, I'm strong as a mule." They lifted the sculpture in tandem and maneuvered it toward the door with him walking backward. "You've been real productive this summer," she commented.

He hadn't thought about it until she said it. Art was something he did every day. Sometimes more effectively than others, but he continued nonetheless. "Lots of my ideas fizzle, but it's true, I've finished more pieces than usual the past few weeks. Have you seen the girl that goes with this sculpture? She's the original inspiration for this series."

"Watch it," she said, as they neared the exit and his shoulder brushed against the doorframe.

"Let's set it down over there." He gestured at the concrete slab where he did his outside work. Cautiously, they lowered the sculpture to the ground. "Thanks, that was heavy."

"My pleasure." She grinned, as though she truly relished the physical exertion, wiping the back of her hand across her brow, stopping a bead of sweat from rolling down her nose.

"Want something cold to drink?"

"Water would be nice."

"Coming right up." He started over toward the trailer and she came alongside of him. "Why don't you have a seat," he said as they neared his two shell-shaped purple chairs. "I'll bring it out to you."

"Women aren't allowed in your kitchen?" She had her hand on the rail and one foot on the steps leading to his door.

"Only when it's clean." He looked at her hand and noticed she didn't wear a wedding ring. The first time they met, she'd introduced herself as part of a "we" who were building the house on the ridgetop. Married or not, she presumably had a man in her life.

"In other words, not today." Restrained laughter curved her lips in an enticing smile.

"That's right."

"Maybe next time." It wasn't a question. She obviously expected him to invite her inside at some future point.

When he came back out, she was perched by the sculpture of the little girl in the rocking chair and appeared to be carrying on a conversation.

"Here you go," he said, handing her a frosty glass of iced water.

Chloe stood up and toed the rocker, setting the sculpture into motion. "Nice piece."

"Thanks. I like it too."

She seemed ready to say something else but took a sip of water instead. The rocking chair had almost stopped moving and she bent over to give it a little push as she might a child in a swing to keep it going. "I ran into another jogger out here last week. He said he bought one of your pieces a few months ago."

"Must have been Howard. He fell in love with a rooster I made. Keeps coming by to see what I've got new."

"That makes two of us. I detour over this way about once a week, but I haven't seen you around except that one time."

"I wait tables at night, so I tend to sleep late."

She was almost as tall as he was, and when she nodded her head, her ponytail brushed against his shoulder. "A job to pay for what you most love to do."

He liked how she put it, making it sound as though working at the restaurant supported his creativity rather than merely paying the bills. "Can't make a living selling junk."

"This isn't junk." She said it so adamantly that her words sprayed into the air.

"What else would you call it? All the pieces come directly from the junkyard or the dump."

"So you're nothing but a recycler, huh?" Her eyes searched his, insisting on the truth. "We both know what you've done is turn trash into art."

"Not the kind of art many people want to buy."

"How do you know that?"

He shrugged. "You see anybody rushing out here to scoop it up?"

"That's like an actor expecting a director to knock on his door. People don't even know you exist. You need to get your work out there where they can see it."

Her fervor amused him. She talked the way people in LA had, convinced the big time was just around the corner. He'd tried to play the game too, but found out he had no patience for the unspoken rules. If he had to kiss ass to sell a sculpture, he might as well wait tables. "You're seeing my work, but you're not buying it. Why would anybody else?"

She again knelt down by the sculpture of the girl in the rocking chair, rubbing at the welding seams as though to test whether they held tight. Then she looked over her shoulder at the carburetor figure. "You say these two pieces go together?"

"The woman's meant to be her mother." He pointed at the rebar piled up outside his studio. "Eventually there'll be a father figure too. And I'm toying with ideas for a son, a brother for Rocker Girl."

The steering wheels had been a diversion, a way to free his mind, allowing it to roam, looking for images for the boy. He'd been thinking about his own childhood, the days spent longing for a father, and had decided to create a foursome, a boy who belonged to a cohesive family.

"I always wanted a brother," Chloe said. She picked a flower from among the weeds and put it in Rocker Girl's lap. "I was an only child on a huge farm, and I used to pretend I had a younger brother named Ben. He was my favorite playmate for years."

She had her back to him, but Parker heard the dreaminess in her voice as she remembered her imaginary brother. Maybe Rita was right and these sculptures would end up too sentimental, a trite appeal to people's emotions.

Chloe abruptly stood up and walked over to his pile of rebar. Searching through it, she lifted a long piece and carried it over to the sculpture waiting to be sandblasted. "Grant Wood à la the nineties," she said, putting her arm around the woman and raising the rebar in her other hand as though it were a pitchfork. Then she laughed. "Could be a portrait of my family. My dad's a skinny guy and my mother's as plump as this woman."

Chloe set the rebar aside and wandered over to some of the older sculptures, the rusted ones he'd left in a more crude state. Her wispy body appeared less real than the metal figures. An ethereal presence floating between immobile but solid beings. She lingered by the piece he'd made earlier in the summer, a melding of the two styles, the Buick bumper's chrome gleaming seductively, like a woman awaiting her lover on a set of old rusty bed springs.

Wondering what she wanted, Parker took a long drink from his glass of iced water, the coolness filling his mouth. She examined all the pieces closely, as though considering buying one, except she didn't ask about prices. Then again, as somebody who could afford a custom house on the hill overlooking his shabby trailer, cost was probably not a factor in her choices.

"Ever heard of New Visions?" she asked, coming back to where he still stood by the steps.

"You saying I need to forget the metal and move on to plastics?"

She had a piece of ice in her mouth and grinned as she bit into it. "No, I much prefer your metal work. The plastic, at least at this stage, is too simplistic. I was talking about the gallery, New Visions."

Like her name, it sounded familiar, but he couldn't place it. "I don't keep up with the local art scene."

"I thought I saw you when I had the opening for Jake Williams' work."

It all came back to him. Last fall, Jake had taken time off from the restaurant to get ready for a show at a new gallery that featured emerging artists. The owner had sold three of his five large abstracts and wanted to give Jake another show this year. Her hair had been longer then, and she had seemed less sure of herself.

"So you're a gallery owner."

"That's right. And, after you've completed them, I'd like to do a show with your four family pieces."

"A one-time deal?"

She reached into her glass with her long fingers, pulled out the last ice cube, put it into her mouth, and rolled it around on her tongue. "Depends what you do afterward."

"And what about you?" he asked. "What can I expect from you if I agree to let you represent my work?"

She threw her head back, her chin at a proud angle. "I have a growing clientele and I sell well."

Eager though he was for recognition, Parker had turned down a couple of gallery prospects in the past, particularly ones that carried a stable of artists with whom he would have been embarrassed to associate himself. Along with sales, he wanted his work to win the respect of people who understood and appreciated good art. Jake's work attracted people with highly sophisticated taste. If Chloe showed other artists of a similar caliber, he'd be tempted to go with her. "Give me a couple of days to think about it."

"Playing hard to get?"

He leaned against the railing, and let his eyes do a quick traverse of her body before looking her in the face. "I'm relatively easy. How about you?"

She set the empty glass down so hard on the metal stairs that he expected it to shatter. "I treat my artists with respect and I insist on the same from them." She propped a foot on the bottom step, tightened up her shoelaces, and then tossed her head back. "When you're no longer afraid to let other people see your work, let me know."

Before he could respond, she took off, running down to the arroyo. He watched as she raced through the sand, disappearing around a bend, the bottoms of her shoes the last thing he saw.

But he knew he'd see her again, and soon.

|| **RITA** || Rita stood off to the side as Ramón, Parker, and Miguel debated the best way to strip the rear axle assembly from one of the '52 Chevy trucks she had in the yard. Watching them made her think of light bulb jokes. One man really could have done the job, but three made it more entertaining. She restrained from taking part in the process, leaving it for the men to share. It particularly pleased her to see Parker joining in the effort.

"I know it's a bitch," Ramón said, "but once you start having differential problems, it's simpler to replace the whole unit."

Out of their league, Miguel and Parker nodded in deference to Ramón's mechanical know-how. "I just want to be sure none of us gets crushed doing it," Miguel said.

"That's why there are three of us," Parker said. And they resumed discussing how best to go about using the hoist.

Rita's attention drifted to the east, where the aspens rippled the mountains in gold. They had turned early, yellow banners unfurling across the slopes as the last days of September shortened. Fall had come suddenly, the summer disappearing, and with it, the last vestiges of open space. Drew Stinson had sold his first lot, and the new owners had already poured the foundations for a large house.

Miguel came and stood by her, his eyes following hers across the road. "Hurts, doesn't it?"

She nodded, feeling a real closeness to this man who so often echoed her thoughts. "Parker suggested I erect a tall wall, blocking my view of them and their view of me, and maybe then they'd let me stay, but that would be like living in a jail cell."

Miguel put his arm around her and gave her shoulders a squeeze. Ever since that day on the ridgetop, when he'd told her about the death of his wife and son, they'd taken small, cautious steps toward each other. This, however, was the first time he'd hugged her, and his touch flooded her body with warmth, the familiar smell of metal on his fingers, his arm curved around her back.

He let go of her too soon, saying, "Maybe there's a way to go about it that'll feel less confining."

For a moment, she thought he meant their slowly unfolding relationship, then realized he was still talking about how she might keep the junkyard. "What do you have in mind?" she asked.

Miguel patted the hood of a nearby Ford Mustang. "Shall we sit?"

"That long of a lecture, huh?" She sat next to him on the hood of the car, their hips not quite touching.

Pulling his feet up on the bumper and crossing his arms on his knees, Miguel began with a question in his voice. "Ramón says for years, before anybody else bothered, you were draining oil and antifreeze from all the cars, pumping Freon out of the air conditioning systems, even recycling some of the tires to a guy who shreds them for road beds."

"What was I supposed to do? No way I'm going to pour contaminants onto the ground."

Miguel nodded. "When I said it would be a waste of money to fight Drew Stinson, it was because I assumed he could close you on environmental grounds."

"Now you're saying we have a chance?" Her excitement propelled her off the car. She stood before Miguel, eager to hear how he'd win her case.

"No, Rita, that's not what I was trying to say." The dismay on his face foreshadowed her own. "We still don't stand a chance against him in court. He'd find ways to drag it out until we couldn't afford to go on any longer. But . . ." Now Miguel also stood, a positive note in his voice. "Since what he wants is lack of visibility, and since you run an operation in keeping with the new environmental ordinances, you can stay in business if you relocate behind that hill." He pointed to the rise that hid Parker's trailer.

"Parker put you up to this, didn't he?"

"No. When I talked to him about it, he said you wouldn't do it."

"He tell you Stinson would pay me to hide the junkyard?"

"Stinson offered you money to move it back there?" His eyes searched hers. "Why didn't you tell me? It's the perfect solution."

Rita sighed and dug her hands into her pockets. "Call me stubborn, but I want to keep the junkyard where my father put it."

"You can't, though. That's the thing. If you keep fighting, insisting nothing change, you'll be the one who loses."

She knew he was referring to more than her troubles with Drew Stinson and Joe Oakes. As she and Miguel skirted intimacy, part of her held back, clinging to her independence, not giving in to her desire for him. Like a skier poised on the edge of a cliff, she craved the run, but feared the outcome. Meanwhile, the house on the hill became a daily larger reality and soon another would appear across the road. Ironically, as the world closed in on her, she felt increasingly lonely.

Miguel took her hands in his, rubbing them as though to take away a chill. "Parker says you're afraid he'll sell his land once he has a public right of way."

"He told you that?"

Miguel sat back down on the Mustang, letting go of her hands. "Yeah, but I don't get it. How can you think Parker would betray you like that?"

Propping a foot on the bumper, Rita gazed off toward the Jemez Mountains. She could recite a long history of men who'd betrayed her, men she'd once trusted. "Parker's young. He wants the things money can buy. If he sells his property, he can continue making unsalable art while appearing to be highly successful."

"I've talked to Parker. Nothing is more important to him than his sculptures. He wouldn't trade living in that trailer of his and doing what he wants for all the wealth in the world."

"But the land. The land means nothing to him. If somebody offers him enough money for it, he can just as easily do his sculpting elsewhere."

"I don't think so. Like I said, he and I've talked." As Rita wondered when the two of them had talked, Miguel continued. "Parker and I both went out to California expecting it to be the answer to our dreams. The golden land of opportunity. And that it is, but it's also a big, heartless state that shuns failures. We came home because New Mexico is like a mother who always takes you in no matter what. We may not have your reverence for the land, but we know it sustains us."

"Except you live in town, and Parker would be just as happy doing the same."

"No, he wouldn't!" Miguel grabbed her shoulders, his face blazingly earnest. "Rita, you've got to trust the people who care about you."

"Are we still talking about Parker here?"

It amazed her how easily Miguel blushed. His hands fell back onto his thighs, letting her go. "All of us are trying to help you, Rita. Your tío, Parker, Ramón. Me. But you push us away, insisting you're strong enough to take care of yourself."

"It's how I've survived all these years. On my own."

She had a hand pressed against the car and he reached over and began to outline it, his finger dancing against the surface of her skin. She felt as though her hand would fuse to the metal with the heat he stirred. When he finished, he looked up at her. "Aren't you tired of being alone?"

He saw her too clearly, this man she barely knew, surmising her secrets yet somehow, still showing interest in being with her. If she let him get too close, he could hurt her more than she'd ever been hurt before.

"So what did you and Parker do?" she asked. "Get drunk together and come up with the answers to all my problems?"

He shook his head, smiling all the while. "We drank not one, but three or four cups of tea together. Nothing like caffeine to loosen the tongue." His smile grew softer, and his eyes seemed to wander back to their talk, fondness filling out the lines in his face. Then he looked at Rita again. "The boy loves you. That much is obvious. I'm surprised you ever got to date any man, as much of a grilling as he gave me."

"Did you tell him you're coming to dinner tonight?"

"Why? Is he going to be our chaperone?"

His ability to perceive her thoughts proved sometimes quite embarrassing. She had indeed considered inviting Parker to join them, using him to keep some distance between her and Miguel.

She ran her finger over the Mustang hood ornament, too bashful to look him in the eyes. "No, it'll just be the two of us tonight."

Miguel put his hand over hers, stilling her jitters. "We'll have to go slow. I'm out of practice."

His honesty drew her to him. This man made no show of bravado; he dared admit his nervousness. "I'm not in any hurry," she said.

III

The dogs barked, their tails wagging with excitement, as Miguel knocked at the door. "Look who's here," he said, scratching them behind the ears with one hand, while holding out a bouquet of white roses with the other.

It had been years since any man brought her flowers, and the heady scent made her giddy. "They're beautiful."

"So are you," he said, thrusting his empty hands into the back pockets of his jeans. He'd gone home and cleaned up before reappearing for dinner. A brown corduroy shirt turned his eyes into pools of amber.

She nervously ran a hand down the side of her skirt, hoping she hadn't overdressed for the evening. It was a simple velvet skirt, but it accented her waist, and the red blouse brought out the highlights in her hair.

"Let me put these in a vase." She walked over to the trastero.

"Are the colonial pieces from your grandparents?" he asked, looking around the room.

"Just this trastero and that chest." She pointed to the trunk they used for a coffee table. When Elaine had insisted that Tío buy new living room furniture, Rita's father had quickly claimed the old family pieces. He'd added them to his own assorted collection of antiques, a collection she'd supplemented over the years. Thus the room also held a ladder-back rocker, a barber's chair, a fifties Heywood couch, for which she'd made pillows out of bold orange and red fabric, plus a couple of rustic end tables. "A bit of a hodgepodge."

"I like it. It says a lot about you."

"You mean that I'm a junk collector?"

"No, that you value the old, while making way for the new," he said, gesturing at the TV and VCR tucked into the corner. "You're a contemporary woman who still honors some of the old traditions. It's an intriguing mix." He took a step toward her, as though magnetized by the very traits he'd described.

"I better put these in water." She carried the roses into the kitchen and Miguel tagged behind her, playing with the dogs.

"Smells like a seaport in here," he said.

"When I asked, you said you liked shrimp." She panicked, thinking of the hours she'd spent struggling with her grandmother's paella recipe, only to have him dislike it.

"I love shrimp. Same's true for chips and guacamole." He pulled out a chair, sat at the table, and dipped a tortilla chip into the bowl of guacamole. She saw the tremble in his hand and realized he was just as nervous as she.

"How about a beer?" she asked.

"A beer would be great."

She pulled two beers out of the refrigerator and sat across from him at the table she'd covered with a Guatemalan weaving to hide the nicks and scars of years of use. Several men had sat at that very table, but none had raised her hopes as much as Miguel. She lifted her Dos Equis. "A toast to the end of differential problems."

He clinked his bottle against hers. "To a nice evening with a beautiful woman and what smells like a great dinner."

"I better check and see how it's doing." She started to rise from the table, but Miguel laid his hand over one of hers.

"How about taking a sip of your beer first?"

She let out a shaky laugh and settled back into her chair. "I should have warned you, I'm not much of a cook."

Miguel dipped another chip into the guacamole and handed it to her. "Have a bite. It's delicious."

His quiet ways calmed her, and by the time they each had a second beer and finished eating what turned out to be a very tasty paella, she sat with her arms on the table leaning toward him. "When you and Pat were growing up, did you think New Mexico was the end of the world?"

"Not Pat. He wanted nothing more than to get married and run the ranch. But don't forget we had three older sisters, and each of them left home as fast as they could. Pilar only made it as far as Albuquerque, and Consuelo to Colorado Springs, but Aurelia fled all the way to Spain and hasn't been back since. As for me, I couldn't wait to go to college. I saw it as my ticket out of here, not recognizing the difference between a career and a life."

"I'd planned on going to college, too. I was going to be a librarian."

"You?"

"Don't laugh. I had good enough grades, but I . . ."

Miguel reached across the table and lifted her chin. "Hey, I've never doubted your intelligence. I just have trouble picturing somebody as high-spirited as you shut up in a library."

"Yeah, but I love to read."

"What else do you love?" he asked, still holding her chin.

She lowered her head so that her lips brushed against his thumb. "I love the feel of your hands." Then she clasped his hand to her neck, and slid it down toward the open V of her blouse, a warm tide brushing her skin.

He played with her top button, then stood up. She rose from her chair and took a step toward him. He fingered her blouse again, his eyes on hers as he undid the button. His slow, deliberate movements stirred a flush over her entire body. Then he brought his lips to hers in a kiss that began gently, tasting, testing, before giving into avid yearning.

When he cupped his hand around her breast, a sound of pain and longing broke from his chest. She took his hand and led him to her bedroom.

|| JOE || The crisp air of morning had given way to a summery afternoon warmth, and Joe rolled down the car window. As he pulled up to the junkyard, he saw Rita, too, taking advantage of the nice weather, sitting on her front porch reading. She barely lifted her head from the book, looking right past him, as though nothing but a mosquito had disturbed her, then she resumed reading.

Joe considered backing up and relinquishing his plan. Instead, he turned off the motor and got out of the car, taking time to look around while greeting the dogs who ran up to him. Construction workers had begun the framework for a house across the road. It was going to be obscenely large. He had seen it too many times—gargantuan misshapen houses, meant as triumphant declarations of wealth. Joe felt sorry for Rita having to live next to one.

"What do you want?"

He turned around to find her still sitting on the porch, but with the book closed over her finger.

"What're you reading?"

She set the book aside and stood up, her mouth hardening into a scowl. "I'm sure you didn't come here to discuss literature, Mr. Oakes."

"Joe."

"Joe." The way she said it, his name came out even shorter than usual, chopped in half. She stood with her hands on her hips, a stern contrast to the softness of the old adobe house behind her, its rounded edges smoothed by the years. "How about telling me why you're really here."

He gestured at his car. "I need a side-view mirror. Couple of kids broke mine off." When he'd stepped outside that morning to get the newspaper, he'd found the mirror lying in the driveway, the metal twisted and the glass smashed.

"Did you see them do it?"

"No."

"Then how do you know it was kids?" She walked down the steps, toward his car, and grabbed the antenna, bending it from side to side, on the verge of snapping it in two. "Lot of adults plenty angry at you rich Anglos moving in and taking over the town."

"I'm not rich. And I've done all I could to adapt to this place. I didn't come here to create another LA. I came here seeking a refuge."

She bent the antenna toward her, then let it go, watching it oscillate. "Did you bring a screwdriver?"

"What?"

"One of these," she said, pulling a screwdriver out of her shirt pocket and brandishing it in his face.

"Believe me, I know what a screwdriver is."

"Costs more if I have to pull the piece for you." She strode toward the junkyard, her dogs right at her feet, and he debated whether to follow too, or wait. Finally, reminding himself of why he was really there, he rushed to catch up with her, hurrying past row upon row of metal, an army of soldiers ready to defend Rita.

"Hard to believe it's the end of September already," he said, coming up alongside her.

"Need to go down this aisle." She cut a sharp turn in front of him.

He quickly moved aside to make the turn too and found himself facing the Sangre de Cristos, aspens ribboning the slopes in gold. "Such an amazing time of year, isn't it?"

Rita stopped walking and looked up at him. He hadn't realized quite how short she was, especially without her cowboy boots. Yet when she put her hands on her hips and threw her head back, the hostility that ran through her dispelled any notions of frailness. "What is it with you and the chit-chat?"

Some of it was nervousness, but he was also looking for a way in, a way to find out what she and her boyfriend were planning. He couldn't afford Leroy's advice to wait until next year to sell his lots. He needed to make sales now, while the weather was beautiful. Before long, people would be in town for Thanksgiving and then Christmas, with fantasies about having a home here. He had to take advantage of the season. Nobody fell in love with Santa Fe in the spring, when horrendous winds blew and nothing bloomed. "Can't help it. I think fall is our prettiest time of year."

For a moment, she softened, he saw it in the way her mouth relaxed, her lips losing their harsh line, curving into fullness. "I hadn't pictured you as a nature lover."

"Why else would I move out here?"

"To play king of the mountain." She resumed walking, charging through a row of Hondas. Singling out a Civic that had been rear-ended, she began detaching a side-view mirror. "This model isn't as old as yours, but it should do the trick."

"Old as my car is, I'll probably be a regular visitor here."

"Don't you have a mechanic?"

"I've got a great mechanic, but I prefer to do the minor repairs myself. Hell, I would have brought a screwdriver if I'd known this place was a 'you-pull.' You're the last of a dying breed."

"That's right. I'm more of an antique than that car of yours. Practically an endangered species." She handed him the mirror. "That'll be fifty-five dollars."

He thought the price a little high, but reached for his wallet. He had the cash, but needed to prolong the transaction. "Do you take Visa?"

"Couldn't stay in business if I didn't accept charge cards." She headed back in the direction of her house. "The card machine's in the shop."

Joe quickened his pace to keep up with her. Tall though he was, his long legs had to work to maintain her speed. If he didn't hurry, he'd lose his chance. "Santiago told me you and your dad used to picnic on that ridge."

She whipped around so fast that he almost bumped into her. "You may own that ridgetop now, but you cannot possess my memories."

She acted like he'd fingered a family photo and dirtied it. "I didn't mean to get personal. It's just . . ." How could he put it so she might listen? "I guess what I'm trying to say is I think I understand why you resent me. It must have been very hard to let the place go."

"How can you possibly understand? You rich people buy whatever you want. You've never been forced to let go of a family heritage."

"I'm not rich, Rita. I . . ."

"Maybe not in your world, but in mine anybody who can afford to pay over half a million dollars for a piece of property is rich."

That he couldn't afford it was the very thing he couldn't tell her. "I'll be paying for that place the rest of my life. Had to take out a huge loan to do it. And it isn't just me. My girlfriend is splitting the cost." He didn't mention that Chloe was only splitting the cost of the house. The land she had left in his hands, expecting him to turn a profit. "It's a stretch for us, but we decided it was worth it to live someplace secluded."

He couldn't tell whether it was the sun that made Rita squint, or something she was considering as she stared at him. "Secluded? How secluded can it be if you have neighbors in shouting distance?"

He knew she wasn't referring to herself, but to the further development of the ridge. It was a trap, a way of getting him to admit his plans, but he wouldn't, not until he had a more sure sense of whether she would fight them. "We're living in town now, with absolutely no space around us. That ridgetop is wide open. Bigger than anything we ever imagined."

"The openness is fast disappearing." She gestured at the house under construction across the road.

"At least my place is a modest size," he reminded her. "And I've designed it so that it'll blend in with the hillside." From where he stood, even now, a drab gray awaiting its stucco coat, the house wasn't obtrusive, its low profile barely noticeable among the piñons and junipers.

"Your house could be three times its size, stick out like a sore thumb, with half a dozen more of them perched alongside you, and it wouldn't make any difference. Once you put a house on that hill, you destroyed it."

She took off at an even faster pace than before, but Joe let her speed ahead of him, finally assured of her position. As she disappeared into her shop to run his card through the machine, he looked up at the ridgetop and let out a loud breath, like the sound of compressed air released upon opening a tightly capped jar. Tomorrow he would file for approval of the subdivision, knowing Rita wouldn't fight it, that she had resigned herself to having houses on the ridgetop.

|| **RITA** || After Joe left, Rita returned to the porch steps and picked up her book but couldn't read. His visit kept intruding, gnawing at her attention. She had the feeling he'd come for something other than the mirror. He'd listened too attentively, like a birder, his ear alert for a rare call.

Puzzling over what Joe had really wanted, she gazed across the road without seeing. She didn't hear another car approaching until just before it turned into her driveway. The sight of Drew Stinson's BMW brought her to her feet. Where was Miguel? He'd said he would arrive well before her meeting with Stinson, who kept pressuring her to get rid of the junkyard. The man had an imperious attitude that both incensed and alarmed her, especially when he flashed his perfectly matched teeth in a smile, as he did when he got out of the car.

"Afternoon, Rita. Catching some rays?"

The dogs bounded over and snarled at Stinson, rare behavior on their part. They posted themselves in front of Rita, making sure he didn't get too close.

"Rays?" she repeated, noticing that he had a small Band-Aid on the bridge of his nose. An odd place for an injury. She gestured at the building site across the road. "Can't say I was out here admiring the obstruction of my view."

Stinson looked over his shoulder at the ongoing construction, then turned his gaze toward her junkyard. "Imagine that as your only vista."

"If they don't like my junkyard, they should live someplace else."

"My clients don't think that way. They set their mind on having something, and they get it. And what they want is a flawless view from here to the Jemez Mountains."

Willing herself to control the anger that constricted her throat, Rita pivoted to look at the range of mountains behind her. They lacked the majesty of the Sangre de Cristos, but when the sun set, the sky above them often blazed in a glory of color. The mountains, with their succession of peaks and valleys that had withstood windstorms, floods, droughts, and fires, lent her strength. She shrugged as she turned back to face Stinson. "Guess your clients will just have to overlook my mess and lift their eyes to the heavens."

"That's not their style. They're going to insist your mess disappear." Like a frayed fuse, he smelled of burning plastic and hot metal. He ran his finger over the bridge of his nose, circling the bandage. "I'm still willing to pay you to move your junkyard out of sight."

Rita stretched her arms over her head, exaggerating a yawn. "Haven't you heard? We Spanish are a lazy bunch. We don't like to work any more than we have to. I'm quite happy leaving my junkyard exactly where it is."

"Move it, or lose it." The steel edge of his voice exposed his determination to get rid of her.

"Go ahead and try!"

His lips scrunched and moved from side to side, as though engaged in a tug of war. "It's in your best interest to reconsider my offer. Otherwise . . ." He left the sentence unfinished, but Rita heard the menace. "I've already sold five lots, and all five parties have signed a petition to close your junkyard. We'll present the matter to the city council the first Wednesday in November."

Rita recalled the city council meeting she'd attended a couple of years ago to prevent a shopping center from going in at the opposite end of the road. The meeting had gotten nasty, with name calling and innuendos about money determining the outcome. No matter how many residents requested the convenience of nearby stores, the council members sided with the realtors who wanted to keep the area less developed, more exclusive. Influential people had indirectly worked in her favor back then; this time, they would outright oppose her.

"How much are you willing to pay?"

Stinson's lips softened into a closed smile, his teeth hidden. "Ten thousand."

Rita disguised her gasp with a clearing of her throat. He'd said it so casually, a number that represented close to a year's earnings for her. She could pay a couple of men a decent wage to move the vehicles and still have plenty left for herself. "I'll think about it."

"You're running out of time. The meeting's less than two weeks away."

"Nine days." She had already run the date through her head, calculating how long she had. Nine days in which to decide whether to let this man buy her cooperation. Maybe he wanted her out of there badly enough to pay even more. "Twelve thousand," she said.

"You drive a hard bargain."

A sour taste rose at the back of her throat as Stinson smiled. Then she heard an approaching vehicle and saw Miguel's truck slowing down to make the turn into her driveway. Despite the dust cloud he stirred up, she felt relief wash over her like a cool shower on a hot day. "I don't think you've met my attorney."

"I didn't know you had one." Stinson's teeth tucked themselves away in a tight-lipped smile.

Miguel pulled in near them and got out of the truck. He wore a denim shirt, jeans, and well-buffed boots. Probably not the image Stinson associated with an attorney, but the sight of Miguel charged Rita.

"Sorry," he said, looking at his watch. "I thought we were meeting at three-thirty, not three."

"I showed up early," said Stinson. "I'm ready to get this over with. There's no need to involve any lawyers."

"Miguel, this is Drew Stinson, the developer of the property across the road. He's offering me ten, maybe twelve thousand to move the junkyard."

"That's too little." Miguel bent down to pet the dogs who circled excitedly around him. "Hey guys, how are you?"

Stinson forced his smile further, all the way back to his molars. "Twenty."

This time she did gasp. The man treated money as though it were a worn-out game of Monopoly, no longer valued, but still played.

"Twenty-five, and we'll give it some serious thought." The quickness with which Miguel volleyed the offer stunned her.

Stinson's smile had disappeared. "You're pushing the limits." He kicked at Flojo, who had been sniffing at his shoes. It wasn't a vicious kick, but one that warned him to back off. "Twenty-five thousand and the junkyard is permanently removed from sight."

"Give us a proposal in writing and we'll consider it," said Miguel.

Stinson again fingered the Band-Aid on his nose, rubbing back and forth over the top of it. "I'll have my attorney draw up the papers."

"I'm not promising to sign anything," Rita said. Twenty-five thousand dollars was a lot of money just to get rid of what he considered an eyesore. She wouldn't put it past him to sneak in a clause that entailed more than making her junkyard invisible.

"We'll look it over and let you know." Miguel reached out and shook Stinson's hand.

She knew he did it to get rid of him, but for her the handshake was a pact with the devil. When Stinson turned to her to repeat the gesture, she bent down and needlessly retied her shoe.

"I'll have the papers for you tomorrow," she heard him say. She waited until he walked away before she stood up, watching as he got into his car. He drove a couple hundred yards to the building site across the road and got back out to talk to what appeared to be the homeowners, people who somberly nodded their heads as he pointed at the junkyard.

Rita leaned back, letting her shoulder rest against Miguel's. "I don't trust him."

"He's not the trustworthy type, but he's anxious enough to get rid of the junkyard that the deal will be straightforward."

"You really think so?" She'd heard too many incidents of people signing papers that gave away more than they had ever intended. Obtuse language tricking them out of their land.

"I'll look it over carefully to be sure," Miguel said. "But there's too much at stake for him to risk losing your consent."

"Consent." She shook her head. "I wouldn't consent to any of this if I didn't think he could wipe me out."

Miguel nuzzled her hair, his lips close to her ear. "You're going to come through this okay."

As his hands slid down her hips, she found herself believing him. The tautness in her spine loosened and she leaned back, her shoulders resting against his chest. Her mind whispered that she'd done this before, let her body betray her, trick her into thinking a man would somehow make her life better. That was the trouble with sex. It lulled her into complacency.

"Let's go inside," she said. After all, a woman could only fight for so long, and then she needed a reprieve.

|| JOE || "No peeking!" Chloe swatted at Joe's hand as he fussed with the bandanna she'd tied around his eyes. "It's a surprise."

"But I can tell you're driving us up to the house."

"Yes, but you don't know what's waiting there for you."

Being blindfolded reminded him of a childhood birthday game—hit the pot—with voices calling out "hot, hot, hotter," as he moved forward on his hands and knees, the chants echoing his own excitement as he neared the prize. When he was young, forty had sounded boringly old, but now that it had arrived, he found himself anticipating a good stretch of years. Soon he and Chloe would be living up here, a more settled time than he'd ever known, with her at his side.

"Almost there," she said, reaching over and squeezing his hand.

In the past week, he'd come upon her a couple of times having low-voiced phone conversations that quickly ended when he walked into the room. At first suspicious, he soon realized she was planning a surprise for him. She loved to create a big fanfare over birthdays, and though it had flustered him last year when she'd encouraged complete strangers in a restaurant to sing "Happy Birthday" to him, he was ready for a special celebration this time. His life had never been better.

"Leave it be," she said when she turned off the engine and he reached up to remove the blindfold.

She came around and opened the door, helping him out of the car. A breeze fluttered the bottom corner of the bandanna, lifting it off his face, offering a glimpse of the dirt beneath his feet. He stepped cautiously as she guided him across the uneven terrain.

"This is like one of those psychology games I had to play in college."

"And you lived to tell the story, so relax." She was leading him over to where the patio would be, he could tell by the feel of the setting sun on his face. "I've got something here for you to sit on," she said, putting his hand on a wooden plank.

It felt like the wide armrest of an Adirondack chair like the kind his

grandparents had had. "Is this my present?" He reached for the blindfold, only to have her hands stop his.

"Hold your horses." She coaxed him into a sitting position, his legs
at a slant, his back firmly supported. "One more sec." She moved away
from him. "Okay, now you can take it off."

He lifted the bandanna and found her expectant smile. She sat in a
white Adirondack chair that matched his. "You talked so wistfully about
them that I couldn't imagine anything more perfect for out here."

It was true that he'd spoken nostalgically about summers at his
grandparents' house, whiling away entire afternoons reading in their
porch chairs, but it wasn't the kind of gift that warranted a blindfold.
She could have just brought him around the house and had the chairs
waiting on the patio. "So why all the secrecy?"

"Because," said a man's voice behind him, "she didn't want you to
see my car parked out front."

"Wayne!" His best friend boasted a grin that hadn't lost its youth-
ful vitality in all the years they'd known each other. Although dressed
in an Armani suit, Wayne sported the tan and deep wrinkles of a man
who loved the outdoors, his brown hair bleached to the color of sand.
"What're you doing here?"

"Oh, ancient one," Wayne said, salaaming. "I had to see for myself
how you were getting along in your dotage."

"Look who's talking. You're the same age I am."

"No way! I'm a year younger."

"For all of another month. Then you turn forty too."

"Forty, not forty-two." Wayne folded his arms around Joe in a tight
clasp. "Good to see you, you old fart."

Joe returned the bear hug, embracing this man who'd been a constant in his life no matter what else happened. They'd gone in very
different directions since they first met in college, Wayne racing to
the forefront with a software company, marrying a stockbroker, and
having two kids. Yet they'd stayed in touch. Wayne had spent a long
weekend with him after the divorce, forcing Joe to go jogging every
morning, both of them drinking too much at night as they reminisced
about the past and spoke of what they wanted from the future.

"I didn't expect to see you again until ski season," Joe said. Then

Chloe's ulterior motives struck him. She'd speculated that since Wayne brought his family out to Santa Fe for a week of skiing every Christmas, he might want to build a vacation home on the ridgetop. Joe had told her the place wasn't suitable to Wayne's needs, but she'd murmured something about it not hurting to ask.

"Did Chloe put you up to this?" He looked around but couldn't find her. Not knowing about the illegalities involved, she didn't understand that there was no way he could sell one of the lots to his best friend.

"Yeah, she thought I'd be a bigger surprise than a couple of chairs."

"But no matter how much I insisted, he refused to be gift wrapped," Chloe said, reappearing with a folding chair. She gave him such an open smile that it convinced Joe she intended nothing more from Wayne than a surprise birthday visit.

Wayne settled into the canvas chair she'd brought out for him. "This is the life," he said. It was a mild end-of-October evening, the sun still warm as it neared the horizon, illuminating the mountains to the east. "Quite a view you've got yourselves up here."

"Isn't it spectacular?" Chloe reached across and took Joe's hand, entwining her fingers with his on the armrest. His grandparents used to sit like that on summer evenings in their Adirondack chairs. He'd given up on ever having the closeness they'd shared, but tonight it seemed possible, as Chloe leaned toward him, her eyes searching his, making sure he was happy.

"You two lovebirds are missing an amazing sunset." The land shimmered as wispy clouds turned a deepening shade of pink. "We never get skies like this in Silicon Valley."

"We have beautiful sunsets all the time," Chloe said. "You should move out here."

"Wish we could, but most of my clients are in California. Same for Tess. We'd both lose too much business if we relocated."

"How about a vacation home? Great place to stay for the winter holidays. The family can go skiing. And you can't beat our summers."

Joe gave her a hand a light squeeze, cautioning her not to go any further.

Wayne sighed, looking at the Sangre de Cristos. "I bet there's some great mountain biking around here."

"You into that now?" Joe asked. "If you're staying through tomorrow, I know where we can rent a couple of bikes."

"That'd be great. My flight isn't until mid-afternoon. We could put in a few miles. Maybe up that trail we skied down last year."

"Tesuque? You gotta be kidding. Skiing down that sucker was suicidal enough. Going up it would kill me. I know a better trail. Aspen Vista. Less treacherous, but awesome this time of year."

Wayne gazed at the mountains, their slopes a golden wash. "Wherever we go up there'll be fine with me. You don't know how lucky you are to have it all so close. I've got to drive hours to get anything comparable."

"Mountain biking, horseback riding, river kayaking, rock climbing," Chloe chanted. "We've got it all."

"Way to keep a man young," Wayne said.

"Ever consider having a second home here?" Chloe asked.

"Chloe, don't."

She let go of Joe's hand. "Just asking."

"Interesting that you'd ask," Wayne said. "Tess has been talking about us buying another house as an investment. She says that real estate is exactly what the phrase implies—real. A tangible object for your money. Unlike the stock market. She's anticipating a crash and wants us to put money into a second home."

"She's wise," Chloe said. "Houses are a sound investment."

Despite the cooling weather, Chloe still wore sandals, her toenails a bold red. Joe put his foot on top of hers and pressed lightly. Without looking at him, she pulled her foot out from under his as though he'd stepped on it accidentally. He put his foot on top of hers again, and pressed a little harder this time, watching as her eyes widened in disbelief.

"Yeah, a second home is probably the way to go," Wayne said.

Chloe looked at Joe, chewing on her lower lip, waiting for him to make the next move. But he couldn't. It wasn't right to take advantage of a friendship to further his own goals. "A place on the coast would be nice," he said.

"Forget it! We get enough foggy weather in Palo Alto as it is. Besides, I'm not a beach person. Give me sunshine and the mountains any day."

"Tahoe?" Joe sought the places he remembered liking when he'd lived in California, ignoring the way Chloe peered at him with utter incredulity. "Or how about the Mammoth area?"

"Too many earthquakes there. And Tahoe's gotten too crowded." Wayne settled more deeply into the chair, stretching his legs out in front of him. "Chloe's right, though. This place is damn near paradise."

"Property isn't as expensive here as it is in California." Chloe tucked her feet under the chair, free of Joe's restraint. "You could easily buy a nice piece of land and build a house."

"Where are we going for dinner?" Joe asked.

"Tess has been talking along those same lines," Wayne continued, as though Joe hadn't said anything. "She was thinking more in terms of a small town in Colorado, but I can see where Santa Fe would suit us better. Not so limited. The kind of place where we could retire after the kids leave home."

Chloe remained silent. Joe had seen her do the same thing with her art clients, giving them time to wander in the direction where she'd led them, letting them think that on their own, they'd reached the decision to buy.

Joe stood up. "Did you make us reservations somewhere, Chloe?"

"Starving, Birthday Boy?" Wayne asked, glancing at his watch. "A client recommended Geronimo's. Only time available was seven-thirty. So we've got a while yet. How about a tour of this house of yours while there's still enough light to see it?"

Dusk cast a beautiful glow, softening even the rough, unfinished portions of the house. Although little of the interior work had begun, the layout itself offered incredible vistas in every direction. Chloe trailed behind them as Joe escorted Wayne from one room to the next. "God! There's that view again!" Wayne angled straight toward the living room's picture window. "Even in the winter, you'll be able to sit and watch sunsets."

"Joe specifically designed it that way. We bought this hill because of the views and he made sure we didn't lose any of them."

Wayne turned to Joe. "You bought the whole hill?"

"Not quite. Just the top."

"The only part that counts." Wayne let out a low whistle. "Must have cost you a bundle."

Joe wanted no reminders of how much the hill had cost him, an expense well beyond the money he owed the bank. "Come see the rest of the house." He led Wayne toward the master bedroom with its southeastern exposure that would catch the first light of morning.

Chloe opened the French doors. "We're going to put a small patio over here, so we can have breakfast outside in the summer."

"Way to go," Wayne said. "You really should have been an architect, Joe. You've thought of everything."

The praise soothed Joe's tormented conscience. He didn't like what he'd had to do to afford this house, but he loved what he'd done with the site, maximizing its potential.

"Had to do these views justice," he said, gesturing toward the mountains.

Wayne turned around to take in the vista, nodding appreciatively. "Lot of land left up here. You going to keep it all to yourselves, or let other people share the bounty?"

Joe ran his boot back and forth across a nail that lay on the floor, the metal rasping against the concrete. He could feel Chloe looking at him, her restraint palpable. If he didn't say something soon, she would take hold of the conversation and steer Wayne into making a purchase. "I'm waiting for the city to approve subdividing the land into three more lots."

Wayne got down on his knees, his hands folded in beseeching prayer. "Oh great real estate baron, in the name of our college fraternity and years of friendship, please let me have first choice."

Chloe let out a gleeful laugh, as though Wayne had already bought a lot.

"Better get up before you ruin your knees," Joe said, only to have Wayne prostrate himself like a Muslim offering prayers to Allah.

"I offer up my pain as a way of winning your approval. I beg of you, please show me the lots you have available."

Wayne had never worried about making a fool of himself, and his humor had been the first thing that drew Joe to him, leavening his own seriousness. "You can look all you want," he told his friend, "but I don't think you'll want to buy up here."

Groaning as he stood up, Wayne put a hand on his back and

exaggeratedly hobbled as they made their way outside. "This old geezer needs to establish a nest egg somewhere."

They walked through all three of the sites, with Wayne showing a marked preference for the one at the eastern entrance. "It's situated so I can still see the sunsets, and get an incredible vista of those mountains." He rubbed his hands together as though it were a done deal. "So how much you going to rob me of?"

"I'm not." He'd seen Wayne's California house, with its five bedrooms and four bathrooms. "These lots are too small for you."

"Not if we're only going to live here a few weeks out of the year. And, all too soon, the kids will be gone. When Tess and I retire, we don't want to shuffle around in a place that echoes with emptiness."

"Even then, you'll want something larger than this." For all his exercising, Wayne was a big man, solid and broad as a semi-truck. He took up room, needed space. A small house like Joe's wouldn't suit him.

"What's the matter, you don't want us as neighbors?" Genuine hurt sounded in Wayne's voice. It was the first time Joe had seen him uncertain whether he was liked.

"Joe's awful, isn't he?" As she might with a sniffling child, Chloe rubbed Wayne's back, making small circles with her hand. "You should've heard him try to talk me out of renting the space for my gallery." She glanced at Joe, one eyebrow raised in a jagged point, annoyed by his hesitation. "He's afraid somebody will blame him if they're not a hundred percent happy with one of his properties."

"You mean it isn't some personal vendetta that's keeping him from selling this place to me?" Wayne looked at Joe, waiting for him to explain.

How could he tell him that the entire project was on ground shakier than the earthquake faults in California? Wayne didn't have Chloe's ethical scruples, but he was his closest friend, one who deserved an honest deal. "The subdivision hasn't even been approved yet. For all I know, it could fail to go through."

"I don't understand. You got permission to build your house. What's the hold-up with the other lots?"

"I've asked him the same question," Chloe said, her indignation causing frown lines in her forehead. "Seems to me they should have approved the entire project right from the start, instead of jerking us around like this."

"The city moves in mysterious ways." Joe looked at his watch. "If we have an seven-thirty reservation, we should probably head back into town. Give us a chance to have a drink before dinner."

Wayne put a hand on his arm, restraining him from walking away. "I get the feeling you don't want me up here."

"Having you as a neighbor would be as good as it gets," Joe said. He had missed having a close friend, a man whose very presence drained the tension out of him. "But I don't think this is the place for you. Santa Fe, yes. But not up here. You need a larger lot so you can build a house big enough to suit you."

"Don't tell a fat boy that he needs to buy bigger pants!" Wayne spun away from them, facing the mountains, his arms folded protectively over his stomach. He'd once told Joe that as an overweight kid, he'd become the class clown to avoid being picked on. Although he'd been trim since college, he couldn't shake the image of himself as a Baby Huey, an enormous klutz of a cartoon character.

Now Joe, too, gazed at the mountains, thinking about how they welcomed him every time he came up here, their massiveness shrinking his own concerns. He never thought of Wayne as having troubles, but who was without worries?

"If you lived up here," Joe said, "you'd have to share that view with me."

"I'd invite you over for a brew and we could stare at it to our hearts' content."

"It doesn't come cheap, even for a best friend."

"I'm not asking you for a bargain. I'll pay the going rate. Hell, having you down the road will feel like being in college again. A fountain of youth. That's how you should package this place."

Chloe took Joe's hand and wrapped it around her hip before whispering in his ear, "Told you it'd be easy."

Joe shivered, the night suddenly cool as the sun slipped out of view. If anything went wrong with the lot approvals, he'd lose not only her and all his money, but also his closest friend.

|| **RITA** || With her Dodge Ram dangling from the back hoist, the tow truck barreled along the dirt road. Rita sat next to the driver, looking out at Parker's sculptures, not seeing the man lying in the road until it was too late. His arms outstretched like Jesus on the cross, pebbles instead of thorns around his head, her father screamed her name as the front tire rolled over him.

She awoke with a crushing pain in her chest, as though she, not her father, had been pinned under the weight of the tow truck. Her body clammy with sweat, she threw off the bedcovers and tried to slow her breathing. Darkness still filled the room, though it was already past six. In a couple of hours, the men would arrive to move the junkyard. The business her father had cherished, and she had promised to sustain, soon hidden like a piece of pornography.

Slipping her feet into a pair of slippers, careful not to trip over the dogs, she made her way across the floor and into the kitchen. The dim light of the range hood guided her steps toward the coffee machine. She waited as, drip by drip, the acrid smell of coffee filtered through the room. The dogs whimpered, and she let them outside, the air chilly against her bare legs. Rather than face the harsh glare of the overhead light, she worked in the shadows, filling the dogs' bowls with dry food and replenishing their water before letting them back into the house. Then she poured herself a cup of coffee and went into the living room, where enough embers remained in the woodstove to start a fresh log burning.

She sat in the old barber's chair by the front window and brought her knees up under her chin, pulling the flannel nightshirt down to her toes, trying to get warm. On those rare occasions as a child when she'd gotten up early, she'd found her father sitting in this very chair, his cigarette glowing in the dark. He was the one who'd shown her the beauty of this time of day, prior to dawn, when the night slowly gave way to morning.

The nightmare still clung to her, and she considered turning on the lights to chase it away but knew she needed to sort through her emotions. A combination of anger and sadness weighed upon her. The vision of her father lying in the road, willing to sacrifice himself rather than lose the junkyard, made her question if she'd given in to Stinson too easily. She'd let Parker and Miguel convince her that the only way she could keep the place was by tucking it out of sight. But what would have happened if she'd insisted on going to court? Wasn't it possible she could have won?

Agitated and cold, she got out of the chair and stood in front of the woodstove, letting the heat burn the back of her legs, then turning to let it work on her front side. She wondered if it was too late to change her mind. The movers were scheduled to arrive at nine. Scrambling around in the dark, unable to find the phone book, she finally turned on the lights and located it under a pile of papers. She dialed the number and waited through several rings before acknowledging that not even a machine was going to answer her call.

Not that it mattered. She really had no choice but to go through with the move. Exhausted from a poor night's sleep and years of struggle, she leaned her head against the wall, the coolness of the adobe seeping through her hair. A shiver coursed along her spine, alerting Flojo, then Loca, both of them standing at her feet, excited, thinking it was time for their walk.

"Okay, okay," she said. A walk would do her good, clear the nightmare from her mind, and strengthen her resolve to get through this day without falling apart. "Let me get dressed first."

November had been uncommonly warm, but the mornings held enough of a chill to warrant a hat pulled down over her ears and a jacket buttoned up to her chin. By the time she stepped outside, the sun had begun to lift itself from behind the Sangre de Cristos, and a solitary bird chirped in the distance. Rita and the dogs set off in the direction of Parker's trailer. She would loop behind his place and head toward her uncle's before circling back home. A good, long walk to air out her mind and get her blood moving.

A light burned in Parker's kitchen, but knowing he never got up early, she assumed he had left it on overnight. She angled toward the arroyo behind his trailer, and then stopped, shocked to see him with Joe's girlfriend. The two of them stood to the east, gesturing at the hill that graced Parker's property.

The woman lifted a camera to her face and aimed it at the hill just as the sun began to peek over the top. The rising sun glinted off her blonde hair and she lowered the camera, turning to speak to Parker. He stood close to her, nodding his head, absorbing every word she said. When she held both hands out in front of her, as though to measure the width of the hill, he put his hands over hers and extended her arms further apart, encompassing a bigger area.

It was like they were talking about building something up there. Furious, Rita stormed up to them. "What are you two doing?"

Parker immediately let go of the woman's hands, his breath forming little clouds as he spoke. "Hey, Mom. You remember Chloe."

"Good morning." She smiled at Rita while putting the lens cap back on her camera and slipping it into her purse as though it were perfectly normal to shoot photos of an empty hill first thing in the morning. "I need to run, Parker. I'll let you know how the photo turns out."

"There's no doubt in my mind. It'll be awesome," he said, following her over to a nearby Miata. "Things will be chaotic around here for a couple of days, what with moving the junkyard, but by next week we should be able to get going on it."

"I'll give you a call." As she opened the car door, she looked over her shoulder. "Bye, Rita. See you around." Her little car took off in a spurt, bouncing over a couple of ruts before hitting the recently graded road.

"What was that all about?" Despite her worst premonitions, Rita couldn't believe that as soon as he'd gained legal access to his land, Parker had made arrangements to sell it. But obviously that was why Joe had sent Chloe, relying on her sexiness to persuade Parker to relinquish the best piece of his property, the small hill that rose like a soft swell in the land.

"I was going to wait to tell you," he said. He hung his head, his hands folding and unfolding a piece of paper.

"Tell me what? That you've sold out!"

His head jerked back in a whiplash. "I did not. She's a reputable dealer."

"How could you sell the land when you told me you wouldn't?" It was too much. The very day she had to move the junkyard, he parted with the prettiest piece of their property.

"Damn you!" He balled up the paper in his hands and threw it at her. "This isn't about you! You or your goddamn land. Can't you think about anybody besides yourself? You've got a son. Me! This is about me!"

His face contorted just as it had when he used to throw temper tantrums, yelling that he wanted a daddy, flailing at her with his little fists, his words searing her heart.

But Parker wasn't a child anymore. He stood before her a grown man, capable of hurting her beyond repair. "So, you've gotten even. Is that what this is all about? I wasn't a good enough mother, and now you're getting revenge. Selling . . ."

"Stop!" He put his hands on her shoulders and gave her a little shake. "You've got this all twisted." The anger had evaporated from his voice, replaced with an annoyingly patronizing tone. "I haven't sold anything. Not until . . ."

"Not until I'm dead." She hammered on his chest with her fist. "You could have at least waited until I died to sell that hill."

He grabbed hold of her hand, stopping her from pounding him again. "Mom, it's not land I'm selling. It's sculptures."

"I saw her, Parker. She was taking pictures of the hill. Buying the ridgetop wasn't enough for Joe. Now he wants this hill too. If you . . ."

"I don't know who you're talking about. This has nothing to do with some Joe. It's strictly between Chloe and me. She owns an art gallery and is giving me a show."

"What?" Rita's hand fell to her side as Parker let go of it.

He bent down to retrieve the ball of paper he'd thrown at her, uncrumpling it to reveal a sketch of four of his pieces on the hill. "We wanted to see how it looked at sunrise before we went through the trouble of moving the sculptures up there for a publicity shot."

She took the wrinkled piece of paper from him and stared at the drawing, sorting through what he'd told her. "You're saying she's only interested in that hill to show off your art?"

"What else would she want it for?"

His sculptures were good, but Rita suspected Chloe had other motives for giving him a show. Motives that might or might not have to do with the land.

"Can you believe it?" Parker grabbed her hands and swung them back and forth. "My sculptures are finally going to fly."

Rita couldn't remember the last time she'd seen him that jubilant, a goofy grin on his face and his legs bouncy as a kangaroo's. Life would show him plenty of disappointment further down the line. For now, let him think Chloe only had his best interests at heart.

"Talent like yours had to take off at some point," she said.

With unexpected tenderness, he leaned forward and kissed her cheek. "Thanks for being the one who has always believed in me."

Even as a teen, he'd shown such a keen interest in art that she'd trusted him to find his way through any ensuing dilemma. But his recent hunger for recognition scared Rita. She'd seen the avid way Chloe looked at him, ready to possess him. Thinking she held his ticket to success, he could easily give away more than he'd ever intended, and end up with none of what he'd wanted.

"The movers will be here in a little while. I need to take a walk before we get to work."

She turned to head down to the arroyo, but Parker put a hand on her shoulder. "You going to be okay, Mom?"

"Sure," she said, shrugging off his hand, but not daring to look at him, tears threatening to surface. She whistled for the dogs to resume their walk with her. If she moved quickly, she could still put in a couple of miles before heading back home. A couple of miles to fortify herself.

The sand in the arroyo slowed down her pace, the ground slipping away beneath her, grabbing at her feet like quicksand. Yet she loved this part of the walk, the piñons and junipers standing above her, their roots visible in the crumbling embankment as they held on to the eroding land. They reminded her of what it was to endure, and she vowed that she too would hold on to this land for as long as possible.

When she made her way home, though, she was dismayed to spot two large flatbed trucks pulling into the yard. She never wore a watch, but she knew it wasn't nine yet. Even with her delay at Parker's, it couldn't be much past eight.

As she drew nearer, she discovered Miguel talking to six men, who shuffled their feet as he spoke. He gestured at the buses on the far perimeter. "You'll want to take those first and put them along the . . ."

"Stop!" she said, storming up to him. She turned to the two brothers, twins, who owned the trucks. "You weren't supposed to be here until nine."

"Realized it might take longer than we originally thought," said the slightly leaner twin. "Decided we better start early."

"And you?" She turned to Miguel. "What're you doing here?"

Her words held the sharpness of a slap, and it was the first time she'd seen the pain in his eyes as a reflection of how she, rather than a past memory, had hurt him.

"I stopped by in case you needed me," he said.

"I don't need anybody running my business, telling these men what I want done."

Miguel shrugged. "They were ready to get started, and since you weren't around, I repeated what you'd told me about . . ."

"Maybe I changed my mind."

"And maybe you're so upset that you're not thinking straight." Miguel eyebrows drew together in a line, ready for any fight she threw his way.

One of the men started whistling an irritatingly chirpy tune. She glared at him until he stopped. Then she turned to the twins. "What're you waiting for? I'm not paying you to stand around and do nothing."

This time it was the fatter of the twins who spoke, holding a hand up like a cop directing traffic. "Look lady, we got to know what you want moved, and where, before we start doing anything."

She wanted to yell that she wasn't a lady, but she'd already made enough of a fool of herself. "Like he told you, the buses have to go first. Line them up fifteen feet in from the arroyo, like a fence."

"Better chain your dogs," one of the men said. "Don't want one of them getting run over."

"My dogs know to stay away from moving vehicles."

Miguel called Flojo and Loca to him. "The man's right, Rita. In the middle of all the lifting, it would be easy for something to fall on them."

His logic pissed her off. He always had to intervene, play the role of the intermediary, too quick to offer help. "My dogs have never been tied up. They're likely to choke themselves."

"They'll be fine. You're just upset." Miguel's impatience darkened his eyes.

"How would you like to be chained up?" she asked, her frustration verging on tears.

His eyes gave way to a soft golden light, and he tentatively reached out to run a finger along her neck, just above the collar of her jacket. "How about if I put them in the house, where they can run free?"

She bit down on her lips to keep from crying, and nodded her head.

"Come on guys." Miguel whistled. "Let's go get some cookies." He emphasized the last word, and the dogs eagerly trotted ahead, waiting for him to open the door.

Meanwhile, the six men had already gotten into the trucks. Rumbling engines shook the ground. She felt the vibration under her feet as the trucks backed out. Then, suddenly, they stopped, the men looking at her in what appeared to be fear.

A loud honking broke through the sound of the idling engines. She turned to see a dozen lowriders heading toward them. Rita recognized the lead, a gold Chevy Impala, as Ramón's. The cars circled around the two flatbed trucks, blocking their exit. Out of the cars came a menacing bunch, all men except one woman who looked as fierce as the others, each of them standing with arms folded over their chests, defying anybody to cross their path.

Miguel came back out of the house and hurriedly walked over and high-fived Ramón. "Hey, bro! What's up?" he asked.

"Thought Rita might need a hand."

"It's okay, Ramón," she said, wiping away her tears. She was getting overly sentimental, like an old grandmother, crying anytime somebody tried to help her. "This way we won't lose the junkyard."

She hadn't noticed until now that women sat in the cars. Teresa opened the passenger door of Ramón's Impala and got out, coming over to give Rita a hug. Other passenger doors opened, and more women filled the yard, some of them with children, and all of them with containers of food in their hands. "We're going to invade your kitchen," Teresa said. "The men can help with the moving while we ladies cook, and then later we'll have a party." As if on signal, Los Lobos blared from a boom box.

This time, Rita didn't even attempt to stop the tears, seeing all these people there to help her when she most needed it. Women she didn't even know, mothering her as her own mother had never done.

She felt a hand on her shoulder. "It's going to be okay, Mom." Parker, his eyes puffy from too little sleep, gave her a hesitant smile, a smile uncertain of its welcome. He was the one who had urged this relocation, promising to stay despite the new road that made his property imminently more saleable.

|| **JOE** || His body a tangle of jittery nerves after hearing there had been a delay in approving his subdivision, Joe walked from city hall over to Chloe's gallery, the air crackling with a pending storm. An art moving truck drove off as he neared, the gallery's front door still propped open despite the cold. Inside, a man hovered next to Chloe, his hip almost touching hers as they pondered a group of ugly metal sculptures. Intently discussing the arrangement, they hadn't heard Joe enter the gallery.

"I'd have trouble choosing," Chloe said, her voice soft, almost dreamy, as though entranced.

Her rapture bewildered Joe. The pieces had a cold austerity to them, polished to a high sheen, like factory assembled vestiges of humans, minus flesh and blood.

"How about if we scoot the boy a little closer to his dad?" Chloe asked.

"Like a harmonious family?" Irony edged the guy's voice but Chloe nodded, the two of them sharing an unspoken language. Joe watched as they moved the sculpture, their bodies in synch, lifting and pushing. Perfectly matched, both of them tall and willowy.

He was young, close to Chloe's age, with curls spilling over his collar adding a sexy dishevelment to his appearance. "Only thing missing is a dog," he said. "Then it could be a Norman Rockwell scene."

"Don't downplay the uniqueness of what you've created, Parker. This work is incredible."

"You really think so?" he asked. Joe hated him for soliciting more praise.

"I wouldn't have asked you to show with me if I didn't value your work." She laid a hand on his forearm, looking intently into his eyes.

"What have we got here?" Joe asked, stepping into the room.

"Joe!" Chloe showed surprise, but nothing else, upon seeing him. "You're just in time to meet my newest artist." She came over and tucked her arm into his, leading him across the room to the man who wore a familiar, dismissive smile. Joe had seen it on the faces of many young men who sized him up as too old for Chloe. "This is Parker Vargas. He lives just down the hill from our new house."

"So you're Joe." The man shook hands but his eyes held a green coldness.

It took Joe a few seconds to connect the name with where Chloe said he lived. "Any relation to Rita Vargas?"

"She's my mother."

Joe had pegged Rita at about his age, but if this was her son, she must have been a kid when she'd had him. And now here the man stood, challenging Joe's hold on Chloe, just as his mother had challenged Joe's right to build on the ridgetop.

"Well, that makes us neighbors then. You'll have to come up for a tour of the house after we get settled." Chloe still had her arm entwined in his and Joe lifted her hand to his lips and kissed it. "We expect to be very happy up there."

"We'll have to invite you and your mother for a barbecue," Chloe said, misinterpreting Joe's words as genuine friendliness.

"I doubt Rita would accept," Parker said.

"Why not?" Chloe's face bore the imprint of his rebuff, stamped pink like she'd been slapped.

"Rita thinks . . ."

"She thinks that ridge is hers," Joe said, steamrolling across Parker's words.

Parker tinkered with one of the sculptures, tilting its head in a listening pose. "It's like the way I feel about my sculptures. No matter who buys them, I still think of them as mine." He crossed his arms over his chest, defiance flickering in his eyes as he looked at Joe. "My mother will always think of that ridge as hers and she'll do whatever she can to keep it from being overbuilt."

"She doesn't need to worry," Chloe said. "We'd never overbuild up there. We're only . . ."

"Chloe's parents lost part of their farmland after several bad crops, so she knows what it's like to feel protective of a place. You can assure Rita that we'll do that ridgetop justice."

Parker knelt down by a sculpture of a girl in a rocking chair and pulled a bandanna out of his back pocket. As gently as he might rub the cheek of a real child, he wiped a smudge off the mirror that formed her face. The bandanna still in his hands, he stood back up and tied it in a couple of knots, his hands quick and ever moving while he talked. "Time for me to head over to the restaurant."

Joe took note of his pressed white shirt and black slacks. "You wait tables?"

"That's right. Gotta eat somehow." Parker's eyes shifted to Chloe, lingering, flagrantly appreciating her. "I'll see you Friday night."

Chloe left Joe's side and wrapped her hands around Parker's, preventing him from tying more knots in the bandanna. "It's going to be an awesome show."

Parker darted a look Joe's way before leaning in close and kissing Chloe's cheek. Joe knew it was the vogue way of saying farewell; nonetheless, it made his body tense to see Chloe's blonde hair brushing against Parker's face.

Finally Parker pulled away from her. "Thanks," he said, his voice low and sexy. Then he raised an arm in a mock salute. "Nice meeting you, Joe." The bemused smile had again returned to his face, the smile of a would-be conqueror.

Chloe didn't even wait until Parker closed the door to say, "Isn't he wonderful? I'm incredibly lucky to have found him."

Joe kicked at a woman made of carburetors, stubbing his toe on the solid base. "This stuff looks like junk."

"I forget, you've never cared for assemblages." Chloe fondly rested her hand on the head of the boy sculpture, dismissing Joe's criticism.

"I also don't care for men who take their time kissing you good-bye."

"Come on, Joe! He only air-kissed my cheek." Her hand had slipped down to the shoulder of the boy, gripping it, causing the sculpture to totter.

"I saw the way he kept inching closer to you while the two of you were pushing those sculptures around. And you played right into him."

Where Chloe's cheeks had blazed earlier, they now blanched, turning a pale, almost blue, ivory. "You can imagine all you want, Joe. But you're the only one I love."

He wanted to wrap his arms around her, hold her until the icy chill left the room, but her frozen stance demanded an apology before she would let him touch her. He crossed over to the figure of a skeletal man, closer to Chloe but with the sculptures standing between them. "I can't help it, Chloe. I see other men hanging around, and I get scared that I'll lose you."

She walked away from him, putting more distance between them before pausing at the window that overlooked the small parking area. Poplar trees divided the lot from the neighboring house. Only a few brown leaves remained on the trees, and Joe watched as one slowly drifted to the ground. Yet another fell before Chloe spoke. "Other men mean nothing to me. The only way I'd leave you is because you drove me away." She turned around, her back to the window, the soft light of autumn bathing her in glimmer.

Her beauty brought out his longing. "It's not your love I doubt, Chloe. It's me. I'm scared that one day you'll look at me and see there's not much here, that you'd rather be with somebody who's more successful or more artistic."

"You just don't get it, do you?" Chloe glanced up at the ceiling and the wooden vigas that he'd uncovered from beneath a layer of sheetrock. "You're an artist in your own right. You take old houses and give them new life. I still remember when you first showed me this place. The pride you took in it. How you wanted to be sure I was somebody who would treasure its uniqueness. It's the way you care for what you love that keeps me with you."

He crossed over and took one of her hands in his, lifting her from the windowsill. "If you'd let me, I'd care for you better than I've ever cared for any house."

Before he could kiss her, she put a finger to his lips. "You're the only one coming between us, Joe."

‖ RITA ‖   Outside, the temperature had gone down with the sun, but Rita's bedroom still held some of the day's earlier heat, and a soft light pooled under the lamp on her nightstand. Clad only in lacy red underwear, she moved onto the warmth of the throw rug before stepping into a pair of black leather pants. She had to stand tall and suck in her stomach to zip them up.

"Now that's a sexy outfit," Miguel commented, still lying in bed.

"Aren't you going to get ready?"

"It's more fun watching you." He bunched the pillow behind his head and sat up a little higher, giving himself a better view.

It was so much simpler for men. They could go from work to a party without changing clothes. Miguel only needed to put back on what he'd worn to the house and he was all set for the evening, whereas she still hadn't come up with the right outfit.

"I feel like a snake ready to shed her skin."

"So wear something else."

"Easy for you to say." She stripped off the pants, letting them fall into a heap on the rug. The floor was cold on her bare feet as she stood in front of the closet, pushing hangers aside, futilely searching for something suitable.

"My wife used to call what you're going through 'clothing weirdies.' She'd try on a dozen outfits before she'd finally settle on something, and even then she'd say it didn't feel right."

"I'm not your wife!" Seizing a broomstick skirt of lush green silk, Rita decided it would have to do.

The kiss on the back of her shoulder caught her by surprise. Miguel wrapped his arms around her waist and pressed his face against her hair. "I know you're not my wife. You're Rita, and that's who I want."

She leaned against him, her back warmed by his naked chest, her hips receptive to the hardening of his penis. Turning around within the circle of his arms, she murmured, "We'll be late."

"There's no such thing as late." He pulled her down onto the bed.

The first time they'd had sex, tears had washed down his face. Now he laughed, a low sound, almost a giggle. The laugh embraced her, amplifying her own pleasure. Making love with him felt like an intoxicating tumble of floating and falling.

"It'll take me forever to get these knots out of my hair," she said afterward.

"Here, let me." He took the brush from her and began unsnarling the tangles. As he combed through her hair, she glanced in the mirror. He wore a look of such devotion that it both thrilled and scared her.

"You'll take forever," she said, snatching the brush out of his hands and ripping through the remaining knots.

"What's the hurry?" He had his jeans on, but was still shirtless and without shoes.

"I want to get there early, before it's too crowded." She picked a couple of stray hairs off the front of her chenille sweater. It was a rich brown, but the sweater looked a little plain. Rummaging through her jewelry box, she pulled out a turquoise heishi necklace her father had given her. It would match her turquoise boots and calm her nerves. It would be like a milagro she could touch anytime the event proved too much for her. She'd only attended a couple of gallery openings in the past, and she distinctly remembered feeling out of place. At least this time she would know more about the art than the other people there. Not that she knew how to use the pompous vocabulary that some fancied, but she should be able to hold her own tonight, or so she hoped.

"You're working that necklace like it was a string of rosary beads." Miguel clasped her hands and brought them to his lips, pressing a kiss against her fingertips. "The secret is to have a glass of wine as soon as we get there."

"A glass of wine won't do it. I've never been comfortable chitchatting with strangers."

"So have two glasses, kick back, and listen to them rave about how talented your son is."

"Just soak up the praise?" Rita knew it wouldn't be that easy, but at least Miguel would be there with her. His composure would help carry her through the evening.

"If you're too uncomfortable, we don't have to stay long. The important thing is for Parker to see you there."

She recalled Parker's excitement that afternoon, the way he'd burst into her kitchen waving the *Pasatiempo* with its feature article about his opening. "My first real show, Mom!" The formal invitation stared at her from the dresser, a photo of all four sculptures posed on the hill that divided his land from hers.

"If people buy the sculptures, do you think Parker will get cocky?" she asked Miguel as they were leaving the house.

"Cocky?" He opened the passenger door of his truck and waited for her to get in before walking around to the driver's side. "Don't forget your seat belt," he said, fastening his own before putting the key in the ignition.

"Cocky," he repeated. "Laura's mother used to use that word." His wife had been an English professor and the only one in her family to go to college. Her parents, her mother in particular, Miguel had said, held her education against her, claiming Laura thought she was better than her brothers, who had both taken blue-collar jobs. "She was afraid Laura would turn her back on the family, but she never did. She was always the one they could rely on to help out anytime there was a problem. Parker's the same way. Success will make him all the more generous."

The problem with success was it entailed trading one's soul to the devil. It was an anachronistic thought; Rita knew that, yet it was one she could not rid herself of. Maybe it was a result of being raised Catholic, categorizing everything as either good or evil, with nothing between the two extremes. Much of her resentment of rich people stemmed from a similar belief that to become wealthy you had to be unscrupulous. To what lengths would Parker go to achieve success? Rita could well understand the concern Laura's mother had had. She feared Parker, too, would change so much that remoteness would arise between them.

Even though the gallery was in a semi-residential area, cars filled the streets and Miguel had to park several blocks away. "Looks like a good turnout," he said as they walked up to the converted house with its windows fully lit and people spilling out the front door. Rita clasped his arm tighter, making sure they didn't get separated in the crowd.

She searched for Parker and saw him off to the side, near his sculpture of the girl in the rocking chair, his hands going in and out of his leather jacket, the one he saved for special occasions. He was a mixture of sophistication and untamed wildness, a hub of raw energy. She wanted to go over to him, but he stood talking to a cluster of people and she was afraid of getting in his way. She would wait until later, when he was alone, to congratulate him.

Miguel led her over to a table where a man with a fey way of speaking asked whether they wanted wine or bottled water.

"Two glasses of wine, please," Miguel said.

"I might not need two."

"One's for me, so we can toast Parker's success." He thanked the man and led her to a relatively empty corner in the otherwise jammed room.

"You must be very proud," Miguel said, clicking his plastic glass against hers. "Parker told me you've encouraged his art from the very beginning."

"It's not like I could I have stopped him, even if I'd wanted too. Sculpting is an addiction for him, something he can't shake." She sipped her wine and looked around the crowded room. People kept squeezing through the doorway, most of them dressed to impress. Some didn't even bother to look at the art; they were there to socialize. Many of them seemed to know Chloe, who made a point of introducing Parker, drawing him into her world of rich people.

"Need me to get you a refill?" Miguel asked.

"Not yet." She'd almost emptied the glass but held off from drinking more. "Do you think Joe Oakes convinced his girlfriend to carry Parker's work, thinking then I wouldn't fight him if he tries to put more houses on the ridgetop?"

Miguel glanced over at Chloe. Her hands sliced through the air as she talked, like a conductor leading a large symphony. "She doesn't strike me as the type to let somebody else dictate her business decisions."

Rita sipped the last of her wine, watching Chloe work the room. She had left Parker's side to talk to an older couple who stood admiring his sculpture of a young boy. Engaging them in conversation, she alternated between listening intently to anything either one said and replying with great animation, her hands dramatizing her points. Then the man said something that prompted her to give him a dazzling smile. She steered the couple back to Parker, who shook their hands and tilted his head as though having trouble hearing what was being said, before he, too, burst out in a big smile.

"If I'm not mistaken," Miguel said, "that couple just bought a sculpture." He tossed his half-full glass of wine into a nearby trash can. "Let's go find out."

"I could use some more wine first."

"Sorry, I should have given you mine." He took the plastic glass from her hand, then gently stroked the fingers she had unknowingly twisted around her necklace. "You're going to break that if you're not careful." She let go of the beads as he leaned forward and gave her a light kiss. "I'll be back as soon as I can." He walked over to the table and waited in line for the server to refill her glass. The line moved slowly, but Miguel showed no sign of impatience, looking over his shoulder once to give her a reassuring smile.

"Rita! I didn't know for sure if you'd be here." Joe Oakes raised a glass of amber colored liquid as though saluting her.

"And I didn't know you were serving hard stuff."

"I'm not. This is my private reserve. Irish whiskey. The best. Would you like some?" His words had a slight slurring around the edges, blurring the line between animosity and amnesty.

"Here's your wine," Miguel said, moving in close, like a bodyguard.

Joe's eyes darted back and forth between the two of them. Then he grabbed Miguel's hand and vigorously shook it. "I'm Joe Oakes. You must be the attorney who's been looking over my house plans."

"That was several weeks ago. I'm busy with other things now."

Rita wondered if she imagined the look of relief on Joe's face. He took another sip of his drink, his eyes searching the crowd for somebody. "Place is filling up. Wouldn't have thought this many people would be interested in junk art."

"Interested enough to spend big money on it," Miguel said.

"Some people have money to spare. Throw it around like it was nothing." Joe's feet remained in one place, but his upper body swayed from side to side as though buffeting a storm.

"If you'll excuse us, we're going to congratulate the artist on his sales." Miguel wrapped an arm around Rita's shoulders and maneuvered past Joe.

"You make it sound like Parker sold more than one sculpture."

"See that red dot?" Miguel pointed to a circle at the base of the woman made of carburetors. "That means somebody already bought that one."

Ten thousand dollars, the tag said. Parker had explained that the gallery kept forty percent of any sale, but that meant he'd still made six thousand dollars off the one piece alone. She craned her head, but couldn't see the amount listed for the boy. "Just a sec," she said to Miguel and detoured over to the other sculpture. Twelve thousand! Smaller, but more intricately made. That must account for the higher price. If it had sold too, then Parker had made more in an hour than she made in a year.

"Isn't it wonderful?" Chloe leaned past her to place a red dot near the boy's feet. "I'm so happy for him."

Chloe's joy encompassed more than the money she'd made from the sales. Rita could see it in the way her hand lingered on the sculpture, her fingers wrapped around the boy's ankle. Even that first time she'd appeared at Parker's trailer, Rita could tell she liked his work from the way she touched it. Yet Rita distrusted her as only a mother can distrust a woman with the potential to emotionally devastate her son. "I hope you continue to do well by him."

Parker walked up, grinning. "Can you believe it, Mom?" He put his arm around Chloe, his grin growing even bigger. "Chloe said she could sell my work, but I didn't expect her to be this good." He squeezed Chloe's shoulder affectionately, then let her go.

A few feet away, Rita saw Joe glowering in their direction, an ugly twist to his mouth. He gulped down the rest of his whiskey and marched toward them. Rita looked around for Miguel but couldn't find him in the swarms of people. Joe pushed past Chloe and jabbed Parker in the chest with his index finger. "Not bad for a first show, huh?"

Parker stepped back, avoiding another jab. "Not bad at all."

"Some people don't know how good they've got it." Joe's voice carried an implicit, but inexplicable, menace. Although slightly shorter than Parker, he had more bulk and Rita could see his back tightening for a fight.

Then Chloe reached over and ran a finger down his neck. Almost instantly, the rigidity in Joe's back disappeared. "If all goes as planned," Chloe murmured, "we should sell the other two pieces by the end of the month. A big success for all concerned."

"Congratulations," Joe said, more to her than to Parker. "I'm sure all the parties concerned will welcome the money."

"I know I will." Parker's words seemed straightforward, but Rita suspected they implied something else, some kind of underlying threat. "I'm looking forward to coming out ahead of the game for a change."

"Don't we all," Joe said.

"Excuse me." Chloe waved at a woman dressed in fur. "There's a collector I'd like Parker to meet." She hooked her arm in his and led him away.

Joe lifted his glass to his lips, his eyes watching them move across the room. Then, realizing he had nothing left to drink, he gestured at Rita's equally empty glass. "I could use another whiskey. How about you?"

Not wanting any favors from him, she started to say no, but found herself craving the taste of something stronger. "Why not?" she said and followed him into Chloe's office. Only a desk and two chairs occupied the small room, letting Rita breathe easier, as though she'd stepped outside, away from the throngs. The wood floors had a warm glow and art books filled what looked like former pantry shelves.

"Great house, isn't it?" Joe said, filling her glass as she scanned the room. "One of my better remodeling jobs, if I do say so myself."

"I hate seeing houses turned into businesses. People used to live here."

"Somebody still does. I added a couple of rooms on in the back, and that's where Chloe lives. At least for now. But I know what you mean. Real estate prices have gotten out of hand in this town. I'm just grateful that the preservation laws are such that I can restore these places instead of somebody razing them." He poured himself more whiskey and lifted his glass, toasting the room. "Old houses are the real history of a town. Where people lived, raised their kids, and died—that's what tells you the true story of a place."

His respect for the past confused Rita. Her habit of dividing things into black and white left her at a loss how to categorize Joe. She remembered the day she'd first met him, making fun of himself for urging his old car up a road too rough for it. His face had grown taut since then, the laugh lines around his mouth having given way to a nervous twitch.

"If you love old houses so much, why didn't you remodel one for yourself to live in?"

"I did. It's over by the cemetery. Same neighborhood where Leroy lived as a kid."

Everywhere she turned, Leroy popped up, like a ghost jumping out from behind gravestones. "You expecting him here tonight?"

"Leroy bends in a lot of different directions, but, no, I think art would be too much of a stretch for him."

Rita knew better. Leroy wouldn't hesitate to appear at a gallery opening if he thought it would boost his own prospects. He was a chameleon, changing to fit the surroundings, speaking the language people wanted to hear. She wondered how Leroy had first presented the ridgetop to Joe. Had he touted it as a place with a history, or had he promoted it as a haven, a place to escape the pressures of living in town?

Joe's eyes narrowed at something behind her and Rita turned to find Chloe and Miguel coming toward them, Chloe's hand alighting on Miguel's arm as she tried to stop giggling. When Rita glanced back at Joe, his eyes had hardened into a glare. She'd once had a possessive boyfriend, honored, at first, by his intense feelings for her until his possessiveness tightened around her like a noose. Mesmerized, Rita stared at Joe's expanding chest, his lungs filling with air, as he took a deep breath, presumably fighting to control his jealousy. His hand tightened around his plastic glass until it cracked. He gave her an abashed look. "Forgot I was holding it."

Miguel chuckled as he and Chloe stepped into the room, her face still radiant with humor.

"What're you laughing at?" Joe's demand filled the room with tension. The mirth fled from Chloe, and her neck stiffened, her head raising, like a wary cobra.

Miguel again chuckled. Rita recognized it as a forced sound, an effort to lighten the situation. "We were speculating what it would be like if the sculptures procreated during the night, filling the gallery with assorted junkyard mutants."

"You mean if they had sex?" Joe removed the bottle of Irish whiskey from the top of the desk and tucked it away in the corner of a back cabinet. Rita was standing close enough to notice that his hands trembled.

"It was idle talk, Joe. An amusing anecdote. We overheard somebody wondering why Parker hadn't made a sculpture of a baby, and we did a riff on the idea of a growing family."

"Better be careful," Joe said. "You wouldn't want to overpopulate the place with those things. Might drive down the value."

"I think I'm a better judge of that than you are."

Chloe's chin jutted out and coldness pierced her eyes. Rita had been wrong to imagine her as Joe's pawn. The gallery was Chloe's pride, and she would let nobody attack it.

"Excuse me." A young woman with spiked hair peered anxiously into the room. "Can you tell me where the restroom is?"

Reverting to a smile, Chloe pointed out a hallway in the opposite direction. The woman thanked her and hurried away.

Joe shrugged, holding out his hands in a helpless gesture. "What can I say? I'm a working-class guy. Somebody who earns a living with his hands. I know nothing about art."

"Don't demean yourself." Chloe leaned against the doorjamb and turned to Miguel and Rita, like an actress delivering a monologue to the audience. "Joe didn't quite finish architecture school, but he's immensely talented, as you can see by this gallery. You wouldn't believe his before and after photos. The place was a total shambles when he first bought it."

Rita recalled a friend who'd gotten lost in an unexpected snowstorm while hunting and later had to have a frostbitten foot amputated. She'd run into him with his wife out shopping, and the woman felt compelled to explain that the accident hadn't stopped him from doing anything, bragging about how he'd gotten a permit to collect firewood, chopping it all himself. Chloe displayed a similar need to bolster Joe's confidence, reassuring not only him, but everybody else that he was a fully capable man.

Miguel's eyes surveyed the room before nailing Joe. "I'm surprised you opted to build a new house, given how talented you are at remodeling."

"That was my doing," Chloe said. "I wanted to live out in the country. We probably could have found an old ranch house somewhere, but it would have been too big. We wanted something small. Easy to maintain." She winked at Joe. "This is an opportunity for Joe to really prove his talent."

Joe smoothed back his silver hair, looking slightly embarrassed but also fortified by her praise. "The house isn't a showpiece by any means. Grandeur never interested me. What I designed was a relatively modest home that's customized to our needs."

"And stuck it on a hill that used to be pristine land!" Rita's words shot through the room, startling her almost as much as everybody else. It was like accidentally firing a gun, having thought the safety lock was on, only to hear a bullet ricochet.

Chloe crumpled against the doorjamb. "If it hadn't been us, it would have been somebody else. And at least we won't overdevelop. Joe could have put four more houses up there, but he limited it to three."

"Three?" Miguel said it calmly, his hand on Rita's arm, holding her back as he might a bull ready to charge.

"You lied," Rita said, pulling her arm free from Miguel's restraint and stepping up to Joe. "You told me yours would be the only house up there."

"You must have misunderstood." Joe retrieved the bottle he'd stashed away earlier. A mirror hung above the cabinet, and as he poured another glass of whiskey, Rita saw the corner of his mouth twitching. He glanced up and his eyes met hers in the mirror, a moment of naked fear, before he looked away. He downed the whiskey and turned to face the three of them. "Chloe and I've always intended to subdivide the lot to finance our own home. It just took me a while to get around to filing the papers."

"That's not what they said at city hall," Miguel countered.

"You know city hall. They can't tell their head from their ass." Joe no longer slurred his words. A raw anger had surfaced. "They've been giving me the runaround since day one."

"Our realtor made it sound like it was going to be a piece of cake, but Joe's had to go through all kinds of rigmarole to get his plans approved."

"Rigmarole?" Miguel repeated. "You mean people's insistence that the subdivision be legal?"

"Of course it's legal. Joe would never do anything illegal. I can't even get him to wander off the trail when we go out hiking, that's how rule bound he is." She said it with utter conviction, her eyes never darting to Joe for reassurance.

Rita, though, looked at him and saw a man desperately seeking cover. Chloe believed him to be totally honest, but he had deceived her somehow, as he had all of them, about the subdivision. His twitching mouth reminded Rita of a cornered jackrabbit. With nowhere to run, he stayed still, hoping not to be noticed. And in that moment, Rita felt sorry for him.

|| **JOE** || The shoe repair shop sat behind a tire store and a health food store, with a parking lot full of potholes. Driving across it, even at a crawl, bounced and jostled the car. Joe parked but didn't get out. Leaning back against the seat, he closed his eyes, almost dozing in the warmth of the sun that streamed through the window. Then his phone rang, snapping him alert.

"Joe! Everything go okay last night?"

He hedged, unwilling to tell Wayne of the neighborhood association that had shown up at the city council meeting to contest the subdivision. Gilbert had said not to worry, that kind of thing happened all the time—people with what he called the not-in-my-backyard syndrome, raising a stink about any nearby development until they realized there was nothing they could do about it. "We barely got heard," Joe lied to Wayne. "The proposal before ours took most of the night and they had to reschedule us for two weeks from now."

Wayne sympathized, saying to give him a call as soon as the deal was approved and he'd wire his earnest money.

Joe slumped over the steering wheel. The lies kept piling on top of him, each one weighing more than the next. So heavy that his very walk had changed, his feet rasping against the ground, scuffing the earth, bringing him here to this abysmal parking lot to retrieve a pair of boots with worn-out soles.

When he stepped into the repair shop, he came to a dead stop upon seeing Rita, her back to him, waving a pair of red boots in the air and exclaiming, "You've resurrected them!"

The man at the counter smiled sheepishly as he took the boots and put them into a paper bag. "How often have I patched this pair now?"

"I've lost count. But each time, when I've thought they might be done for, you've given them new life."

The man nodded at Joe. "Be right with you, sir."

Rita glanced over her shoulder. Her eyebrows shot up in surprise when she saw him. "Can't you afford to buy new shoes?"

"Give me a break, Rita. You've seen my car. I hold on to the things I love, just like you do."

The words carried more hostility than he'd intended. They erased the smirk on her face and caused her to clutch the bag with her boots closer to her chest, as though he might try to grab it. "You better take good care of that hill, that's all I have to say."

She again thanked the shoe repairman and then rushed past Joe like a subway train, leaving him stranded with no means to get where he needed to go.

"Do you have a ticket, sir?"

"What?"

"Are you here to pick up a pair of shoes?"

"My boots, yeah. The ticket? Just a minute, I've got it here somewhere." Joe reached for his wallet, wishing he had a ticket out of the mess he'd got himself into. "Brown cowhide," he said, handing a yellow stub to the man.

Row upon row of shoes, each with yellow tickets, lined shelves to the side, and it took the man a moment to locate Joe's. When he brought them to the counter, he turned the boots upside down, showing him the bottoms. "I essentially had to give you new soles. They should hold up quite a while."

"Mind if I sit down and put them on?" he asked after he paid. His loafers pinched the little toe on his right foot.

The man gestured at some chairs, not waiting for Joe to sit down before he returned to his workbench and picked up a woman's high heel. Humming softly, he attached a rubber tip to the front of the shoe. He had a premature stoop to his shoulders, his back bent with honest work, not countless lies. He called out a friendly good-bye as Joe left the shop.

It was almost five and Joe's stomach growled, reminding him he hadn't eaten all day and had nothing at home for dinner. Leaving his car in the pockmarked lot, he walked over to Wild Oats. He would pick up something he could stick in the microwave. Normally he preferred to cook simple meals of grilled meat or fish and a salad, but lately he had little interest in food.

Nor had he seen Chloe the past two days. Nervous about yester-day's hearing for the subdivision, he'd told her he had a cold and didn't want her to catch it. Another lie. But he was afraid if she spent the night he would wake her with his sleepless flopping around on the bed like an out-of-water fish. She would want to know what was wrong, asking questions he couldn't answer except with more lies. So he kept his dis-tance, not even answering the phone when it rang that morning.

But when he finished his errands and turned onto his street, he saw her white Miata in his driveway. If he made a quick right, she wouldn't even know he'd driven by. He could go away, not come back until after she'd tired of waiting for him and left. Except, before he could do it, she came around from the backyard, dragging the hose with one hand and waving at him with the other.

He had no choice now but to face her. He pulled into the driveway and forced a note of levity as he got out of the car. "Hey, Farmer Chloe. Just can't keep you from getting your hands dirty, can we?"

Rather than smiling at his attempted humor, she looked concerned as she laid the hose at the foot of a tree. "If you want apricots next year, you have to give this tree some water now and then."

She could just as well have been talking about herself. He had neglected her too. Chloe wasn't a needy person, but she wanted a man who would share his feelings with her. And while he could tell her about the little things—who he'd had lunch with, the busted water pipe at one of his rentals, the quote he got on the kitchen tile for their house—eventually something would come up about the subdivision and he would have to lie to her, the lies tumbling out of his mouth like an avalanche of stones, piling up higher and higher, forming a barrier between them.

"Feeling better?" she asked.

"Still a little peaked," he said, resorting to one of his mother's words.

Chloe laid her hand on his cheek. "No fever, but you are kind of pale." She nodded at the Wild Oats bag in his arm. "Hope whatever you bought will keep until tomorrow. I made us chicken soup. Good for whatever ails you. Why don't you go on in, and I'll join you in a sec, after I turn on the water."

She had also baked a fresh focaccia, the fragrance of rosemary and basil filling the house. Joe put his deli meal in the refrigerator for another day and opened a beer. Sitting at the kitchen counter, he prepared his story. She would ask about the city council meeting last night and he needed to assure her everything was fine.

When she came in, her smile looked forced, her eyes taking note of the bottle in his hand. He expected her usual welcoming kiss, but she walked past him and went over to the sink to wash her hands. "Beer's not exactly what the doctor would order for somebody who's sick."

"I'm pretty much over it," he said, raising the bottle to his lips. "Chicken soup should do the trick."

"I forgot to warn you—it's green chile chicken soup. A bit of fire to burn out any residual germs."

"I noticed you also made my favorite bread." If he could keep the conversation light, maybe they could skim right over last night's city council meeting. He would downplay the neighborhood's resistance. Do like Gilbert and shrug it off as a common occurrence. A minor delay. No big deal.

"Earth to Joe! Where are you?" He hadn't seen her cross over to him, her eyes searching his face.

"I was just thinking how good this meal is going to taste. I haven't eaten much of anything the past couple of days." He took her hand and swung it playfully. "It's great to have you here."

"You're the one who asked me to stay away." She toyed with a curl near his ear, tucking it back in place. "Next time you get sick, we'll be living together in our new house, and there'll be no escaping me."

He detected a cautionary note, a warning that in the future she would not let him hide from her. But he had watched his father over the years, sitting at the dinner table or in front of the TV with Joe's mother, fooling her into thinking he was right there, while slipping further and further away, until the marriage had become a hollow casing where once there'd been a solid core. It scared him to think he might be doing the same thing, his lies eroding the closeness he had with Chloe. She was so trusting, believing he'd been sick these past two days.

"I didn't want you to catch what I have."

"So you said." She tossed her head, her hair swinging back from her face. "How'd the hearing go last night?"

Finding his beer already gone, he stood up to get another, keeping his back to her as he opened the refrigerator. "We ran into a little bit of trouble, but nothing that won't take care of itself." He twisted the cap off the bottle and took a long sip before rejoining her. "The people at the bottom of the hill claim there'll be too much runoff from an additional three houses."

"Is there?"

"Absolutely not." He set the bottle down on the counter harder than he'd intended, the glass chattering. "That's why I'm putting in ponds, to prevent that very thing from happening."

"Then why didn't the council approve it?"

"Oh, they will, but first they have to listen to all these people's complaints. Leroy says it's nothing but sour grapes. They're sorry they have houses at the bottom of the hill instead of on top. You never heard such a group of whiners."

"Whiners?" Her eyes narrowed, assessing him like she did a piece of art, judging his merit. "I know if I lived at the bottom of the hill, I'd hate to see a row of houses going in above me."

"Chloe, you're the one who wanted to live up there!"

She turned away from him and rubbed at a smear on the toaster. It was an annoying habit of hers, needlessly cleaning when she was upset. He wanted to still her hand, tell her to get a grip, to trust him.

"Say something," he demanded.

She quit fussing with the toaster and brushed her fingers against her thigh, her eyes wide now, as though trying to take him in fully. He faltered under her gaze and looked aside. "The article in today's paper said that neighborhood association was going to hire a lawyer."

"Fuck! Why did you asked me what happened, if you'd already read about it?"

"I wanted to hear your side."

"My side? You mean our side. Don't forget there are two of us."

This time, instead of the toaster, she went for the countertop, her fingernail scraping at a piece of dried food, picking at it like a scab. "I don't want to live up there if it means being surrounded by people who resent us."

Not a violent man, Joe suddenly found himself wanting to shake her, yell that she was the one who'd gotten them into this mess. Instead, he reached for his beer, clenching the bottle, his fist absorbing the coldness. "They'll get over it. It's human nature to resist change. They want everything to stay the same, but the world doesn't work that way."

Slowly, sadly, she shook her head. "You're the one who's changed. What happened to the man who respected tradition?"

"Tradition? An empty hillside has nothing to do with tradition. The place is waiting to be developed. If it hadn't been me, it would have been somebody else."

Chloe took a step back, her brows scrunched together. "You didn't used to think that way. Ever since you bought that hill, you've become . . . harder, somehow. Less compassionate." Her lower lip trembled. "I wish I'd never asked you to build up there."

|| **RITA** || The houses in Miguel's south Capitol neighborhood sat so closely together that they made Rita claustrophobic. Although the sun had already set, Miguel hadn't drawn his living room curtains and enough light filtered out the window to guide her across the gravel yard. The night air carried the fragrance of piñon, and as she stepped onto his porch, she could see logs burning in the kiva fireplace. Tapping lightly on the door, she walked inside.

Miguel, a dishtowel tied around his waist and his hair disheveled, came through the doorway of the kitchen just as a saxophone murmured seductively from the stereo speakers.

"Sounds like music to lure a woman to bed," she said, loving the way his lips curved into a smile at the sight of her.

"When words fail, we lawyers resort to other methods to get our way." His kiss tasted of olives and his fingers smelled of garlic.

"You've been nibbling while you were cooking." She kissed him again, welcoming the heat of his body.

He playfully chewed on her lip. "I had to have something to tide me over until you got here."

She began to move them toward his bedroom, the saxophone reaching a crescendo in the background. "Not so fast," he said, his hands on her hips, keeping her from pressing against him. "I want to wine and dine you first. Then, after we make love, maybe you'll fall asleep in my arms."

The saxophone drifted into a new cut, a soft, floating melody. Dreamy music that made her long to stay the night, but she knew the noises of town would keep her awake and sooner or later, as always, she would leave for the quiet of her own bed.

"Hey, King," she said, reaching down to pet Miguel's German shepherd. Half deaf, he'd only now come into the room. He walked with the stiff gait of an aging, arthritic dog, but he always greeted her with the affection of a puppy. "Have you missed me?"

"We both have," Miguel said, leading her into the kitchen. Except for the expensive stereo system and a vast collection of CDs and books, his living room held the minimal amount of furniture—a futon, in case a friend spent the night, and a comfortable chair cozied up to a floor lamp for reading. The kitchen, however, had a complete range of accessories from red pots that hung on the walls to electrical gadgets that lined the countertops. Small, like the rest of the house, the kitchen should have felt cramped, but its fullness testified to Miguel's love of food and invited others to join him.

A folded newspaper lay on what he called his cooking island. The headline "Slippery Slope" caught Rita's attention and she began reading what turned out to be an article about a hearing on Joe's request to subdivide the ridgetop.

"I thought you were keeping an eye on things!" Her frustration echoed off the walls. She'd relied on Miguel to let her know when there was a public hearing.

"I was going to tell you but then I decided there was no point in both of us going."

"You went?" She stared at him in disbelief.

Miguel lifted a glass of wine to his face. He took a long sip, then lowered the glass, still holding it close. "I made a point of being there."

"Why didn't you tell me?"

Miguel set down his glass and moved over to the stove, where he finished chopping garlic, the blade hitting the wooden board with an aggravating steadiness. Slow and deliberate, he scraped the garlic into a pan on the stove. Hot oil sizzled and he turned down the gas flame before answering her. "I didn't want to see you getting all worked up again."

"So you kept the meeting secret from me?"

Miguel turned on the stove fan, its whirring noise drowning her words. Then he stirred a can of tomatoes into the pan, dropped pasta into a pot of boiling water, and set a timer before joining her at the counter, where he took her two hands in his. "I figured I'd attend the meeting for both of us and see whether anything came up that we could use against Oakes."

Rita slipped her hands free of his. Struggling to control her anger, she forced herself to look around the room. The kitchen barely had enough space for their two chairs. The whole house was tiny. Normally it felt big enough because Miguel had so few possessions, but tonight she felt squeezed, the simmering tomato sauce and boiling pasta steaming up the dark windows as the night closed in on them.

"I should have been there," she finally said.

Miguel popped an olive into his mouth, chewed it solemnly, and nodded. "It was probably wrong of me. But I wanted to save you the pain of listening to Joe go over all the details."

"Save me?" She picked up the paper and shook it at him. "What did you save me from? It's all right here."

"Yes, but you didn't have to sit there while he glorified what he was doing. Or witness Gilbert lying about how they'd followed all the required procedures. It infuriated me. And you would have gone through the roof."

Rita glanced at the article again, skimming through it for the details. It confirmed that Joe wanted to put in three more houses. A photo showed a woman angrily pointing her finger at the city council members. "What's this about the people on the other side of the hill? Is it true they'll end up swimming in sewage?"

"They claim there'll be a lot of trouble with erosion, but Joe's taken all the necessary precautions to prevent that from happening."

"You sound like you're on his side."

"Rita." He said her name with a tone of complete exhaustion. "We've been through all this before." A look of such pious condescension filled his face that she wanted to slap him. "We know Joe's hiding something or he would have been up front about his plans to subdivide the land. But we can't nab him for what's in keeping with city code."

"Then we have to find out how he cheated."

Miguel rubbed his forehead, a sure sign that he had a headache. "I've gone over the rules and regulations so many times I've got them memorized. Whatever trick they pulled, the Sena brothers have covered it up so well that nobody can see it."

Rita remembered the day Leroy had officially bought the ridge, walking her out of the bank to her truck, assuring her nobody could ever build up there. She could forgive him for selling lots on the other side, but she would not let him get away with people living on top, looking down at her. "The article says this neighborhood association brought up enough complaints that the city had to postpone any final decision until the next meeting."

Miguel shook his head. "Rita, don't get your hopes up." He stood and took the colander off the wall and set it in the sink. After glancing at his timer, he turned around with his arms across his chest. "Much as I'd like to, I don't think we're going to be able to stop him."

She could see that he wanted her not to get involved, to let him handle things, but she couldn't. He wouldn't fight hard enough. "I have to be at that next hearing. I know more about that ridge than anybody."

"And you love it too much."

The timer buzzed and she exploded. "Too much? Don't talk to me about loving something too much! That land has been in my family for generations. I will not stand by and let Joe Oakes destroy it."

Miguel emptied the pasta into the colander, the steam rising like a cloud around his head. His back to her, he spoke in a muffled voice. "He's already destroyed what you love." When he turned, he raised his empty hands. "One house or four. What difference does it make?"

"I can't just stand by and let him get away with it."

Slowly, Miguel nodded his head, apparently trying to comprehend the logic of something he didn't understand. The fury rose in Rita as he calmly emptied the pasta into a bowl, ladled the tomato sauce over it, and carried it into the other room. When he came back into the kitchen and got a salad out of the refrigerator, he finally looked at her. "You can lose touch with life," he said, "if you hold on to something that's already gone."

Rita could barely restrain herself from grabbing the salad and throwing it on the floor. "How dare you talk to me about holding onto something that's already gone. You with pictures of your dead wife and son filling your bedroom. And you wonder why I never spend the night? There's no room in your life for me!"

Miguel's freckles paled and he gripped the salad bowl tightly. "I'll put the pictures away. I didn't . . ."

"Don't bother. I don't need some man who pretends he's protecting me and then doesn't do a damn thing to stop the biggest threat in my life."

"What threat?" Miguel slammed the salad bowl down on the counter, knocking over his wine glass. "You use the land as an excuse to keep anybody from getting close to you."

"Your idea of closeness would suffocate me. I'm better off by myself." Grabbing her purse off the chair, Rita walked past the table with its lit candles and rosemary-scented pasta. She slammed his door behind her and got into her truck, tears washing over her anger as she drove home alone.

|| **RITA** || The morning after their fight, Rita couldn't seem to get the house warm enough. She grabbed a flannel shirt from her bedroom chair, not giving it much thought until she turned the collar up around her neck and caught his scent, pungent and earthy. She closed her eyes and inhaled him. No other man had smelled as good to her as Miguel.

Shivering, she wrapped the shirt tightly around her, but then removed it, searching for something warmer. She found a wool sweater and pulled it over her head, its itchiness a friction of heat against her skin. She had slept poorly, and that made her susceptible to chills. Over and over, she'd rehashed her argument with Miguel, sliding in and out of dreams, reawakening in the dark of night, aware she'd left the only person who'd ever understood her more fully than she understood herself.

Too tired to bother dressing up for Mass after walking the dogs, she exchanged her jeans for a pair of black slacks. Her walk had failed to console her, but maybe prayers and hymns would. She drove into town, barely aware of what she was doing, the truck almost as reliable as the dogs in leading her along a habitual route. When she entered the cathedral, with its years of collected souls, her mind quieted. The familiar words of the service, repeated effortlessly, erased her thoughts.

Rita waited until the church had pretty much emptied before she rose to leave. Slowly making her way down the aisle, trailing her hand along the wooden pews, it wasn't until she neared the door that she noticed Miguel in the last row. His head bent down, shoulders slouched, hands in his lap, he didn't see her. A man who said he no longer believed in God, but there he sat, slumped with defeat, pleading for reprieve. Instinctively she reached a hand out to him, her heart craving his touch in return. Yet her feet moved on, pulling her away from him before he noticed her presence.

Outside, the winter wind slapped her, a brisk reminder to get a grip on her feelings. She buttoned her coat and folded her arms against the cold, hurrying to her truck. Once she got inside, though, she simply sat there, keys in hand, breath fogging up the window. She wondered if Miguel had come to Mass in the hopes of seeing her. He'd shown no signs of searching among those who left, but he'd appeared forlorn, abandoned. Was it only his wife and son he missed, or did he regret Rita's absence too?

She leaned forward, resting her head on the steering wheel, the hard plastic as painfully cold as the rest of her body. She thought she'd resigned herself to loneliness, accepted it as inevitable, but Miguel had shown her what it was like to meld your life with somebody else's, fusing your differences with closeness.

"Stupid, stupid, stupid," she said, hitting her head against the steering wheel with each repetition of the word. Her fingers stiff from the cold, she had trouble inserting the keys into the ignition. Wishing she'd thought to bring a pair of gloves, she considered sitting there until the heater warmed up the cab, then decided against it. Best to keep moving. Stillness fostered regrets.

At home, she attempted to clean house. Straightening up the bedroom, she came across one of Miguel's books, a collection of short stories about growing up in northern New Mexico. She remembered the night they'd snuggled in bed and he'd read a story aloud to her in Spanish, everyday experiences transformed into poetry. Now, lying down by herself, she thumbed through the book until she found the story they'd shared. She was unaccustomed to reading Spanish, and it took her a while to pick up the rhythm, the cadence gradually lulling her into sleep. When she awoke, she reopened the book and slipped into the next story, reading one after the other, until the dogs insisted she get up and feed them.

Flojo gobbled his food, as was his tendency, hovering near Loca, who ate with a delicacy befitting a princess. Rita herself had no appetite. She'd attempted a piece of toast for breakfast, the remains of which sat on a plate on the kitchen counter. Too much coffee, however, had left her queasy and she opened a can of chicken noodle soup, thinking it might settle her stomach. Toast and soup, the food of a sick person.

The stories she'd read lingered in her head, the characters so familiar she wished she could discuss them with Miguel. Instead, she sat by herself, and as she lifted the soup spoon to her mouth, the emptiness of her life struck her. Unable to eat, she poured the soup into a container and put it into the refrigerator, convinced she'd feel better tomorrow.

Huddled under an afghan and clutching a mug of herbal tea, she sat before the TV, letting the mindless shows and barrage of advertisements numb her. When she could no longer keep her eyelids open, she clicked the remote and stretched out on the couch. It felt less empty than her bed.

She awoke late the next morning, stiff and groggy. Although she'd slept through the entire night without awakening, fragments of dreams now flitted about her, disturbing her with their persistent but tenuous presence. A pair of Miguel's dime-store reading glasses also haunted her, lying next to the couch, stirring up ghostly visions of the ways he had been filling her life.

Grabbing a paper bag, she resolved to rid herself of any reminders of him. From the bedroom, she gathered up the book of short stories and the bolo tie he'd worn when they'd last gone dancing. She pushed the memories aside, unwilling to recall how happy she'd been that night. In the living room, she found a Charles Mingus CD that Miguel had brought over one morning to listen to as he made brunch for her. Few though they were, each of his things aroused images, sensations of lost intimacy and laughter.

The sooner she rid herself of all his stuff, the sooner she could begin putting her life back together. The flannel shirt went into the bag last, but not until she'd pressed it against her face, breathing the unforgotten pleasure of his body.

She waited until ten, when she knew he'd be at his office, to go over to his house. The sight of his truck in the driveway threw her until she remembered that he always walked to work. She'd toyed with the idea of writing a note but couldn't find the words to express her regrets. Rather than say she was sorry, she would leave the bag on his porch, letting him know she expected no more from him.

King stood looking out the front window and barked at the sight of her. She would have liked to give him a last hug, but she'd buried her key at the bottom of the bag. Placing it on the porch, she murmured good-bye and hurried back down the steps, her eyes already swimming.

"Wait!" Miguel called.

Rita turned and found him standing in the open doorway, stubble on his face, his hair unwashed and standing on end as though he'd raked through it countless times with his fingers. He wore an old Berkeley sweatshirt, the letters barely legible, over plaid pajama bottoms and a pair of sheepskin slippers.

"Are you sick?" Her concern slipped out before she could help it.

"Only in spirit." He opened the door wider. "Come on in?"

"I need to go." She began backing away from him. "I just stopped by to drop off some things you'd left at my house."

"Just a couple of minutes?"

His eyes crusty from lack of sleep, she saw the plea reflected within them. "How about out here on the porch?" she relented. "It's warm in the sun."

"Not to mention more neutral territory." He closed the door behind him, joining her outside.

As they sat down on the top step, Rita made sure to keep several inches between them. He must have been running a fever, though, because heat emanated from his body. His hands, small boned and delicate, hands that she loved, rested on his knees, and she wanted to reach over and run a finger over the bumps of his knuckles.

"I blew it," she said.

"We both did." He rubbed his legs as though they hurt. "I want to apologize for the things I said the other night."

"No need. You were right. I've been holding on too tight to something that's already gone."

"Yeah, but as you pointed out, the same's true of me. It wasn't fair to start a relationship with you when I hadn't yet made peace with Laura and Joey's death." He leaned over and played with the tongue of his slipper, bending it back and forth, exposing the fleece, then hiding it. "You deserve a man who's fully there for you."

Rita let her teeth close over her tongue, biting down on it, refraining from saying he'd given more of himself than any other man she'd known. It hurt to still want him, knowing his bed lay just behind them, where they could make love as though nothing had happened. But she wanted more. Although he'd sometimes disappeared into the past, he'd been present enough to show her what it was like to have a bond that transcended the pettiness of everyday life.

"Who knows?" she said. "Maybe by the time you come to terms with being a widower, I'll be free of some of my hang-ups."

He put his head on his knees, turning his face to look up at her, his eyes still sad, but his lips verging on a smile. "That would be nice."

Her fingers clamored to caress his face, to stroke away his sorrow. "It's cooler out here than I thought," she said, and sat on her hands.

"If we went inside, we'd . . ."

"We'd make love," she said. "And we'd pretend everything was okay, but it wouldn't be." Yet she wanted nothing more than to hold him and be held by him. To tumble into his bed, her body pressed against his, burying their fight with kisses.

She stood up to leave.

Miguel stood up too and reached a hand out to her hair, but then stopped and tucked his hand behind his back. His restraint gave her hope. If they could hold back, wait until they'd each sorted through their troubles, maybe they could try again.

|| JOE || Joe couldn't wait any longer. "Eight-thirty here, seven-thirty there," he said aloud, calculating the time difference in California. Telling himself Wayne had always been an early riser, he punched the number into the phone.

Wayne answered with the alertness of a man accustomed to doing business first thing in the morning. "What's the verdict?" he asked.

"Ran into some problems with a neighborhood association," Joe confessed, withholding none of the details of the second hearing on the subdivision. "The city insisted I take a couple more precautions against erosion."

"But it's a done deal?"

Joe heard the concern in Wayne's voice and thought one day he'd have to tell him how close it had all come to falling through. "Yeah, I finally got approval. You can send your earnest money whenever you're ready."

"I've been ready since the day I saw that hill. I'll wire the money as soon as the bank opens." Wayne sighed, a sound that echoed Joe's own pleasure. "I can't tell you how happy this makes me."

"Who would have ever thought we'd end up as neighbors, huh?"

This time Wayne laughed with the fullness of his joy. "Before you know it, we'll be sitting in rocking chairs and reminiscing about the good old days."

Chloe had filled such a yearning in his life that Joe had overlooked how greatly he missed having a close friend. His laughter joined Wayne's. "It doesn't get any better," he said.

"Well, maybe it can." Wayne paused, something he rarely did in the course of a conversation. "Tess and I were wondering if you'd be willing to design the house for us."

"Me?" Joe cleared his throat, too overwhelmed to believe what he'd heard. "You want me to draw up the plans?" He kept his voice as steady as he could, his good fortune coming in such a big wave that he had to struggle to breathe, his heart pounding in his ears.

"I told Tess what you did with your place. She has a real thing about light and lots of windows."

"It would be an honor," Joe said, his legs so wobbly he had to sit down on one of the kitchen stools.

"I was also thinking, since we don't have time to fly back and forth to supervise the building, maybe we could pay you to oversee the construction too?" Wayne posed it as a question.

Winter equinox lay around the corner, the shortest day of the year, a darkness that normally depressed Joe, but he felt as if a brilliant sun had suddenly flooded his life with brightness. After months of agonizing over whether he could get away with building on the ridge, he now had the full go-ahead. He and Chloe would be able to celebrate the New Year in their new house. And he'd be the architect for his best friend's home. "I'll see if I can get Santiago as a contractor. His crew is the best."

"I leave it all in your hands," Wayne said, then clarified that he'd stop by the bank on his way to work and transfer funds directly into Joe's account.

When Joe hung up the phone, he raised his fist in victory. He'd gone into last night's city council meeting braced for the worst. The neighborhood association had hired an attorney successful at halting developments, but she'd only pushed for extra containment ponds to prevent runoff problems. As soon as he agreed to her stipulations, the city had approved the subdivision.

Leroy had taken him out for drinks afterward, and Joe had woken up with a hangover this morning, but it didn't diminish his sense of accomplishment. The bottle of aspirins almost fell out of his hands, however, when the phone by his elbow rang. A glance at the caller ID showed it to be Santiago, and Joe squelched all thoughts of an emergency.

"What's up?" he asked, shaking three aspirins out of the bottle and swallowing them with a gulp of coffee.

"The plasterer is here." Joe could hear a man yelling in the background. "He says the check you gave him for last week's work bounced."

"Got to be a bank error. I'll call and take care of it." Joe knew he'd cut it close, but he'd thought there were enough funds to cover the check. He'd been juggling money, moving it from one account to another, but he must have miscalculated the exact amount somewhere along the line.

Joe heard Santiago tell the plasterer it was a mistake, and the man yelling back obscenities. "He's threatening not to finish the job if you don't show up with cash."

"I'm on my way to the ATM machine now," Joe said, reaching for his keys. The man was one of the finest plasterers in town, and he didn't want to lose him. Despite his hangover, Joe was in such fine spirits that he didn't notice the overcast skies until he stepped outside. The clouds hinted at snow and the air carried a moistness that awoke his hopes. He and Chloe wouldn't move in until January, but he was planning on buying them the biggest tree he could find and opening presents at the new house. A white Christmas would make it all that more perfect.

He parked in front of the federal courthouse, a two-story stone building that asserted its stateliness. As he crossed the street to the bank, he saw Gilbert coming out of city hall. Gilbert had had to stay for another hearing last night and had missed the celebration at the bar.

"Congratulations," he now said, joining Joe at the ATM machine. "Told you it would be a cinch." Gilbert inserted his card into the machine and punched in the necessary numbers.

"A lot closer shave than you led me to believe."

Gilbert took his money from the ATM and stuffed it into his wallet. Then he gazed in the direction of city hall with its naked trees lining the sidewalk. "Different kind of people moving into town. More savvy. We're lucky they didn't figure out what we did with that driveway."

"Good reason to play it straight in the future."

"Too big a profit in bending the rules." Gilbert tugged at the waistband of his pants that fit snugly around his broad belly. "City's still growing. Got to take advantage of it while we can."

"And what happens when somebody catches you?"

Gilbert gave one last tug to his waistband, his dimple almost disappearing into the fold of his smile. "We'll plead ignorance. Dumb

Hispanics who never learned any better." He raised his hand in a cross between a wave and a salute. "See you around."

Gilbert cut across the street at an angle, jaywalking and nodding hello to the city cop who slowed down to let him pass. The man had no compunctions about breaking the law, whereas Joe, despite all the money he'd ultimately make on this deal, would never risk an illegal business transaction again. Too much anxiety had accompanied the whole process. Overriding his fear of being caught, facing bankruptcy, and losing Chloe had been the loss of respect for himself. Much as he was going to love living in that house, shame would tinge his pleasure, for he knew he had not earned it honestly.

Driving up to the house, he held his breath as he did every time he crossed over the narrowest section of the road, the hillside falling away so abruptly that a slight misturn of the wheel would send him plunging over the side. If he could have, he would have closed his eyes so as not to see how close he had pushed nature's limits. The hill wasn't meant to accommodate a road, and he knew it. Luckily, the beauty of the house went a long ways toward assuaging his guilt. It nestled atop the hill, blending into the land, a soft shade of brown, the same tone as the earth.

The plasterer had opted to trust him and was in the process of completing the living room when Joe arrived. He'd given the walls a warm umber finish, a golden glow that enhanced the view out the window. The man was more than a fine craftsman; he was an artist with color. Joe apologized for what he called the bank's screwup and promised he'd soon have another job for him.

Mexican music reverberated from the other end of the house, where a small crew worked on the master bedroom. Santiago stood in the kitchen, chatting with two men laying tile. "I need to get out to another site," he said to Joe. "These guys are fine on their own."

Little remained to complete the house. Santiago only stopped by occasionally to check on the progress of the final details, spending most of his time now overseeing the start of somebody else's house. But he assured Joe he could begin construction on Wayne's in March. "Shoot, if this warm weather continues," Santiago said, as they both walked out the door, "we might even be able to start by the end of February."

"Looks like it could snow later today." The sky had darkened since earlier in the morning, but the temperature had stayed uncommonly mild, often a sign of a pending storm.

"Radio said it'll pass us over." Santiago got into his truck and reminded Joe he needed to stick around that morning until the kitchen appliances arrived.

The delivery wasn't due for over an hour, so Joe decided to take a walk. He headed toward the other side of the hill, in the direction of Rita's house, finding the path he'd seen her use that first day they'd met, when she'd told him he couldn't build up there.

Last night, after the city council approved his subdivision, she had sprung out of her chair in anger and lectured the entire room about a loss of honor. She couldn't have chosen a more apt word to pinpoint Joe's shame. But he had too much vested in this project to let honor intervene. Although the subdivision had infringed on a minor regulation, in the end it would prove an asset to the community. He intended to demonstrate that people could build exquisite but modest-sized homes befitting the terrain.

As he made his way down the path, Joe glanced back up to admire the way the house looked from that side. He imagined feature articles appearing in various magazines, praising the environmentally sound design of his little development. His life had definitely taken a turn for the better. Joe filled his lungs with the morning's damp air, welcoming the moistness, like a cleansing.

At the bottom of the hill, he skirted past where the junkyard had once sat and continued on down an arroyo. After he and Chloe settled into their new home, he would get a dog. Take it for long walks instead of plodding on the treadmill at the gym. A dog would have as much fun as he would out here, both of them on the lookout for nature's surprises, like the jackrabbit that took off at that very moment, running under a chamisa.

As Joe came around a bend, he spotted the junkyard. He'd noticed it from up above but had never visited it since its relocation. It sat behind a hill, with a trailer off to the side. Next to the trailer sat a white Miata.

Joe told himself that people other than Chloe owned a Miata. He also reminded himself that Parker and she could have business to conduct. Except, normally, her artists met her at the gallery. And today was her day off.

He walked up out of the arroyo to check the license plate—ARTISTS—the personal plate he had given Chloe as a gift when she first bought the car. Telling himself her being at Parker's place was strictly related to her job, he detoured over to what appeared to be a studio, with sculptures and car parts scattered outside of it. Finding the door ajar, he looked inside, thinking he'd catch her there. But the room sat dark and cold, empty not only of people, but also of sculptures.

That meant she had to be inside Parker's trailer. Not looking at his work, but doing what? He heard her laugh as the door of the trailer opened. She and Parker stepped outside, smiling into each other's faces, oblivious to his presence. He watched as Parker leaned in closer to Chloe, his mouth a few inches above hers. "Thanks for coming by."

"Thank you. It's not every day I get an invitation to tea."

Joe's hands clenched into fists, ready to pummel Parker, who merely shrugged, unaware of his existence. "Hated to think of you driving all the way out here for nothing."

Chloe's hand reached out and touched Parker's shoulder, resting there a moment too long. "It was well worth the trip. I knew when I first saw your sculptures that you would take them different places over time. But . . ." She laughed, the kind of pleasure-full laugh that Joe had not heard from her in weeks. "I never would have expected metal totem poles."

"That was only a model. Wait until I show you a full-scale one."

"So where is this new sculpture?" Joe moved away from the metal shed, making himself more visible. "I didn't see anything in the studio."

"Joe! What're you doing here?" Chloe, for once, looked as though she warranted his jealousy, her cheeks flushed with red.

"I was taking a walk. Didn't expect to find you here. You never said anything about a tea date."

"I didn't know I was supposed to give you a list of my business appointments."

"Business? Since when did art sales involve dallying in a man's kitchen?"

Parker sauntered down the steps, leaving Chloe standing by his door. "Actually, we were sitting in the living room. On the couch, if you really want to know. Looking at drawings and a scale model of a new sculpture." He planted his feet, his arms crossed over his chest, as though guarding Chloe.

Joe walked around him and held his hand out to Chloe. "Shall we go? You can give me a ride to the house. Our kitchen appliances are arriving today."

"Will the driveway be wide enough for a truck?" Rita's voice surprised them all.

"Hey, Mom. What's up?"

When Joe turned around, he found Rita leaning against one of Parker's junky sculptures made out of a rusted hot water heater. She affected a casual pose, her hands thrust inside her jean jacket and her chin resting against her turtleneck sweater. But her eyes pinned him, waiting for an answer to her question.

"If you'll excuse us," he said, "we need to hurry before the delivery truck gets there." He took Chloe's hand and tugged her down the steps.

At that point, Rita lost all semblance of nonchalance. She quickly moved across the yard and thrust herself between them and the car. "It's a driveway, not a road. That's how you cheated, isn't it?"

"Everything's legal. The city's already approved the subdivision."

Rita had a look on her face of somebody who had been struggling to understand a complicated idea and then finally got it. "Struck me as I was walking back here. Past where an enormous piñon used to stand. Had to chop it down when we moved the junkyard. City made us broaden the road. Said a road had to be wider than a driveway."

"Mom, don't you think . . ."

"Guess I should have kissed ass at city hall," she said, ignoring Parker. "Got Gilbert to turn a blind eye, overlook the discrepancy."

Chloe's hand slipped out of his. "What's she talking about, Joe?"

It had been one thing to lie by omission, but he couldn't look Chloe in the face and deny what Rita had said. "The city has this senseless rule about roads being six feet wider than driveways."

Parker rumbled through a pile of rusty car parts near his trailer and pulled out a headlight, which he began to dismantle, his hands moving the entire time he spoke. "The same rule we were forced to comply with when we moved the junkyard back here. Had to chop down that gorgeous tree Rita was talking about, so we could make our driveway officially a road."

"But there isn't enough room to widen a driveway on the ridge, is there?" Rita asked. "It drops off to nothing in one spot. That's why you had to lie and say you were only putting one house up there. Hoping none of us would notice when you filed for the subdivision."

"What difference does it make?" Joe kicked at a tailpipe lying near his feet. "If a driveway is wide enough to get to our house, why shouldn't it suffice for three other houses along the way?"

He heard Chloe's sharp intake of breath. "What they're saying is true?" She stepped toward him, forcing Joe to look her in the eyes, eyes filled with a mixture of incredulity and disgust.

"Chloe, it's a ridiculous law. If I hadn't broken it, somebody else would have."

"You lied to me, Joe." She said it quietly, but anger tightened the skin across her cheekbones, stretching it to the point of tearing.

"It was the only way we could afford our house." He reached for her hands, pleading for her to understand, but she pulled away from him.

The distance between them had become unbridgeable. He had betrayed her faith. It had nothing to do with fudging a few feet to get around a city regulation; it all came down to his having deceived her.

"I can't live with a man who lies to me."

Joe knew he'd lost her, as surely as if she'd been killed in an accident. Taken from him in an instant. And the loss hollowed him, sucked the core of his being. He turned and walked away, the sandy arroyo tugging at his feet, pulling him down.

|| **JOE** || Joe changed his clothes, opting for a more formal appearance to show his respect. Somber colors, such as he would wear to a funeral—dark gray wool slacks and a navy blue blazer. At the last minute, he shed the loafers in favor of his cowhide boots, hoping to come across as a local rather than an outsider.

Noticing that the slacks sat too low on his hips, he took in his belt another notch, the pounds having fallen off him in the past month. Without somebody to share his meals, he'd lost interest in eating and had to remind himself from time to time to insert food into his mouth, as he would gas in his car, so he wouldn't cease to function.

Chewing and swallowing he could still do, but sleep evaded him. Like a cross-country runner, he would set off each night, racing for miles, telling himself sleep waited just around the next lap as he folded the pillow yet a different way, trying to make himself comfortable in a bed that yielded little more than a horizontal position for his body.

After surveying himself one last time in the mirror, he reached for his keys, turned off the light, and made his way through the dark house. It lacked the roominess of the one he'd designed on the ridge, but its smallness suited a single man. A man who had nobody else in his life.

He flipped on the porch light and locked the front door, pocketing the keys and setting off at a fast pace, hoping that the evening's brisk temperature would prove invigorating. Ever since Chloe had announced that she could not live with a man who lied to her, Joe had moved through his days as numb as a person with frostbite, unaware of his extremities, his mind fuzzy. Only his heart exerted its presence, beating with a painful regularity, setting the rhythm of his lifeless days.

Wayne had tried to resuscitate him, visiting for a long weekend, just as he had after Joe's divorce. "Another woman will come along soon enough," he'd said, expressing more concern about the potential loss of Joe's subdivision. Rita had joined forces with the neighborhood association and requested a public hearing over the driveway discrepancy. "You've got to fight this," Wayne insisted. "You can't let the city rescind approval of your plans."

Joe rolled his shoulders, squaring them before he walked into city hall, where the bright lights caused him to blink. Clusters of people filled the hallway, chatting about everything from restaurants to who on the night's agenda of scheduled issues had taken advantage of whom. He brushed past the owner of a liquor store complaining about parents trying to put him out of business because his store sat too close to their children's school.

"I was there first," the man said, directing his words at Leroy, who offered sympathy while, at the same time, telling him of a new commercial listing he might want to consider relocating to. Leroy pretended not to see Joe, who passed by close enough to catch the scent of his spearmint gum.

But when Joe walked into the meeting room, Gilbert grabbed his arm and pulled him into a far corner. "That neighborhood association is going to prevent you from developing all of the lots, but I can get you approval for at least one more house."

"How?" Joe was curious what Gilbert had come up with now. He and Leroy had already offered to pay Joe fifty thousand to conceal their part in the fraud.

"There's this law that's older than most of the ones on the books, and it allows you to connect two family dwellings with a driveway instead of a road."

Gilbert's little fat hand still held on to Joe's arm, desperate to strike a bargain. "I don't have any family," Joe said, shaking himself free of the other man's grasp.

But when he tried to step around him, Gilbert kept spinning out words, like a spider hurrying to trap him in his ever more intricate web. "Your friend Wayne came by to see me, and he says he can come up with papers that claim he's a distant cousin of yours."

Joe ran the numbers through his head. If he could sell even one lot, he might not have to declare bankruptcy. "I'll think about it," he said and made his way past Gilbert.

So many people had squeezed into the meeting room that most of the chairs were already taken, but Joe managed to find one near the back. He wouldn't have wanted to sit in the front anyway, where people would stare at him and whisper speculations.

"Aren't you that developer who lied about only building one house on a hill so you could sneak in more later?" asked the man on his left.

Joe stood up to find another seat, but the man reached out and pumped his hand. "Clever strategy."

Stunned, Joe sank back down into the chair. The man turned to a woman and began praising what Joe had done. Sometimes it seemed for every person opposed to Santa Fe's rapid growth, there were two more scheming on how to profit from the real estate boom.

Scanning the room, Joe saw the president of the neighborhood association and its attorney looking smug, standing by front-row seats as people came up and seemed to congratulate them. Heat blasted through the ventilators, making the room unbearably stuffy. Joe considered removing his jacket, but the navy blue set off his silver hair and gave him what he hoped was a dignified look. So he left the jacket on, the sweat rolling down his armpits, wetting his shirt and making him clammy.

Clammy and thirsty. His mouth a desert, Joe craved water but didn't want to risk losing his seat. He could see a fountain in the hallway, humming contentedly against the wall, chilling the water within it while he sat sweltering. He considered asking the man next to him to save his place, but then Rita entered the room.

She had dressed the part of the hardworking poor. A worn pair of jeans with frayed cuffs bagged on her small frame and her once black sweatshirt spoke of the many washings that had faded it to gray. She even displayed a cross on a necklace, pleading her piety. Joe immediately regretted his own choice of clothes. He had thought it best to appear professional; now he thought it to his detriment. Rita's presence would lead everybody to think a broad spectrum of people opposed the subdivision. It wasn't merely a wealthy neighborhood fighting him, but also a poverty-stricken old-time Hispanic.

Acid soured Joe's stomach and rose through his chest, searing its way up his throat as he watched Rita move to the front of the room, where the attorney had used her briefcase to reserve two seats next to the president of the neighborhood association. Rita greeted both women with overt friendliness. As she shook their hands, her eyes swept over the crowd. Joe gave a curt nod, insisting that she acknowledge him. Rita returned the nod with the solemnity of a duelist meeting her opponent.

Joe couldn't help thinking a duel might have been a more appropriate way to end all this, except the fight wasn't really between him and Rita, or even between him and the neighborhood association with their expensive legal recourse. The battle lay within himself. Reaching under his jacket, Joe touched the folded letter in his left shirt pocket. Chloe had sent it earlier in the week, and he carried it as a reminder of what he needed to do tonight.

The mayor called the meeting to order. Joe's case was second on the agenda. He stood for the pledge of allegiance, his mouth too parched to do more than shape soundless words. When he sat back down, he noticed the quiver in his hands. Entwining his fingers, he pressed his palms together, like a prayer, to still his jitters.

The first matter on the agenda pertained to a house built three feet taller than regulations allowed. "It's too late to do anything about it now," the builder/owner said.

"Cut it down to size! Cut it down to size!" chanted a group of voices from the middle of the room.

Recently, a pair of scissors had been spray painted on the house along with a dotted line. Though Joe normally disapproved of vandalism, this particular piece of graffiti had won his begrudging respect, for he'd heard the builder bragging about having disregarded the rules. Yet he never expected the city to do as it did that night and force the man to lower the height of his home.

"That'll teach you, you asshole!" somebody yelled.

The sweat chilled on Joe's ribs and his heart clenched in his chest. How much animosity would he meet with his case?

The mayor read out the name of Joe's subdivision, Punta de Vistas. Gilbert, who sat at a table in front of the room, shuffled papers, his chin wobbling in a nervous tremble, as the attorney for the neighborhood association explained about the driveway being too narrow to accommodate additional houses.

"You can stop right there!" Joe called out as he climbed over the legs of the half dozen people to his right and made his way to the front of the room while the attorney protested his speaking out of turn.

"Mayor, city council members," Joe said, overriding the woman's words. "I can spare everybody here a lot of time."

He heard the silence behind him. Could almost feel the people leaning forward in their seats as they might at a strategic moment in a sports event. "I withdraw my request for approval of the subdivision."

The silence expanded, enveloping Joe in absolute quiet. Then somebody cleared their throat, and a chair squeaked, followed by a growing murmur of voices as the full significance of his words settled upon the room. The mayor pounded a gavel on the table with repeated emphasis, finally dimming the noise. "Explain your request."

Joe asked for a glass of water. He needed to be able to swallow before he could continue. The councilor who represented the down-town district, a woman who had championed his remodeling projects, handed him her unused glass. The cool liquid passed down his throat, easing the way for the words that knotted his chest.

Joe again slipped his hand under his jacket, resting it upon Chloe's letter. She had written that he had given away what he most valued when he traded his honesty for a house that could no more hold a ray of sun than it could a woman who had once trusted him.

Joe turned and faced the entire room. "I initially applied to build only one house on that ridgetop, hoping, when I later requested approval to subdivide the land, nobody would notice that the road wasn't wide enough to serve three more houses."

"It was an oversight on the part of the city," Gilbert interrupted. "We never noticed the difference. It's so slight. Only six feet."

"Six feet," Joe said, "is the height of a man." He found himself standing taller, the truth straightening his back. "An honest man would not stoop to lying about his intentions."

His eyes ran over the room, seeking the faces of those who showed support for what he'd said and avoiding those who frowned and fidgeted in their seats, uncomfortable with his statement. His eyes came to rest upon Rita. He remembered their first meeting on the hill, when they'd talked about his old Honda, sharing a belief in living simply. "I let greed overcome my better judgment."

An old hippie, his beard and ponytail threaded with gray, stood and raised a fist. "Amen, brother."

"You tell them!" shouted a woman.

One by one, people began clapping, the noise of their hands filling the room with an almost danceable beat, overriding the mayor's pounding gavel as they cheered Joe.

‖ RITA ‖   The day after the city council meeting, Rita climbed the ridge. When she crested the top, she gasped, surprised by the For Sale sign, its brilliant red metal glinting in the noon sun. Like a raven checking roadkill to be sure it's dead, she skittered around the sign. After seeing how much the place meant to Joe, she had never expected him to let go of it.

At last night's hearing, he'd appeared too thin, loss etched into the hollows of his cheeks. Rita had noticed, though, that when he interrupted the proceedings and walked up to the mayor, he no longer dragged his feet and his shoulders had lost their slump. In admitting to his lies, he had regained his dignity.

Rita, in turn, had expected to feel a sense of vindication when she climbed the hill today. Instead, an overwhelming weariness bore down on her, making it difficult to lift her legs as she walked up the steep incline. Now, standing on top, she felt the toll of her long fight and the emptiness of her purported victory. Her legs gave out from under her, and she sank onto the low wall that surrounded a small patio.

Although nobody had ever lived in it, the house felt haunted. Rita gazed at the patio, a small intimate space that faced southeast—a perfect place to await the dawn. French doors opened onto the patio from what she presumed to be the master bedroom. Curious, Rita stood up, walked over, and tried the handle. Finding it unlocked, she went inside, her feet brushing along the tile floors. Wandering from one room to the next, she saw how beautifully Joe had designed the house, letting in the views, opening up the rooms to as much light as possible. Though not much bigger than her own house, it had a spaciousness that allowed her to breathe easier.

The living room also had French doors, and on the back patio sat two wooden chairs with arms wide enough to rest a cup of coffee while you read, or a beer as you savored the sunset. The chairs beckoned to Rita, and she made her way outside, the patio protected from the wind and surprisingly warm in the midday sun. The back of each chair angled in such a way as to invite her to lean back, stretch out her legs, and relax. She pulled her sunglasses out of her jacket pocket, put them on, and stared at the sun glistening off the snowy face of the Jemez Mountains. Never would she have imagined that Joe's house could elicit a greater appreciation of the surrounding beauty.

"Want to buy it?" he asked.

Joe's voice gave Rita a start. He stood on the other side of the patio wall, presumably insisting she leave, but she was too tired to lift herself out of the chair. "I can see why you wanted to live here," she conceded. "It's magnificent."

"There isn't a better view in all of Santa Fe."

"Not just the view. The house too. You capitalized on every angle."

"Capitalized." Joe straddled the low wall, seeming to collapse, just as she had earlier. "Now there's a truly American motto for you. We take advantage of every opportunity that comes our way, never stopping to realize we might be paying too high a price."

The sad irony in his voice convinced Rita of his remorse. She'd originally assumed he was only out to make money, but the night of Parker's opening, when she'd watched Joe's behavior around Chloe, she'd recognized his desperation, his willingness to risk everything, including his own values, in an attempt for love.

Now he sat on the wall, staring at something behind Rita, and when she turned to see what it was, she noticed how the windows of the living room curved around the patio, almost like an embrace. She realized Joe was memorizing every feature of the house, saying good-bye before letting go of it.

"I may have accused you of building where nobody should have built," she said, "but you enfolded nature in each and every room of this house. If I were rich, I'd hire you as my architect."

His bitter laugh reverberated, so unlike the laugh she'd heard him give that day his car had gotten stuck making its way up the hill. "High praise from a woman who made sure I can't afford to ever build another house in this town."

Rita removed her sunglasses and looked him straight in the eyes. "I wasn't the woman who made you go against your principles."

Joe stood, and Rita instinctively pulled her knees up to her chin in a protective huddle. He took a step toward her, then halted, his eyes full of anger. Abruptly, he turned away and looked out toward the Jemez.

Rita, too, gazed that way, watching as the corded muscles in Joe's neck loosened in the unwinding silence. Eventually he spoke, his back still turned to her. "It was such a minor rule I broke, an arbitrary one really, nothing of major significance. But it ate at me. Made me hate myself."

When Joe turned around, his face reminded Rita of her father's after the priest heard his last confession, peace finally overriding the pain. "I tried to convince myself this house would keep Chloe." Shaking his head at his own foolishness, Joe plopped down in the chair next to her.

Rita stretched out her legs again, her dusty pink tennis shoes not far from his scuffed cowhide boots. "We have the opposite problem. I drive men away by insisting on my independence."

"Is that what happened to that attorney fellow? I wondered why he wasn't at the hearing."

At the reference to Miguel, Rita's eyes stung with the saltiness of too many unshed tears. "He warned me that even if I stopped you from building more houses up here, I'd never regain the joy this place once held for me."

Joe crossed his legs at the ankles, one foot rocking atop the other. "Was he right?"

"More so than I realized." She leaned forward to see the realty sign alongside the house, with Leroy's name and phone number visible to anybody coming up the driveway. "I would have thought you'd be too pissed off at Leroy to let him be the one to sell the place."

"I didn't have the heart to do it myself. Besides,"—Joe gave her a wry smile—"if anybody can sell the place for enough money to bail me out of bankruptcy, it'll be Leroy."

Rita remembered the night Leroy had knocked on her door, bringing a jar of chokecherry jam his mother had made and conveying his condolences, while convincing her she needed to sell the ridgetop to buy more medical care for her father. "Leroy has a knack for profiting from other people's misfortunes."

"Maybe, but I can only blame myself for this mess."

When she'd first seen the sign, Rita couldn't fathom why Joe had decided to sell the house. But that was before she'd walked through it, almost voyeuristically, witnessing the passion that had gone into the layout, rooms folding into each other like a couple who couldn't stay apart. To live here would be a constant reminder of Chloe's absence. Just as for Rita sitting at the kitchen table, or even in the living room, and particularly lying in bed, brought home the vastness of her own loneliness.

Rita stood up, and Joe raised an eyebrow. "Don't you want to hang around?" he asked. "Scare off any prospective buyers?"

"No, I'll stay out of your way this time." Rita hesitated a moment, then stretched a hand out to Joe. "I've finally accepted that the ridgetop is no longer mine."

Joe remained seated, but he shook her hand, his attempt at a smile no match for his grief. "We both lost, didn't we?"

"That we did." As she left, walking into the wind, she folded her arms across her chest to block out the cold, her jacket straining across her back, shrunk to the point of tightness, just like her life. Rita stepped over the wall and began making her way down the hill, wondering how to keep her world from becoming any smaller, to dare something bigger.